D0188628
NIGHT
OWLS

SIMON & SCHUSTER

First published in Great Britain in 2015 by Simon & Schuster UK Ltd
A CBS COMPANY

First published in the USA as 'The Anatomical Shape of a Heart'
in 2015 by Fiewel and Friends, an imprint of Macmillan

3 5 7 9 10 8 6 4

Simon & Schuster UK Ltd
1st Floor, 222 Gray's Inn Road
London
WC1X 8HB

www.simonandschuster.co.uk

Simon & Schuster Australia, Sydney
Simon & Schuster India, New Delhi

A CIP catalogue record for this book
is available from the British Library.

PB ISBN 978-1-4711-2530-0
eBook ISBN 978-1-4711-2531-7

Printed and bound by CPI Group (UK) Ltd, Croydon, CR0 4YY

Simon & Schuster UK Ltd are committed to sourcing paper
that is made from wood grown in sustainable forests and supports the Forest
Stewardship Council, the leading international forest certification organisation.
Our books displaying the FSC logo are printed on FSC certified paper.

To Max Brödel and SHOK-1, two wildly different artists who both make anatomy beautiful

1

THE LAST TRAIN WASN'T COMING. IT WAS ALMOST midnight, and for the better part of an hour I'd been clutching my art portfolio and what was left of my pride at the university hospital Muni stop alongside a handful of premed students, an elderly Chinese woman wielding an umbrella like a weapon, a chatty panhandler named Will (who lived in the hospital parking garage), and an enthusiastic drunk street preacher who either wanted to warn us about a fiery apocalypse or sell us ringside tickets—maybe both.

"A two-car N-Judah train broke down in Sunset Tunnel," one of the medical students read off his phone. "Looks like we're stuck riding an Owl."

A collective groan passed through the group.

The dreaded all-nighter Owl bus.

After hours, when light-rail train service ends in San Francisco and most of the city is sleeping, Owl buses take over the surface routes. I'd ridden an Owl only once, right before summer break started. My older brother, Heath, had mistakenly tried to cheer me up with tickets to a sing-along of *The Little Mermaid* (glow sticks, shell bras) at the Castro Theatre, and after a midnight dinner at a greasy spoon, we'd missed our regular train. Owl buses are slower, dirtier, and filled with people leaving parties, clubs, and closed bars—automatically upping the chance of encountering fistfights and projectile vomit. Riding an Owl when Heath was with me was one thing; risking it alone was another, especially when no one knew where I was.

Yeah, I know. Not the brightest idea in the world, but I didn't have cab money on me. I chewed a hangnail and stared up at the fog clinging to the streetlight, hoping I didn't look as anxious as I felt.

Just for the record, I'm not supposed to take mass transit after 10:00 p.m. That's my mom's scientific cutoff for avoiding violent crime. It's not arbitrary. She's an RN and works graveyard at the ER right across the street three or four times a week (where she was at that very moment), so she knows exactly when the gunshot victims start wheeling in. And even though Heath has the same curfew, I'm plenty aware that my Victim Odds are higher because I'm small and female and not quite eighteen. So, sure, I might be a statistical easy target, but I don't usually prowl the city after midnight, giving my precious teenage life the middle finger. I mean, it's not like I was taking *that* big of a risk. It wasn't a bad part of town, and I'd been riding Muni since I was a kid. I also had pepper spray and an itchy trigger finger.

Besides, I was sneaking around for a good reason: to show my illustrations to the professor who runs the anatomy department and convince her to give me access to the Willed Body Program. At least, that was the original plan. But after waiting hours for someone who never showed, the whole thing was looking more like a stupid waste of time.

As the med students bet on the arrival time of the Owl bus, Panhandler Will gave me a little wave and made his way over. Fine by me. I'd feel safer with a familiar face between the drunken preacher and me; he was making me nervous when he breathed fire in my direction.

"Hey, man," Will said as he approached.

Man? Before I could answer, he'd shuffled on by as if he hadn't even seen me. Wow. Snubbed by a homeless guy. My night was getting better and better.

"What up, Willy?" a male voice answered cheerfully. "Pretty late for you to be working."

"Hospital rent-a-cops are making the rounds. Just waiting for them to clear out."

Curiosity got the better of me, so I turned around to see who'd snagged Will's attention—some shadowy guy leaning against a telephone pole. Will was blocking my view, so I couldn't make him out all that well, but the two of them chatted for a moment before Will even noticed me.

"Sad Girl," he said with a toothy grin. That's what he calls me, because he thinks I'm depressed. I'm not, by the way. I'm just pleasantly dour and serious, but it's hard to explain the difference to someone who sleeps in a cardboard lean-to. "How's it going?"

"Not that great," I said. "I don't have anything tonight." Sometimes I give him my change, but if I had any cash, I'd be in a taxi headed home by now.

"No worries. Your old lady treated me to dinner on her way in to work earlier."

That didn't surprise me. Maybe it was the nurse in her, but Mom had a thing about feeding everyone in her line of sight and was practically *obsessed* with leftovers; if it was larger than a grain of rice, it was either stored in the fridge, packed as part of someone's lunch, or distributed to neighbors, coworkers—and now, apparently, the ever-popular Panhandler Will, who had spotted someone else he knew and was already heading over to greet them, leaving me stranded with his shadowy friend.

Anyone had to be better than the street preacher. But it wasn't just anyone. It was a boy.

A boy about my age.

A *really hot* boy about my age.

Loose-limbed and slim, he slouched against the telephone pole, pushing away an unruly slash of dark hair that fell over one eye. He was dressed from head to toe in black, as if he'd landed a starring role in some Italian caper movie and was ready to break into a bank: jeans, snug jacket, knit hat pulled low. Tight black gloves covered his hands, and a scuffed backpack (probably filled with explosive devices for the bank safe) sat on the sidewalk against his leg.

It wasn't until the preacher started up again that I realized I'd been staring.

Together, along with the umbrella-wielding woman, we listened to the preacher's mumbled lines about salvation and light and something I couldn't hear and WHORES AND BEASTS AND FLAMES. Holy fire and brimstone, dude. My eardrums! I gripped my portfolio tighter, but a second later his tirade died down and he leaned against the back of the bus stop as if he might fall asleep.

"Doesn't look like much of a runner," the boy noted in a conspiratorial tone. Had he moved closer? Because, wow, he was tall. Most people were, from my petite, low-slung vantage point, but he must've had a good foot on me. "I think you can take him if he tries to swipe your case. Artwork?"

I glanced down at my portfolio as if I'd never seen it before. "Artwork, yes."

He didn't ask me why I was carrying artwork around a medical campus. He just squinted thoughtfully and said, "Hold on, let me guess. No still life or landscape. Your skeptical eyes say postmodern, but your boots say"—his gaze swept down my black skirt and the knee-high gray leather covering my calves—"savvy logo design."

"My boots say 'stood up for a meeting with the director of the anatomy lab.' Dr. Sheridan was supposed to meet me after her last lecture." It ran from 7:00 to 9:00 p.m., and after it was over, I'd waited and waited, watching a dwindling number of grad students exit the building. And even when she finally called to apologize at eleven and claimed she'd had a family emergency, I got the distinct feeling she was too proud to admit she'd forgotten.

"And my artwork isn't postmodern," I added. "I draw bodies."

"Bodies?"

"Anatomy."

That's my thing. I'm not one of those cool, creative kids in my art class who make skirts out of trash bags and paint in crazy colors. Not anymore, at least. For the past couple of years, I've limited myself to pencil and black ink, and I only draw bodies—old or young, male or female, it makes no difference to me. I like the way bones and skin move, and I like seeing how all the chambers in a heart fit together.

And right now, my anatomy-obsessed mind was appreciating the way my new acquaintance fit together, too. He was a walking figure study in beautiful lines and lean muscle, with miles of dark lashes, and cheekbones that looked strong enough to hold up his entire body.

"I'm the person who actually enjoyed dissecting the frog in ninth-grade biology," I clarified. Not to sound tragic, but that particular piece of trivia had never won me crowds of friends, so I'm not sure why I was tossing it on the table. I think I was just juiced up on a fizzy boy-candy rush.

He made a low whistling noise. "We had fetal pigs, but I got to opt out and do mine on the computer. Philosophical reasons."

He said this like he wanted me to ask what those reasons were, and I took the bait. "Let's see, squeamish about dead frogs—"

"Philosophically opposed," he corrected.

"Vegetarian," I guessed.

"A really bad one, but yes." He pointed to his coat collar. Pinned there was a small button that read BE HERE NOW.

I shook my head, confused.

"It's my philosophical excuse. Zen."

"You're a Buddhist?"

"A really bad one," he repeated. The corners of his mouth curled into an almost-smile. "By the way, how long ago was it that you dissected this frog? Four years? Two years . . . ?"

"Are you trying to guess my age?"

He smiled all the way this time, and one attractive dimple deepened in the hollow of his left cheek. "Hey, if you're in college, I'm totally fine with that. I dig older girls."

Me? College? I let out a high-pitched, neurotic laugh. What the hell was the matter with me? Thankfully, the bad muffler on a van turning the corner muted my hyena cackle. After it passed, I gestured toward him with the pepper spray canister attached to my keychain. "Why is a vegetarian Buddhist dressed like a jewel thief?"

"Jewel thief?" He peered down at himself. "Too much black?"

"Not if you're planning a heist. Then it's the perfect amount, especially if you have a Hamburglar mask in your pocket."

"Damn," he said, patting his jacket. "Knew I forgot something."

The sidewalk rumbled beneath my boot heels. I glanced up to see the digital N-OWL sign on the windshield of the bus that was pulling over to our stop. Cool white light glowed from the windows.

"Miracles of miracles," the boy murmured. "The Owl actually arrived."

I stood on tiptoes to see what I'd be dealing with. Looked like some seats were filled, but it wasn't sardine-packed. Yet.

A line was already forming at the curb, so I rushed to outpace the medical students and the drunken preacher. Was the boy getting on, too? Not wanting to appear obvious, I resisted the urge to turn around and, instead, dug out my monthly pass. One swipe over the reader at the door and I was inside, hoping I wasn't alone.

2

THE FIRST RULE OF RIDING PUBLIC TRANSPORTATION late at night is to stick close to the driver, so I staked out a prime spot up front, on one of the long center-facing bench seats. You're supposed to reserve them for the handicapped, pregnant women, and the elderly, but since the woman with the umbrella had already claimed the adjoining seat on the other side of my pole, I wasn't too worried about it. I wedged my portfolio behind my calves, quickly scoping out the rest of the bus for any other risks. To my great relief, drunk preacher was nowhere in sight.

But someone else was.

As the bus doors squealed shut, hot boy plopped down across the aisle in the seat facing mine and tucked his backpack on the floor between his feet. He blew out a dramatic breath and slouched in his seat before jerking up a little, pretending to be surprised to see me. "You again."

"Your target seems to be in my neighborhood. I hope you're not planning to rob my house. We have no jewels, Mr. Burglar."

"'Jack the Burglar' has a nice ring to it. Maybe I should give some serious consideration to this career path."

Jack. Was that his actual name? Under the fluorescent glare of the bus lights, deep shadows etched the valleys of his cheeks and the crevice beneath his lower lip. He had a devil-may-care thing going on in the way he teasingly held back his smile.

"You knew the homeless guy, Will," I said, going into Sherlock Holmes mode as the bus rumbled away from the curb. "That means either you live around Parnassus or you've got a connection to either the hospital or the campus."

"I will eliminate one of those things for you," he said. "I don't live here."

"Hmm. Well, you're not going to med school."

"Let's not be judgmental. Some jewel thieves could have surgical skills."

"But you made that 'older girls' remark, which means you're in high school, like me—"

"Like you? A-ha!" he said merrily. "I'll be a senior this fall, by the way."

"Me too," I admitted. "So if you're not taking classes at Parnassus, I'm guessing you know someone who either goes to school here or works in the hospital. Or possibly you've been visiting someone in the hospital."

"Nicely logical, Sad Girl," he said. "Hold on. I wasn't the only person who knew Will. He said your 'old lady' gave him dinner, so he knows your mom. And since you're now worried I'm going to burgle your house—"

"'Burgle'? I don't think that's a real word."

"Sure it is. Burglar here, remember?" he said, raising a gloved hand. "Anyway, you and your mom might know Will, but you don't live near the hospital, either. Inner or Outer Sunset?"

"Yes," I said, avoiding a real answer.

Undaunted, he tried another approach. "You never said why you were meeting with the anatomy director who didn't show. Are you trying to get an internship or . . . ?"

"No, I was just trying to get permission to draw their cadavers."

One eye squinted shut. "As in corpses?"

"Bodies donated for science. I want to be a medical illustrator."

"Like, drawings in textbooks?"

I nodded. "And for pharmaceutical companies, medical research, labs . . . it's super competitive. Only five accredited masters programs, and to get in those, you need any advantage you can get. A couple of local museums are cosponsoring a student drawing competition in late July, and I want to win it. There's scholarship money up for grabs, and a win would look good on my college applications."

"And drawing dead bodies will help you win?"

"Drawing *dissected* bodies will."

He made a face.

"Da Vinci drew cadavers," I said, using the same argument that had failed to win my mom's approval when I announced my intentions to follow in the Italian painter's footsteps. "So did Michelangelo. The Sistine Chapel panels are filled with hidden anatomical paintings. If you look closely at the pink shroud behind God in *The Creation of Adam*—you know, the one where God is reaching out to touch fingers with Adam?—the shroud is actually a diagram of a human brain."

"Wow. You weren't kidding about the frog thing, were you?"

"No." I scratched the back of my head; the pins holding up a tangle of braids above the nape of my neck were making me feel itchy. "All I want to do is draw cadavers after hours. I wouldn't be bothering anyone or getting in the way. But now I have to come back Wednesday before her lecture. Hopefully she actually shows this time." Was I talking too much? I wasn't sure, but I couldn't stop. I get chatty when I'm nervous. "At least next time I won't be risking my life on the Owl talking to strange boys."

"Feeling alive is always worth the risk."

"Feeling alive is merely a rush of adrenaline."

He chuckled, and then studied me for a moment. "You're an interesting girl."

"Says Jack the vegetarian Buddhist jewel thief."

His lazy grin was drop-dead dangerous.

You know, I always felt like I was pretty good at flirting—that it was the boys I'd flirted with who just weren't good flirtees. Jack, however, was an excellent flirtee, and my game was on fire tonight. His gaze flicked to my crossed legs . . . specifically to the few inches of bare knee peeking between my skirt and boot.

Crap. He was definitely checking me out. What should I do? Earth to Beatrix: This was the night bus, not a Journey song. Two strangers were not on a midnight train going anywhere. I was going home, and he was probably going to knock over a liquor store.

When it came to romance, sometimes I was convinced I was cursed. Don't get me wrong: I'm not one of those "woe is me, I'm so plain Jane, no boys will ever look my way" kind of girls. Boys looked (like now). A few even stared (seriously, like *right* now). It was just when they got to know me—or saw my oddball medical artwork—that things usually went south.

Too weird for jocks, and not weird enough for hipsters, I was neither freak nor geek, and that left me stranded in no-man's-land. I was fine being a misfit—really, I was, even when someone scribbled "Morticia Adams" on my locker with a Sharpie this winter. I mean, first of all, even though we sort of share a last name, Morticia's is spelled with two *D*s, and I doubt whoever defaced my locked had the brain capacity to know the difference, but whatever. And second, I actually look more like the Addams daughter, Wednesday—the apathetic girl with the headless dolls—than Morticia, mostly because of my hair. I always braid it, and I know a thousand and one quirky styles, from Princess Leia buns to Swiss Miss to Greek Goddess, or tonight's masterpiece: Modern Medieval Princess.

But the funny thing is, I actually like *The Addams Family,* so whoever christened me with that nickname wasn't really crushing my feelings. I definitely didn't lose sleep over it. And it's not like I'm completely socially inept, either. I have a couple of friends (and by "a couple" I mean exactly two, Lauren and Kayla, both of whom were spending the summer together in a warmer part of the state). And I've had a couple of boyfriends (and by "a couple" I mean I dated Howard Hooper for two months, and Dylan Norton for two hours during an anti-prom party in Lauren's basement).

So, okay. My calendar wasn't exactly full, and I could never wear black dresses at school without people snickering behind my back, asking me where Gomez was. But I figured I could ditch all that in college, where I could reinvent myself as a sophisticated art student, bursting with wit and untapped joie de vivre. My limitless conversation starters about skin and bones would seduce the heart of some roguish professor (who almost always had a British accent and was also a former Olympic-trained swimmer—but only for the body), and we would run away together to some warm and fabulous Mediterranean island, where I would become the most celebrated medical illustrator in the world.

In this daydream, I was always older and more clever, and it was always sunny. But here I was, on a cool, foggy night, sitting on an Owl bus feeling . . . I don't know. Feeling like maybe I didn't need to wait through senior year to make it to some fantasy island on the other side of high school.

Maybe I could seduce a dangerously good-looking boy on a bus right now.

His gaze lifted and met mine. We stared at each other.

And stared.

And stared . . .

A strange heat sparked inside my chest and spread over my skin. It must've been contagious, because two pink spots stained his cheeks, and I'd never seen a boy like him blush. I didn't know what was happening between us, but I honestly wouldn't have been surprised if the Owl had burst into flames, veered off the road, and exploded in a fiery inferno.

Bus stops came and went, and we didn't stop staring. The older, wittier me was one second away from leaping across the aisle and throwing myself at him, but the real me was too sensible. He finally broke the silence and said in a soft, desperate voice, "What's your name?"

The woman with the umbrella made a low noise. She gave me a disapproving frown that put my mother's to shame. Had she been watching us the whole time?

"Shit." Jack pulled the yellow stop cord drooping across the window and bent over his backpack. Irving and Ninth. A popular stop. Mine was still several blocks away, which meant one thing: My night bus fantasy was ending. What should I do? Ignore the umbrella lady's warning and give him my name?

What if I never saw him again?

The bus jerked to a sudden stop. Jack's backpack tipped sideways. Something rolled out from a gap in the zipper and banged into the toes of my boots.

A fancy can of spray paint with a metallic gold top.

I picked it up and paused. The way he tightened up and ground his jaw to the side, there might as well have been a neon sign over his head that flashed NERVOUS! NERVOUS! NERVOUS!

I held the spray paint out. He stuffed the can in his backpack and slung it over one shoulder. "Good luck with your cadaver drawing."

My reply got lost under the news ticker of recent headlines scrolling inside my head. All I could do was quietly watch his long body slink into shadows as the door shut and the bus pulled away from the curb.

I knew who he was.

3

SINCE SCHOOL LET OUT IN MAY, GOLD GRAFFITI HAD been popping up around San Francisco. Single words painted in enormous gold letters appeared on bridges and building fronts. Not semi-illegible, angry gang tags, but beautifully executed pieces done by someone with talent and skill.

Could that *someone* be Jack? Was he an infamous street artist wanted for vandalizing?

The remaining leg of the ride blurred by as I recalled everything I'd heard about the gold graffiti on local blogs. I wished I'd paid better attention. I definitely needed to do some research, like, *right now.*

When the bus got to my stop on Judah Street, I raced off, eager to do just that.

I live in the Inner Sunset district, which is the biggest joke in the world, because it's one of the foggiest parts of the city. Summer's the worst, when the nights are chilly and we sometimes go for weeks without seeing the sun. But apart from the fog, I like living here. We're only a few blocks from Golden Gate Park. There's a pretty cool stretch of shops on Irving. And we're just down the hill from the Muni stop. We live on the bottom two floors of a skinny, three-story pale yellow Edwardian row house and share a small patch of yard in the back with our neighbor Julie, a premed student who rents the unit above us. She's the one who got me the appointment at the anatomy lab.

I jogged up a dozen stairs to our front door. As I fumbled for the house key, a taxi pulled up to the curb. My brother jumped out and quickly paid the driver before spotting me.

"Mom's on her way home!" Heath called as he raced up the stairs, imitating an ambulance siren. He was dressed in a tight jacket, tight jeans, and an even tighter black shirt with silver studs that spelled out 21ST CENTURY METAL BOY. He also reeked of beer, which is why I didn't believe him.

"Where have you been?" I asked.

"Me? Where have *you* been?"

"Picking up criminals on the night bus."

He made an "uh-huh, whatever" sound as he combed his fingers through spiky hair the same shade of brown as mine. Standing one step above, I was almost taller than him; we both took after my mom in the height department. He glanced at my skirt and boots. "Hold on. Why are you dressed up?"

"It's a long story. You smell like a brewery, by the way. Are you drunk?"

"Not anymore," he complained. "Hurry up and let us in. I'm totally serious. I saw the paddy wagon pulling out of employee parking when my cab passed the hospital."

The paddy wagon is my mom's ancient white Toyota hatchback. It has two hundred thousand miles on it and a dent in the fender.

"I paid the cabbie extra to run a red light so we could outrace her. Grrr!" he growled impatiently. "Any day now, Bex."

Bex is what my family and friends call me, as in short for Beatrix, and Bex only—not Bea, not Trixie, and not any other way that can make my nightmare of a name sound even more old-fashioned than it already did.

While Heath prodded my back, I unlocked the door and we hurried inside. Even though our apartment takes up two floors, it's officially only a one-bedroom. My mom has that bedroom, and Heath lives below on the bottom floor in Laundry Lair, which is technically a tiny basement space attached to a one-car garage. And my room is *technically* the dining room, but we eat at the kitchen table or on the couch in front of the TV—"like pigs," my mom says, but the shame doesn't stop her.

The no-shame gene runs in the family, because it also doesn't stop my twenty-year-old brother from squatting here at home instead of getting his own place. And because he is still four months away from being legal, my mom would kick his ass if she knew he'd been sneaking into clubs with a fake ID. Again.

"Why is she coming home in the middle of her shift?" I asked.

"Hell if I know," Heath called back to me as he headed for the bathroom. "I've got to take a piss. Watch at the window and yell when she drives up."

"Forget it. I have to change. She doesn't know I was out, either." I raced into my room and stashed the portfolio next to my drafting table before shrugging out of my coat. Two French doors separated me from the living room. I'd covered all the glass with old X-rays I'd cut into squares, so that when the doors were shut, I had a modicum of privacy. But since it isn't a real bedroom, I don't have any windows, and all my clothes are crammed inside a rickety Ikea wardrobe that won't stay shut.

But it isn't all bad. For light, I have a cool old Deco chandelier that hangs in the center of the room and a gigantic built-in mission-style china cabinet on one wall that I use to display my collections: vintage anatomy books, a 1960s Visible Woman (a clear plastic toy with removable organs), some old dental molds, and several miniature anatomy model sets (heart, brain, lungs). At the foot of my bed is Lester, a life-size teaching skeleton that hangs from a rolling stand. The skeletons are usually expensive, but my mom snagged him for nothing at the hospital campus because he's missing an arm.

Heath skidded to a stop outside my X-ray doors, breathing hard. "Seriously, where were you tonight?"

"Trying to meet with the anatomy lab director, but she never showed."

"That again? Look at you, being stubborn. I thought Mom told you not to bug them."

"I'd already made the appointment," I argued. "It's not like I was breaking into the lab and molesting bodies. I wasn't doing anything wrong." Except defying my mother's wishes, taking the Owl, and flirting with someone who may or may not be a wanted vandal . . . "Not horribly wrong, anyway," I amended.

"God forbid," Heath mumbled. "You really don't know how to be bad."

I got my boots unzipped and tossed them into the rickety wardrobe. "Oh, and you do? Was Noah out with you, or did he even know? If you're cheating on him—"

"Shh! Listen." He angled his head to the side, bracing his hand on the doorway. "Is that the paddy wagon?" he whispered.

The familiar grating thump of the garage door rattled through the floor.

"I was asleep when you got home!" Heath instructed, racing downstairs.

I quickly tossed my skirt under my bed and managed to hop into lounge pants while pulling my doors closed. Right after I shut off my chandelier, Mom's footsteps hurried up the basement stairwell and into the living room. Crap. That was fast. She must be in a hurry.

"It's one in the morning. Where the hell are you calling from?" Mom's voice said over the squeak of her rubber soles. "Never mind. I don't care. Just get to the point and tell me what you want."

Who in the world was she talking to?

"Absolutely not. If you mail something, I will dump it in the garbage. Do you hear me?" Her voice bounced past my room as she headed into the kitchen. Jars rattled. She was in the fridge. Oh! She gave her lunch to Panhandler Will. Guess she was foraging for a replacement. "Too bad. Nothing's changed. Stop trying, and you won't be disappointed. Now, if you'll excuse me, I'm actually working here. Enjoy your flight from *London*." She enunciated the city in a mocking tone. A muffled bang ended the call.

Whoa. She was seriously pissed.

Footfalls squeaked past my room again. "May your plane crash into the fucking Atlantic," she mumbled to herself before jogging down the stairs again. A minute later, the paddy wagon's engine roared to life and she was gone again.

Mom rarely gets angry. Honestly, she pretty much never gets emotional about anything. Ever. It's one of the things I've inherited from her—a no-nonsense personality. No drama, no tears, no yelling. We both operate on a nonemotional setting, unlike Heath, who operates on an unhealthy decadence of shifting highs and lows. He got that from our father, who up and left us three years ago for a strip-club owner he met on a business trip to Southern California. We hadn't seen him since, and to be perfectly honest, I didn't miss him.

Sure, there was a lot of yelling before he left, but after he was gone, Mom pulled herself together pretty fast. She didn't cry when the divorce went through, and she didn't bad-mouth Dad when he never made a single child support payment. The last time I remembered her getting emotional was a couple of years ago when Heath and I suggested we legally change our last names to her maiden Adams out of solidarity.

Anyway, the only person who ever put her in a remotely bad mood was my dad, and as far I knew, they didn't have any contact. She wasn't dating anybody—she was "done with men"—and none of her friends were in London.

So who was she yelling at on the phone?

I cracked open one of the X-ray doors when Heath bounded back upstairs. He held out a palm as he passed, and we high-fived. "Live to puke another day," he said cheerfully, striding back to the bathroom.

"You've got glitter on your nose," I answered.

Whatever smart-ass answer he gave was out of earshot. I had more pressing concerns, so I ignored him and curled up in bed with my laptop. It took me only a few seconds to find what I was looking for—a post on a local city blog luridly titled: "Golden Apple Street Artist: Poet or Attention-Mongering Vandal?"

The blog post detailed what I already knew, but I learned a couple of new things—like that the "burners" or "pieces" (short for *masterpiece*) were executed with both a professional airbrush and a specialty graffiti spray paint that's illegal to sell in the city. I thought of the fancy can in Jack's backpack—definitely not something you could buy at the local home improvement store—and my stomach went a little flippy.

Five words had been painted over the last couple of weeks: BEGIN, FLY, BELONG, JUMP, TRUST. *Begin* was, aptly, the first word, painted in ten-foot-high letters on the pavement around Lotta's Fountain, the oldest monument in the city. The most recent word, *trust,* had been stenciled across the ticket booth roof at the San Francisco Zoo entrance.

The post quoted a police officer in charge of the SFPD Graffiti Abatement Program. He warned that the difference between graffiti and art is "permission," and pointed out that since the cumulative cleanup costs were over four hundred dollars, the artist who painted the golden words would be facing a felony charge.

But that wasn't all. The artist signed all the words with a small golden apple at the bottom of the last letter. And this made the blogger wonder about a connection to a local anonymous "artist collective" called Discord.

Not good.

Members of Discord were known for engaging in antagonist behavior toward the mayor's office and had done tens of thousands of dollars' worth of damage to public property: breaking windows, trashing stores, setting things on fire, and pouring paint on a bronze statue of Gandhi outside the Ferry Building on the Embarcadero. The blogger speculated that the golden graffiti's signature might be a nod toward the Apple of Discord from Greek mythology, which was inscribed with "the fairest" and started a catfight between Hera, Aphrodite, and Athena.

Thinking about all this made me feel as if I were on one of those pirate-ship rides at a carnival, swinging back and forth between excitement and the nagging fear that a bolt would break and the whole thing would slingshot into the sky.

My brother was right about one thing: I didn't really know how to be bad. So maybe I should have just put Jack out of my mind and gone back to my boring sunless, friendless summer.

But that was easier said than done.

The next afternoon, while Mom and Heath were both still sleeping off their respective graveyard shift and club-hopping, I took the regular Muni train to Irving Street, a short walk from the southeast entrance to Golden Gate Park... and one stop from where Jack got off the bus the night before.

It was also where I worked part-time as a glamorous checkout girl in an upscale gourmet market called Alto. Because we catered to the upper crust, everyone but the meat and fish counter employees had to wear a white button-down shirt, black pants, a black tie, and a store-issued black Alto Market apron, which made me feel like a high-end restaurant server—without the benefit of high-end tips.

A lot of people at school complain about their summer jobs, but apart from the black tie, I was sort of okay with mine. It didn't take a lot of effort to run stuff over a scanner. I also secretly enjoyed stacking groceries in bags because it was sort of like a puzzle, fitting the heavy stuff in the right place, and keeping the cold stuff together—a little like replacing all the plastic guts in my Visible Woman anatomy model: strangely satisfying.

Along with all that, the store always smelled like baked bread and fresh flowers, and the piped-in classical music fueled my Sophisticated Older Art Student fantasies. It could be worse.

After clocking in and counting my till, I headed out to my assigned register. The last person who used it had moved the rubber bands and pens around. As I put it all back into place, a dark-haired woman poked her head around a rack of imported candy.

"Good afternoon, Beatrix."

Ms. Lopez is one of the store managers. She's a single mom in her early thirties with an eleven-year-old daughter named Joy. She's been my boss since I started working here last summer. As far as bosses go, she's pretty reasonable and fair, and just plain nice—another reason I don't mind this job.

"Damn . . . looks like we're *slammed* up in here today," I said.

"I can't stop yawning," Ms. Lopez admitted with a smile, crossing her arms over her apron. A small red-and-black pin glittered in the center of her tie, right below the knot. She had a thing for ladybugs and always wore the lucky insect somewhere—socks, sweater, pins. I got her a preserved ladybug encased in piece of Lucite for Christmas; she kept it on her desk in the office. "How did your secret meeting go?"

Ms. Lopez knew all about my art and wasn't weirded out by the idea of my drawing dissected cadavers—another reason why we got along.

"Unfortunately, it was a huge bust." I spilled most of the story but stopped when I got to the part about sneaking home on the Owl bus and meeting Jack. "So, anyway, I get another shot on Wednesday. Lucky for me, I'm not scheduled, so I don't have to beg my boss to let me have the night off."

"Lucky for you, your boss is cool, so you wouldn't have had to beg too hard."

True. "So, what's going on around here?" I asked as I squatted to check my paper-bag supply. "Any good gossip?"

"We're out of the on-sale salmon steaks."

"That's terrible gossip."

She *hmm*ed, trying to think of something juicier. "Oh! That gold graffiti vandal hit the Ninth Avenue Golden Gate Park entrance."

My heartbeat lurched from *bored* to *FIRE!* "Wh-what?" I said, shooting up from behind the cash wrap.

"On the sidewalk. News crews were up there this morning when I was walking Beauty before work. The letters are about as tall as me and sideways stacked." She ripped off a piece of register tape and scribbled a visual aid:

B
L
O
O
M

"Sideways stacked," she said with a hand flourish, complete with perfect red nails that never seemed to chip.

Bloom. I was still in shock.

"It's very pretty and feminine. Lots of curlicues and vines."

"The Botanical Garden," I realized. It was located just inside that particular park entrance.

"Yes, on the walkway leading to the gardens. Police say it's the first time there's been a direct connection between one of the words and the place it was painted. Now everyone is worked up that it's some elaborate Morse code message."

I thought of the button pinned to Jack's coat: BE HERE NOW. Weren't Buddhists supposed to be peaceful? I pictured kindly old men raking patterns in sandy Zen gardens and drinking tea, maybe doing some yoga in the afternoon.

Not defacing public property.

"Whoever is doing this is either very stealthy or very lucky—or both," Ms. Lopez mused. "But luck doesn't last forever. I think it's only a matter of time before someone catches the vandal in action."

That someone could've been me. But now I'd probably never see him again. I mean, all I knew was his first name and his philosophical stance on bacon.

Oh, and something else I'd almost forgotten: our fellow acquaintance.

4

MY SHIFT AT ALTO MARKET ENDED AT EIGHT, BUT INstead of going straight home, I took the N-Judah train to the hospital. It was only a ten-minute ride, and my mom wasn't working that night, which meant I didn't have to worry about crossing paths with her. So I just texted her to say I was running a little late and would catch a ride home with one of my coworkers.

Evening fog was rolling in, but it was still light outside, and the hospital parking garage was fairly busy. I checked out all the places I usually spotted Panhandler Will. But after walking around for twenty minutes, I'd just about given up. That's when I saw him waving at passing cars on the corner.

"Hey, Will," I called out from a few feet away. He sometimes got startled, so I didn't want to give him any reason to freak out on me.

His head turned, and he surveyed the sidewalk with a confused look until he spotted me. "Sad Girl! Why are you wearing a tie?"

"It's part of my work clothes," I told him, holding out an Alto Market bag. "I brought this for you."

"Me?" He warily took it and peered inside. "What is it?"

"Meatloaf, potato salad, and a cupcake." The least froufrou stuff in the deli counter; I didn't think I'd be doing him any favors by giving him imported olives and spicy noodles. "But don't get too excited. It's a bribe. Do you remember when I saw you last night at the bus stop across the street?"

He sniffed inside the bag before looking up at me like he'd already forgotten I was there. "When? Last night?"

"You were talking to a boy who knew you. His name's Jack."

Blank face. This might've been a bad idea.

"He called you Willy," I added.

"Monk!" he said with a grin.

"Monk?" I repeated, wondering if we were on the same page.

"He's religious," Will explained.

"Oh, the Buddhism thing?"

Will brightened. "Yeah."

"That's him," I said. "How long have you known him?"

"Oh, I'm not sure. Years, probably. I see him two or three times a week."

Years. That meant he wasn't just visiting a patient who'd had surgery. "Does he work here or have family that works here?"

"He comes to see his lady friend."

I pictured Jack cuddling up with some busty candy striper, and my heart sank a little—which was silly, because the boy was a criminal, not my potential soul mate.

"Do you know anything else about him? Like his last name? Where he lives?"

Will sniffled and wiped his nose. "I know he takes the N."

"Outbound?" I asked. "Like the bus we were getting on last night?"

"No," he said, pointing in the opposite direction. "He takes it that way."

Okay, that was something. He must've specifically taken the Owl bus to paint the BLOOM graffiti piece in the park. Which meant he didn't live in my neighborhood. But where he *did* live was anyone's guess. The N line stretched across the city and connected to a billion stops.

"Is there anything else you know about him?" I asked.

Will shrugged. "He's pretty funny. Tells a lot of good jokes. Some of them are over my head. But you know, sometimes people smile when they're sad. And sometimes girls who look sad are really smiling."

He pointed at me and winked like he'd just handed me the secret to life. And that would be nice, but it was more likely he'd recently scored pain pills from one of the patients leaving the ER. And when he started whistling what I suspected to be the theme to *The Brady Bunch*, I knew I'd coaxed all I could get out of him, which wasn't much.

And unless I wanted to camp out with Will until he happened to see Jack, I didn't hold out high hopes of seeing him again. The medical campus is a busy place.

Just not as busy I thought.

Two days later, I headed back over for my second chance with the anatomy director. It sometimes seemed like the only times I really needed the train to be on time were the times it was late, so I was already ten times more anxious than I wanted to be. And maybe that's why I wasn't paying attention.

Someone bumped my arm, and my portfolio flew from my hand. "Ow!"

"My bad. I thought you saw me."

A jacket bent over in front of me and picked up my portfolio. When the jacket stood back up, it grew arms and legs and a face that probably competed with Helen of Troy's in the ship-launching department.

Jack.

He looked so different in daylight. A turquoise plaid Western shirt peeked out from the jacket, which was one of those classic black leather motorcycle ones. And when I say classic, I mean actually vintage—like, straight-up 1950s Marlon Brando *Wild One*–style, all lightened along the creases and covered in tiny punk rock buttons. It matched the big black boots beneath the turned-up cuffs of his jeans. No hat covered his hair today, which was dark brown and several inches longer on the top than the super-close-cropped sides and back. That long top was swooped up into a loose pompadour, with fallen tendrils hanging over his forehead and all tousled in a way that was *far* too good to be windblown.

He was all retro and rockabilly and cool. If James Dean and David Beckham had a baby, it would be Jack. That jewel-thief outfit he'd been wearing that first night was a total criminal disguise.

"Jack the Vandal," I said, and not in a cheerful way, either. More like he was my mortal enemy.

He cringed and glanced around. "Can you please not announce that to the world? I liked it better when I was Jack the Burglar."

"So you're not denying it? I mean, you shouldn't, because I know what I saw, and then I find out that you . . . desecrated the Botanical Garden."

"'Desecrated'?"

"You heard me." Okay, I hadn't actually meant to use that word. It's not like I'm *really* into flowers and thought the park was some kind of temple of nature; I was just nervous. But since it was already out of my mouth, I defended it like I was an old woman shaking her fist at scamps and ne'er-do-wells, snatching the portfolio out of his hand to emphasize my righteous anger. But he wasn't fazed.

"Did you see it?" he asked, herding me toward the edge of the walkway with his too-tall body as a group of medical students passed.

"Umm, you mean 'bloom'? I think the entire city saw it."

Joy flashed through his eyes, but he blinked a few times with miles of dark lashes and sobered up. "You're the only one who knows."

"I doubt that. What about your little revolutionary art collective, Discord?"

He shook his head. "I don't belong to Discord."

"That's not what people are saying online."

"Well, they're wrong. I work alone, and no one knows who I am."

Huh. Funny, but I sort of believed him. Or maybe I had a case of temporary hot-boy-influenced naïveté.

"Scout's honor," he promised. "Only you hold my secret identity in your hands, Lois Lane."

Do not be flattered. Do not be flattered. . . . "But not your real one."

"You know more than I know about you."

I ignored that. "What are you doing here, anyway?"

"You said you had another meeting today and that it was before Dr. Sheridan's lecture, so I checked the schedules and guessed the wrong one." He scratched his head in a way that would've been adorable if he wasn't an admitted criminal. "I've been waiting around here for the last two hours. But now that I see you again, it was worth it."

Was he serious? I tried to form a snappy answer, but it came out as one long, strangled vowel. To make things worse, heat crept up my cheeks, so I turned away from him and strode down the cement walkway like I was full of Grand Purpose, not like I was running away. But it didn't matter. Long legs always beat short legs, so it was no surprise when he caught up in a couple of steps.

"I dig the dark-rimmed glasses," he said alongside me, stuffing his hands into his jacket pockets. "They give you a sexy scientist vibe."

"Artist vibe," I countered without looking at him. And I'd only traded out my contacts that afternoon because I thought the glasses made me look older, but he didn't need to know that. And he *definitely* didn't need to know that my heart double-timed a few beats when he said "sexy."

"Can I see what you've got in your portfolio?" he asked.

"Just pencil sketches."

"That's cool. Can I look at them?"

"No."

"Why?"

"Because."

"Because . . . your art isn't good?"

"It's good."

"Prove it," he said, taking one hand out of his pocket to tap a couple of knuckles against my portfolio as it swung between us. "You know, one artist to another. You've seen mine. Show me yours."

Oh, the teasing in his voice—and *oh*, the places I could go with that line. The older, sophisticated Fantasy Me was completely charmed. But the real me was feeling too many pinwheeling emotions wrapped in a center of gooey nervousness. I was also having trouble tearing my gaze away from the scuff marks on the toes of his boots. They weren't plain-old Doc Martens; they looked fancier, like Fluevogs or something.

The entrance to the building that housed the anatomy lab was only a few yards away. I checked the time on my phone. Crud. I had to hustle. Why did he have to show up right now? I needed more time to properly freak out about his being there.

"Will you at least tell me your name?" he asked as I pocketed my phone.

"Why? Afraid I'm going to snitch on you? Is that why you tracked me down?" And why was I being so defensive?

"You don't know anything about me and have zero proof, so what's there to snitch on? It would be smarter for me to avoid you, if you want to get right down to it. Besides, you're the one who tracked me down first."

I stopped in front of the building and faced him. "How so?"

"Willy said the sad girl was asking about me."

That little panhandling ratfink. "Look, I was just curious—"

"Me, too. Since that night on the Owl, I've been having midnight fantasies about meeting hot girls on buses, and that's messing up both my routine and my deep loathing of public transportation."

Was he really saying this? Ignore! Ignore! "I asked Will about you because I wanted to find out if you were really a criminal," I argued a little too loudly. A student exiting the building gave us a curious look. "I have to go. I'm running late."

I tried to move around him, but he blocked me. "I'm a low-level criminal at best. Barely even a reprobate. And I've never been caught, so if a tree falls in the forest, does it really make a sound?"

"Don't make me laugh. I've got an important meeting."

He ducked his head to catch my eyes. "If I make you laugh, will you skip it and go have dinner with me?"

Whoa. Was that a date request? "Look, this is serious. I'm going to be late."

He held up his hands in surrender. "Please, just tell me your name. An email address, phone number—something. Come on, Sad Girl. All old Willy could tell me was that you have a sister and that your mom's a cleaning woman at the hospital."

"Brother and nurse," I corrected, stifling a laugh. "He told me you're a monk and that you have a 'lady friend' who works here."

Jack laughed and said, "Oh, that Willy." Then he abruptly went quiet.

"Do you?" I pressed, silently saying the end of the question in my head: . . . *have a girlfriend?*

"Though it's true that I do visit a female person, otherwise known as a 'lady,' here, and we are, indeed, friends, she would probably kick me in the balls if I ever called her my 'lady friend.' Besides, I'm a monk, apparently."

Hmph. Monk, my ass. The only guys at school who were this particular combination of persistent and beautiful were players. I backed up and pointed to my wrist. "Seriously have to go."

"Give me something, *please.* Don't make me wait out here in the cold stalking you like a creeper."

I took a few more backward steps and opened the door, heart racing. "*Body-O-Rama.* It's an anatomy illustration blog. I'm one of the contributing artists. If you can pick my art out of the lineup, you'll find my contact info there, and you can stalk me online."

He grinned and pulled his leather jacket closed as the wind picked up. "Challenge accepted."

5

MY MEETING WITH DR. SHERIDAN WAS STRANGELY UNsatisfying. Maybe that's because I was still holding a grudge about her leaving me hanging at our first meeting, or maybe it's because I spent the entire ten puny minutes she gave me struggling to keep Jack out of my thoughts.

This wasn't me. At all. I'm the serious girl with straight As. Well, except for the Bs in calculus and that C in freshman PE, which I earned for my "bad attitude" toward Mallory Letson—who happened to be head of the varsity pep squad and Coach's favorite. Never mind that she was talking crap about Heath, who was a senior that year. (For the record, I think Mallory was behind the whole Morticia thing.)

Still.

All Dr. Cold-as-Ice Sheridan said was that my portfolio showed "remarkable talent," and after questioning why I wanted to be a medical illustrator, she just went on to explain that the university was one of the top medical schools in the country and had (standards and practices) or (board members' expectations) or (insurance regulations) to uphold. And that their actual students came first. She promised to consider my request and run it by her colleagues and students. She said she'd have an answer in a week or two.

In a week or two, the summer would be half over and I'd barely have time enough to come up with something else for the student art contest. But what could I do, argue with someone who was doing me a favor? She gave me her business card, so at least I had her email address. I wasted no time writing her the cheesiest, most polite thank-you email in the history of sucking up.

After that, I'm ashamed to say that I spent my entire night checking my artist profile on *Body-O-Rama*, hoping that Jack had gone straight to his computer and searched me out. Granted, my profile pic was an inked self-portrait with half of my face drawn as exposed musculature. But only twenty artists were featured on the site. How difficult was I to recognize? Then again, Jack really didn't know anything about me. Maybe he'd mistaken me for the much cooler girl who painted brightly colored Day of the Dead sugar skulls. In a panic, I read through all the comments on everyone's recent posts, just in case.

Nothing.

And nothing the next day. And the next. But it was the day after *that* when his lack of response was more disappointing than it might've been if it was just another Saturday. Because it wasn't: It was my eighteenth birthday.

And yet, no Jack. Had he given up? I'd even made it easier on him by posting about my birthday plans the day before. It practically screamed, *Look! Here I am!* It was just weird that he was begging me for my name and supposedly waiting for hours to see me, and then boom, nothing.

Was he just busy? Or maybe there was a reason I didn't want to face: that he'd seen my art and decided I was too morbid. It certainly wouldn't be the first time, and even if we *were* both artists, maybe Cadaver Girl and Vegetarian Graffiti Boy were oil and water. I guess I needed to stop pining away for something I didn't even really know if I wanted.

I mean, hello! I was eighteen, baby. I could finally . . . vote and buy all those cartons of cigarettes I'd been pining for. Yippee.

So Mom spent her only weekend day off from the hospital schlepping Heath and me around the city for Beatrix-approved birthday activities. We waited in early-morning fog for forty-five minutes to have milk shakes for breakfast at St. Francis Diner (my favorite) before nerding out at Green Apple Books (where Heath ponied up for a 1960s coffee table book about medical oddities that he'd had on hold for me). We finally ended up at the Legion of Honor, which, in San Francisco, is an art museum—not a brotherhood of knights, or whatever it is in France.

I know a museum may not be everyone's idea of Super Birthday Funtimes, but I really wanted to see this exhibition called *Flesh and Bone*, and it featured one piece in particular that had me salivating: a Max Brödel diagram of a heart. I'd posted a link to it on the *Body-O-Rama* site when I'd blogged about my birthday plans, and, holy smokes, seeing it in person didn't disappoint. Brödel is pretty much the godfather of modern medical illustration. He was a German who immigrated here to draw diagrams for Johns Hopkins School of Medicine in the early 1900s. His illustrations were beautifully detailed and had this weird, surreal quality.

I'd studied his stuff in books and had even copied a few for practice. But seeing the actual carbon-dust-on-stipple-board drawing was breathtaking.

In fact, even after I'd looked at everything else, I went back to that heart diagram for one last look, admiring every detail, including the tiny handwritten labels: AORTA, LEFT VENTRICLE, TRACHEA. It was so completely perfect. And I couldn't help but think he'd drawn it from a dissected heart. If Dr. Sheridan would just let me spend some time in the anatomy lab, I might be the next Max Brödel. I mean, anything's possible, right?

But even though I was currently in muscle-and-sinew heaven, it didn't mean that my family was. Mom kept trying to steer me into one of the permanent collections to see Rembrandt and Rubens: "They're famous, Bex. And so beautiful." Eventually Heath griped and groaned and yawned us into the museum's overpriced cafe for lunch. It was pretty much the same kind of food we had in the deli at Alto Market, so none of it was all that appealing to me. But we ordered, then snagged seats on the patio outside. And because I was a total loser, I checked *Body-O-Rama*'s comments one more time, only to be disappointed anew.

My mom was checking her phone, too. I *so* wanted to ask her about that weird late-night phone call she'd gotten the other day, but I was worried I'd end up incriminating myself. I'm a terrible liar.

"You're eating that, Bex," she said, nudging my shoe beneath the table as she futzed with the fanning dark hair around her temples. She had a pixie cut, which was pretty much just a shorter version of Heath's haircut—only where his was all blown up, hers was blown down. She was tiny, like me, and the elfish thing looked good on her. But as long as I lived with the two of them, I could never cut my hair short, or we'd all look like some freaky family gang, ready to lure strangers into our house with Kool-Aid. Hence the braids.

I made a face at Mom. "The bread's stale."

"It was twenty dollars. It can't be stale."

Heath slung his arm over the back of my chair. "Sure it can. Noah says half the starred restaurants in town recycle bread from other tables."

"Saint Noah is never wrong," I pointed out. Noah was my brother's latest boyfriend, a twenty-five-year-old engineer who had a million-dollar condo in the Castro. He's stable and smart, and even though Heath had yet to bring him home and introduce us, we'd heard so much about him that we were kind of in love with him, too—especially my mom. I think she was hoping he'd be a positive influence on my not-so-stable brother, who had already burned through two community colleges, dropping out once due to boredom and a second time after he got busted at an inopportune moment with an English professor twice his age.

"By the way," Mom said, rearranging her knife on her plate, "you never told me when Noah would be free to come over for family dinner."

"I forgot to ask, sorry. He's been working, and . . ."

And Heath had been sneaking out to drink and see metal shows every other night. I didn't say this—sibling loyalty is a two-way street—but my mom has some weird sixth sense about these sorts of things, which is probably why I have no confidence when it comes to lying to her. Nurse Katherine the Great always knows.

She shot him a dark look across the table. "I swear, Heath, if you screw this up with Noah—"

"I'm not going to screw it up."

"Again," I amended under my breath.

"We were on a break," Heath said.

"Because you were fooling around with that cook."

"Chef," he corrected. "And he was fooling around with *me*. I didn't start it."

"Tell me again, why is Noah with you?"

"Because I'm overflowing with personality and I ooze charm."

I snorted. "You're overflowing and oozing something, all right."

"Please, God," Mom pretend-prayed to the sky. "All I ask is that you swap these children for kittens, and I'll never sin again."

Heath made prayer hands and closed his eyes. "Dear Prince of Darkness, please make sure the kittens piss all over her bed so she'll regret it and beg for us to come back."

I elbowed him in the ribs until he laughed, and then I asked Mom for money. "I'm going back inside for ten-dollar strawberry shortcake," I explained as I accepted her debit card. "You two keep steering us toward the apocalypse while I'm gone."

They continued to joke and laugh as I strolled around tables and a hundred pecking birds, who must've thought this place was some kind of avian Shangri-La, what with all the fancy crumbs being tossed their way by museum patrons. I couldn't blame them. It was really pretty out here, especially beyond the patio; afternoon sun cleared out the fog over the Golden Gate Bridge's famous orangey-vermillion arches stretching across the blue bay. For once, it actually seemed like summer. Though I did feel a little sorry for the tourists who were prancing around in shorts. Come nightfall, they'd be regretting they didn't book their trip in September or October, when it was sunnier.

As I opened the cafe door, a riot of sound drew my attention toward the museum hallway. People were jumping up from their seats, craning their necks to see something. I sidled past one of the museum volunteers and wove between patrons crowding the exit of the *Flesh and Bone* exhibit.

A couple of guards cleared a space around a spotlighted area in the middle of the room. That's when I saw it, scrawled in slanting metallic gold on the gray exhibit wall beneath Max Brödel's heart diagram:

CELEBRATE

Was this, could this . . . ? Who the hell else would it be?

Jack.

Jack-Jack-Jack! His name bounced around my hollow head like a rubber ball inside an empty gym. Celebrate. This was no coincidence. He went to the *Body-O-Rama* website. He saw my post about birthday plans—the one in which I'd posted *a photo of the Brödel.* Humiliation and excitement raced through me in dizzy spirals.

Oh, my ever-loving God . . .

He did this for me.

Important-looking people rushed in with a security guard. Museum administration. One of them was a distinguished older woman in a dress suit, who clamped a hand over her mouth when she saw the graffiti.

Someone was excitedly talking to a couple next to me. "Dressed in black," he was saying. "I didn't get a look at his face, but I thought it was weird he was wearing dark glasses. He had a paint pen or something tucked into his sleeve, and he just strolled up to the wall and started writing, like it was nothing."

The couple gasped and shook their heads.

"Did they catch him?" I asked, butting into their conversation.

"I don't think so," the man told me excitedly. "It all happened so fast. I ran through that doorway to flag down a guard for maybe ten seconds, maybe. He was already gone when I got back."

Holy crap. This was shocking. And stupid. And crazy. Someone else nearby said the police were on their way. My hands shook as I fumbled inside my pocket for my phone. No way in hell was I getting closer, so I zoomed in as best I could and snapped a photo.

Oh, Jack . . . what have you done?

6

IT TOOK US FOREVER TO GET OUT OF LINCOLN PARK because of all the hubbub and traffic. Meanwhile, I was cooped up in the backseat of the paddy wagon, dying to talk about it. But I couldn't—not in front of Mom, who'd already joked that the "coincidence" of the graffiti was bizarre (if not cooler than the birthday sombrero I'd get in a restaurant).

As soon as I could get Heath alone, I was telling him everything. My brother may be a lousy role model, but he's an excellent listener and advice-giver. He'd give me some perspective.

If I didn't die first.

We made a couple more stops before we headed home, but I spent the rest of the afternoon on my phone, refreshing *Body-O-Rama* every minute and checking my email and feeds (still nothing). Now that I knew he'd actually been on the site, it was driving me batty that he hadn't contacted me personally. I did my best to consider everything rationally. I mean, he hadn't actually defaced any artwork. If he had? Watch out, buddy. Never mind the world of hurt he'd be in with the law—I would personally hunt him down and strangle him if he'd screwed with the Max Brödel heart.

But he hadn't. All he'd defaced was a temporary wall—one the museum probably painted over for every installation.

And yet he'd had the balls to walk into a museum in broad daylight and vandalize it. Talk about a jailable offense. Cop cars had descended on Lincoln Park like they were answering a bomb report. Granted, I knew a lot of kids who did crazy things. My own brother had probably broken a million minor laws before he graduated. Unlike me, he knew perfectly well how to be bad, and he was damn good at it. But smoking weed and using fake IDs paled in comparison to citywide infamy.

And then there was the much more personal part of this: the Me factor. What did it mean? Yes, it was my birthday, so clearly it was a nod to that. But for the love of Pete, just send me a *Have a Terrific Day!* message online. No need to bring a felony charge into the mix. Was Jack a secret adrenaline junkie? I could already hear Mom labeling him a troublemaker.

Despite all that, it was—in a way—incredibly romantic. Or maybe I was just romanticizing it. Maybe he pulled a dozen nutball stunts every day before breakfast.

"You okay back there?" Mom asked when we were nearly home, peering into the rearview to make eye contact.

"A little weirded out by everything, that's all." Which was true. "And hungry." In the wake of what had happened, I'd forgotten all about getting my fancy strawberry shortcake.

"I thought we'd pick up Mae Thai for your birthday dinner. How does that sound?"

I sighed with pleasure. "Heavenly."

Mom's eyes crinkled at the corners when she smiled at me in

the mirror. I really hated lying to her, especially when she'd been so nice to me today. This whole situation with Jack was exhausting. If this was what it was like to have a crush on a bad boy, I wasn't sure if I could handle it. I mean, Howard Hooper—aka the only real boyfriend I'd ever had—was kind of a jerk, but not in a tough-guy way. In the way that geeks sometimes are when they look down on everyone who doesn't know the name of every Avenger or what 1337 meant.

Howard Hooper would probably wet his pants if he even day-dreamed about doing something as ballsy as vandalizing a museum in broad daylight.

Where are you, Jack?

When I finally got so frustrated I couldn't handle it anymore, I decided to throw caution to the wind and posted the pic I took at the museum. I added the vaguely troll-rific comment Golden Apple Vandal wishing me a happy birthday.

Once I'd hit SEND, I had a minor panic attack. There it was in my feed, for all 167 people who followed me to see. Okay, almost none of those people actually knew me, so maybe I was overreacting. Besides, I really only wanted one person to see it, because hey, you just can't make an epic public declaration like that and then walk away as if nothing happened.

When we finally got home, a printed note was stuck to the door from some place named Godspeed Courier. "Sorry we missed you, but we need your signature. We'll try again ___." The blank wasn't filled in, and there was no name.

"Bike messenger?" Mom said, hefting steaming bags of takeout. "What is this, Heath?"

"How should I know? I didn't order anything. Maybe it's a birthday present for Bex."

"Right. Because I have so many friends who use courier service."

"Probably the wrong address," Mom said, taking the courier note before heading toward the kitchen.

"Maybe it was meant for Julie."

"Who knows," Mom called back. "I'll ask her about it next time I see her."

"I can run it up to her," I said.

"I said I'd take care of it, Beatrix," she snapped in a very un-Katherine way.

"Sheesh," I mumbled. "Bossy much?"

I remembered Mom's late-night phone call. She'd told the person not to mail anything. Was this what she was talking about?

"I thought you were starving. Come help me get ice in the glasses," she said in a nicer tone from the kitchen before I could read anything more into it.

Besides, I had other things to worry about, like the ding on my phone. One HAPPY BDAY text from Lauren and Kayla in LA (who couldn't even spare enough time to send separate texts or type the *IRTH*). While I was at it, I checked my email. Holy freaking alerts, Batman: The photo I'd uploaded two hours ago had been reposted 503 times, which was about five hundred more times than anything else I'd ever posted. Was I the only person who'd snapped a picture?

"Bex," Mom called again.

"Coming!" Ugh. Maybe posting that photo was a mistake.

My post-museum panicky high faded into a slow buzz after a

movie and massive amounts of Pad See-Ew noodles and lemon-grassy Panang curry. While Mom was in the kitchen, our doorbell rang. It was almost eight o'clock, which was kind of late for some-one to be stopping by. My brain jumped to conclusions and screamed *Jack*, but when Heath swung the door open, it was a uniformed po-lice officer.

The oh-shit look on Heath's face was mirrored on my mom's when she walked into the room balancing a plate of three candlelit cupcakes.

"Evening. I'm Officer Dixon," he said. "Sorry to interrupt your night, but if you don't mind, I have a few questions. May I come in?"

Mom's shoulder's sagged. "Of course. Heath, close the door and sit down. Beatrix, go to your room."

"You're Beatrix Adams?" the cop said.

"Umm, yes?"

"You're the person I'd like to speak with."

"Me?"

"Did you post a photograph online from the account BioArt-Girl?"

My response was caught in some kind of psychedelic slow-motion filter. "Uuuuuh, yeeees, siiiir."

I barely heard Mom, who was politely introducing herself and sounding disturbingly calm as she questioned the officer: What photo? And what was this all about? And how did they get her daughter's address?

Officer Dixon matched her on the supercalm attitude. "We traced the account to an art website and found her Facebook link.

Lincoln High was on that profile. Your address is in the school system database."

Holy crap. All of that was set to private. Wasn't this a violation of my rights?

"Miss Adams," he said to me in a firm tone, "can you please tell me what your relationship is with the person who vandalized the Legion of Honor this afternoon?"

"None!" Why was my voice so high? "I just posted it as a joke. It's my birthday. I saw it and took a picture. It's my birthday," I repeated dumbly. Could I sound any guiltier?

The officer was a brick wall. Completely unreadable. "Did you witness the vandalizing?"

"No." I told him what happened, which was fairly easy because I was actually telling the truth. Mostly. And I thought he believed me, but then he got serious.

"Are you aware of an anarchist art group called Discord?"

"I've read about them."

"Then you know that someone in the group defaced a Rothko painting in the Museum of Modern Art two years ago."

"That was them?"

"Cost the museum thousands of dollars in restoration damage. That's a very serious crime. So if you even suspect you might know someone in your art class at school who might do some graffiti now and then, you need to tell me. Legion of Honor isn't taking this lightly. And if this perp"—Jesus! Jack was now being considered a freaking perpetrator?—"defaces something else, the charges are just going to keep getting worse. Right now, they're looking at one to three years in state prison."

Years?

"And trust me, if this person is connected to Discord, he or she won't be getting mercy from the court, because members of that group are facing felony arson charges, assault on a police officer, rioting—you name it."

"I only read about Discord last week!" I turned around when Mom made a noise. "I swear, Mom. This is craziness. I just posted a photo."

"I believe you, baby."

"Ma'am, did you know that parents can be held responsible, too? You can face fines, jail time, and up to twenty-five thousand dollars in damages if your daughter is found to be connected to Discord."

My future fantasy life in the Mediterranean flashed before my eyes. Jack swore he wasn't affiliated with them. Did I believe him?

"The graffiti isn't connected to her birthday," Mom said. "It was a coincidence." Now she was getting mad, and I would appreciate her anger a heck of a lot more if I deserved her defense. "My daughter is a talented artist, not a troubled teen." Oh, Lordy. "She takes AP classes. She works a steady job twenty hours a week."

"She won an attendance award for not missing a day of school last year," my brother said from the hallway. "She's a total nerd."

Thanks, Heath.

"You're barking up the wrong tree," Mom added.

The officer handed me a business card. It said he was in the SFPD Graffiti Abatement Program. "If you think of anything or remember something about one of your classmates, give me a call. Sometimes I've been able to mediate a solution between the property owners and the perpetrator. Believe me, I'm a good friend to have."

I gripped the card as he walked to the door with my mother, but I could hardly feel the paper. My hands and feet had gone numb. The door closed, and after my mom bolted the lock, she turned around and stared at me with her eagle eyes. The silence was choking me. Even Heath was quiet, a sure sign of damnation.

"Please tell me it was a coincidence," Mom finally said in a low voice.

I tucked my feet between the couch cushions and hugged myself. "All I did was take a photo."

She nodded, but the doubt wafting off her hung around my head like cheap perfume. And why was I feeling so guilty? I didn't do anything wrong. It's not like I *asked* Jack to do it. I didn't even know his last name, for Pete's sake.

"Don't worry, Bex," Heath said. "If anyone's going to jail in this family, it'll still be me."

I tried to smile, but my heart wasn't in it.

"Oh no," Mom mumbled, rushing over to the forgotten cupcakes. Only one of the candles was still lit, and half the frosting had melted and dripped down the black-and-gold bakery paper. She set the tray down on the coffee table. "Hurry up and make a wish."

I groaned and leaned over the table. As I blew out the flame, I wished I could see Jack one more time . . . just so I could boot him in the balls.

7

AS IF A PANIC-SOAKED BIRTHDAY WASN'T A BIG enough pie in the face, the next morning I got an email from Dr. Sheridan's assistant. In the coldest, most banal language possible, grad student Denise wrote that I would "unfortunately" not be allowed to draw inside the Willed Body classroom. But she noted that Dr. Sheridan hoped I'd consider taking anatomy classes there in the future.

I was devastated. And because Heath had already left for work—he's the front-desk guy at a vet office in Cole Valley—I had no one to unload on. I told myself I'd figure something else out. An alternate plan. But at that moment, it felt like the end the world.

It didn't help my black mood that Mom was checking up on me online, reading everything I hadn't disabled after the cop left. Not like I had a cache of boozy party pictures or anything that would get me in trouble, but still. Mildly violating.

Because of all this, I wasn't in the best frame of mind when I clocked in at Alto Market later that afternoon. I'd already deleted the CELEBRATE photo, and in honor of my craptastic day, I posted a new one of my name tag, to the bottom of which I'd added a sticker the backroom workers use for pallets of dented cans: DAMAGED GOODS. Ms. Lopez made me take it off the second I got on the floor, but at least I finally got to talk to someone about the rejection.

"Can't you try another medical college?" she suggested. Today's ladybugs dangled from earrings that peeked between strands of her shoulder-length hair when she moved. "After all, a body is a body on the inside, yes?"

"I suppose I could try."

"What about a veterinarian office?"

Dead cats. Ugh. I'm not squeamish, but drawing someone's deceased pet was miles different from a formaldehyde-preserved frog in a bag. "Veterinarians don't dissect for teaching, and they have to follow laws about disposal." I knew that because of Heath's job.

Ms. Lopez made a face. "What about your mother? Maybe you should just come clean and talk to her about it. If you explain how important it is, perhaps she'll change her mind and help you out."

"No way. She doesn't like to make waves at work, so she'd never pull any strings for me. And I really don't want her to. I want to do this on my own."

When I sighed, she patted me the shoulder. "You'll think of something."

We got a mad rush of customers in the early part of the evening, which helped get my mind off things. But sometime after eight, business slowed to a crawl. I decided to occupy myself with cleaning the magazine racks, so I pulled out stacks of *Food and Wine* and *Organic Spa*. Then I knelt on the floor and started cleaning.

"You missed a spot," a low voice said behind me.

My muscles turned to stone. I stood up and slowly turned around to face Jack, who towered a mere foot away from me. He smelled like fabric softener, and his retro-rockabilly hair curled over one eye. He was buttoned up in a short, fitted black peacoat, the wide collar pulled up a little in the back.

He was beautiful. I'd forgotten just how much. Not only that, he was flat-out *happy*. Glittering dark eyes. Chest rising and falling, as if he'd just sprinted uphill. Enormous grin splitting his face, with that single perfect dimple studding his cheek like a beauty mark.

And what? Now I was smiling right back? *Get control of yourself, Beatrix.*

My shoulders hit the magazine rack. Crap—I'd backed up into it? Maybe he hadn't noticed. "How did you find me?" I said in the calmest voice I could muster.

He pointed to my nametag. "Only two Alto Markets, and this one is on the N-Judah line."

"And you just happened to be in the area."

"Oh, no. I went well out of my way to find you." He knocked the toe of my shoe with the toe of his boot. "I believe your Damaged Goods photo said, 'Summation of my sucky day.' Why are you having a bad day?"

"Oh, I don't know. Maybe it's because a freaking cop showed up at my house last night to question me about the vandalizing inside the Legion of Honor."

"What? Are you joking?"

"Does it look like I'm joking?"

He glanced behind him—nothing but a rack of dehydrated vegetable snacks and Mozart raining down from the speaker above—and swiped a hand over his hair to push it out of his eyes. "Shit. Because of the photo you posted?"

"Mmm-hmm."

"What did you tell them?"

"That your name is Jack, you're seventeen, you're a Buddhist, and they should talk to Panhandler Will for your whereabouts. I also provided a sketch so they could identify you."

He stared at me blankly while his mouth made a little O shape.

I swung around and spritzed the empty magazine rack. "That's what I *should* have told Officer Dickwad. But I didn't."

"Jesus and Mary, it's hard to tell when you're joking."

Spritz. Spritz. Spritz. "The cop threatened me *and* my mom with jail. He's in charge of the vandalism department, and he thinks you're part of Discord."

"I swear to you on my life, Beatrix. I'm not."

Oh, don't think I didn't notice my name on his tongue. I shot him a look.

"Sorry. Miss Damaged Goods."

I grumbled to myself, sighed, and said, "Adams." If the police could track me, what was stopping a professional criminal like Jack?

"Adams," he repeated. "Beatrix Adams."

"Bex," I corrected, because apparently I'd temporarily lost my mind.

Two roselike spots bloomed over the apples of his cheeks. "Bex Adams," he said in a softer voice. "It's so strange that I don't know that already. I feel like I should."

I concentrated *superhard* on wiping away my spritzes.

"Vincent," he said, bracing one arm on the rack beside me.

That name sounded vaguely familiar to me, but I couldn't put my finger on why. "Jack Vincent?"

"Jackson Vincent, if you want to get technical. You know. In case you need to turn me in to Officer Dickwad or something," he joked.

"It's not funny."

"I'm really, really sorry. I just thought . . . damn." He picked at a peeling section on the magazine rack. "I found you right away on the anatomy art site. BioArtGirl. Your self-portrait is crazy good. All your work is incredible. Blows mine out of the water."

"I wouldn't know. All I've seen are some dripping letters done with a paint pen."

"I didn't deface the heart diagram," he argued. "I'm not an anarchist—I love art. And I especially wouldn't destroy something that meant that much to you."

Oh, he'd *definitely* read my post. I mean, obviously he had, but it was weird to have him acknowledging it right in front of me.

"I was trying to . . . I don't know. Get your attention, I suppose. Communicate."

"You could've sent a card."

He struggled not to smile. "I have problems sticking to the Middle Path."

I shook my head, not knowing what he was going on about.

"It's a Zen thing. We try to live in the middle, somewhere between self-denial and self-indulgence. No extremes."

"Wow. Major failure there."

"I told you I was a bad Buddhist."

I didn't say anything for a few moments. "You liked my stuff?"

"That X-ray figure study of the torso with the bones showing through?" He whistled. "Amazing."

Err . . . that was a self-portrait drawn in a mirror, but it only showed one of my breasts, and only one person outside my family had seen those up close and personal, so it wasn't like anyone would know. It was Serious Art, and sort of clinical, but I'd forgotten it was posted, and now I was feeling as if I'd accidently given Jack a *Girls Gone Wild* photo of me flashing my tits. But he wasn't acting weird about it, so I probably shouldn't feel weird about it either. I discreetly wiped sweat off my brow.

"I seriously don't know anyone with that much talent," he continued while I was quietly freaking out. "Now I get why you want to draw the dissections."

"Well, that's not happening."

"Why?"

"Because the head of the anatomy department said I couldn't draw in the lab. No reason. Probably because she didn't want a high school kid running around underfoot. Or maybe because I'm not pumping thousands of dollars of tuition into her school."

"Oh, man. That sucks. Is there anything you can do to change their mind?"

"Probably not. All I know is that the art show I'm entering is a competition for scientific art, and most of the participating students will likely be engineering and chemistry and microbiology geeks, and ninety percent of them will be guys, and if I don't enter something with precision and detail that will blow the judges away, I'll end up losing to a piece of shit Photoshop manipulation of some crappy fractal pattern."

"Guess I see now why you're having a bad day."

"Don't underestimate your part in it," I said drily before pasting on a half-hearted smile for the customer who was ready to check out. Leaving Jack at the magazine rack, I headed to my register and quickly scanned a woman's two-tiered mini cart of organic groceries and imported cheese.

When I was finished, he stepped up to the counter. "I'm *really* sorry."

"You said that already."

"But I still mean it," he said with a hopeful, wide-eyed look.

Those dark eyelashes should be illegal. Sometimes Heath wore eyeliner when he went out, and Jack's lashes were nearly as dramatic. He blinked, and it hit me what was so striking about them.

"Distichiasis."

"Huh?"

"Your eyelashes. A genetic mutation that causes double rows of lashes."

"Oh. Yeah." A hesitant smile lifted his lips. "My mom used to say I had Elizabeth Taylor eyes, but I prefer to think of it as an X-Men mutation. You know, more badass."

I was a sucker for medical oddities. So unfair that his was exotic and alluring. *Do not look at his eyes.* To be honest, I couldn't look at *any* part of him and stay mad, so I deserted him at the counter and went back to the magazines, picking a stack off the floor to set it back in its cubby. He didn't get the hint.

"It was Dr. Sheridan who turned you down at Parnassus?" He picked up another pile and put it in the wrong place.

"Yes," I said, moving the stack down to the second row.

He got out his phone and typed. "I'll fix it."

"Fix what?"

"Just give me a couple of days. I'll get you into the anatomy lab."

"Excuse me? And just how do you propose to do that?"

"I have ways. Don't ask."

"Oh, no. I'm asking."

"Just trust me."

I laughed. "Why in the world would I do that? I'm probably flagged as some kind of potential criminal in the SFPD database, and now my mom suspects I've crossed into Troubled Teen territory. Don't pull me into your drama. I don't need your help."

"Beatrix?" a voice called from behind me.

I spun around to see Ms. Lopez's head peeking out from one of the aisles. "Is everything okay?"

"Yes, fine."

She eyed Jack with suspicion. "Five minutes until register cash-out."

I gave her a thumbs-up before rushing to straighten the magazines. "Please don't get me in trouble with my boss," I whispered hotly to Jack.

He made a frustrated sound. "What's your number? Let me fix this for you."

"Are you kidding? The police are probably monitoring my phone."

"That's ridiculous."

"You're ridiculous," I mumbled.

"Adorably ridiculous?"

"Criminally ridiculous."

"I'll take it." He smiled and stuck a finger out to playfully poke the knot of my tie. He had large boy hands, all sinewy and latticed with faint blue veins, and long, slender fingers. More beautiful bones. I desperately wanted to trace my fingers over them—which was insane. And stupid.

"Please don't stand so close," I murmured.

"I can't help it. I'm strangely turned on by the tie and those Sacagawea braids."

My checks caught fire. Was he making fun of me? And why hadn't he moved?

"Beatrix?" Ms. Lopez called out again.

"Just a moment," I shouted back. "I can't talk anymore," I told Jack, stepping away with a nervous twist in my stomach. "You need to go."

"Digits?" he said, holding up his phone.

"Absolutely not."

"Email address?"

"Yeah, it's Bex at why-won't-you-leave-me-alone dot com."

"I'll message you online, then."

I shrugged as nonchalantly as I could. "It's a free country."

"You're a mean one, Mr. Grinch," he said, backing up toward the doors. They opened with a *whoosh*. He pulled up his collar. "I'll fix it for you. Hand on my heart, Bex Adams, I will fix it."

8

I STARED AT MY PHONE, WHICH WAS PROPPED ON the pencil ledge of my drafting table. Any second now, it would morph into a rabbit and I'd know I'd been dreaming. But, no, it remained a phone, and if I needed further proof I was experiencing reality, I got it from the rapid-fire drumbeats of Heath's metal blasting through the floorboards; he didn't work at the vet's office on Mondays.

The impossible phone call I'd just received was from Dr. Sheridan's assistant Henry. He said the director had "reconsidered" my "query," and could I come in tomorrow night at six? I was assigned to Simon Gan, a physical therapy student who was earning independent research credits with three other grad students who met on Tuesdays and Thursdays from 6:00 to 8:00 p.m. in the otherwise empty lab. I could draw under his supervision unless my presence detracted from their research.

"I promise it will not," I'd told Henry before he thanked me and hung up.

But now that the reality of what was—really!—happening settled in, my brain scrambled to see how this would fit in with Mom's changing shifts and my work schedule. On top of all that, an unavoidable question loomed in my thoughts:

How had Jack done this?

Because, clearly, he'd done something. But what? Threatened to spray-paint four-letter words on the anatomy lab?

I won't lie: The second he left Alto Market, I was on my phone, vetting him. I found his name in the usual places, but his profiles were set to private. I also unearthed a handful of comments made by one Jack Vincent of San Francisco on a couple of comic-book forums and a music venue on Potrero Hill that hosted some indie bands I'd never heard of. But the weirdest thing I found was his full name in a school picture from last year. The thumbnail was too small to see much, but "Jackson Vincent" was standing with a bunch of other kids. The reason I couldn't pull up a bigger photo was because you had to be registered on the site to see it, and the site was a private high school in the Haight. A *really* expensive private school—like, one that costs more than forty thousand dollars a year to attend.

Who the hell are you, Jack?

I supposed it was possible that he didn't actually go there and had just participated in some kind of activity the school sponsored; I'd had artwork displayed at other schools in regional competitions.

Either way, it didn't explain how he'd changed my luck at the anatomy lab.

My mind jumped back to the reason Panhandler Will knew Jack—the so-called "lady friend" working at the hospital. Jack had admitted to visiting someone there and implied that they weren't dating. Or had he? He sort of skated around that, and I hadn't had a chance to call him out on it. But if he had a girlfriend, why was he showing up at my workplace and risking his neck to spray-paint irresponsible romantic gestures for me?

He and his "lady friend" could've broken up. Or maybe they were just good friends. But unless she volunteered there, she had to be older. He *had* said he liked older girls. Crap. Was he some young doctor's boy toy? Was he diddling busty nurses in empty patient rooms? Mom said strange things happened during the graveyard shift; she once walked into a male doctor/male doctor/female nurse threesome a few years back. They were doing it right there on a hospital bed—one that a patient had died on earlier that night.

Super. Now my head was swimming with that image and Jack's face, and all of it overlapped with one of Heath's illegally downloaded gay hospital porn scenes—one that I'd *accidentally* stumbled upon when I used his laptop to look up a pizza delivery phone number. And sure, maybe I watched the whole thing, but it was only for the anatomy. (Sort of. Who could look away from all that dark furry hair? Apparently, the "doctor" just couldn't help himself, either.)

Thanks to Heath's music, I almost didn't hear the doorbell ring. I tiptoed to the front door and peered through the peephole, praying it wasn't Officer Dixon. It wasn't.

After flipping open the lock, I was staring at an out-of-breath guy in black spandex pants and a bike helmet. "Beatrix Van Ass?"

"Van Asch," I corrected. "It's Dutch." And why in the world was he using my old last name? I'd legally been Adams for two years. Now I remembered why I didn't miss it.

"Delivery," he said, pulling a brown-paper-wrapped box out of a backpack strapped diagonally across his chest. "And I'll need your signature."

"Did you come by two days ago?"

"Yep. But hey, not my fault you weren't here. That's stated on the online form."

Don't think he realized I couldn't have cared less. "What is it?"

"No idea." He handed me a digital board to sign.

"Who sent it?"

He twisted his head around to read the board. "Uh, blank. That means the client wants to remain anonymous."

"What if it's a bomb or something?"

"It would've gone off already. Can you please sign?" he said irritably. "I've got other deliveries."

I signed and exchanged the board for the brown box. He stuck around like he was waiting for a tip. I quietly backed up and shut the door in his face.

The box was about the size and shape of a loaf of bread. My name and address were printed on a small label, along with some other stickers from the bike service. I put my ear to the box and listened. No ticking. I shook it. Nothing rattled. So I sat down on the couch and unwrapped it.

Inside the paper was a plain corrugated box, and inside that, bubble wrap. I unrolled it, and a wooden object fell into my hand.

It was an articulated artist's mannequin—you know, the poseable kind, standing on a base. Except this one didn't have a smooth, blank spool for a head and flat disks for hands and feet. It was intricately carved with all the major muscles and tendons. Parts of the body were stained darker than others, and the eyes were painted glass.

It was extraordinary.

A small tag hung from a string tied to the leg. It read: CUSTOM MADE FOR YOU. HAND-CARVED AND DESIGNED IN-HOUSE. TELEGRAPH WOOD STUDIO. BERKELEY, CALIFORNIA.

"Whatcha got?" Heath hung over the back of the sofa. "Whoa. Who sent this?"

"I have no idea. But get this—" I told him all about Mom's weird phone call that night as he inspected the mannequin. "It was sent by a local messenger, but look at the tag. It was made in Berkeley."

"Oh, Bex."

"What?" When Heath didn't answer right away, I panicked. "What? Tell me!"

"Dad just moved to Berkeley a couple of months ago."

That couldn't be right. "He's somewhere in LA—Santa Monica."

"What did the address label say?"

My heart thumped as I showed him the crumpled paper. "No return address. Just Beatrix Van Asch. This is what the bike messenger note on the door was all about."

Heath sighed, sat on the sofa arm, and slid down into the cushion next to me. "I saw an envelope in the kitchen trash when I was I tying it up. It had Dad's name and Berkeley on the return address, so I dug through the garbage—"

"Gross."

"—until I found a card. One of those 'We've Moved!' deals. Dad was informing Mom that he and Suzi had moved to Berkeley."

"Are you kidding? Why didn't you tell me?"

"If Mom didn't tell us, I figured she didn't want us to know. And big deal. So he's closer now, who cares?"

"And sending me extravagant gifts? Is this to make up for not paying child support? What the hell?"

"I don't know, Bex. But the bike messenger note on the door was left on your birthday, so I guess he remembered. Damn sure didn't remember mine."

We both sat there staring at the mannequin for a long moment before I shoved it back into the box. "If that was the person Mom was talking to on the phone, she said she'd throw away anything he sent."

"All I know is, if you're planning to keep it, you better hide it."

"Don't tell her," I warned. "I mean it. *Do not tell Mom.*"

He mimed zipping his lips.

I unzipped them and gave him a quick thank-you peck. Part of me wanted to tell him about Jack, but if I really was the only one who knew Jack's secret, it felt like a betrayal to share it—even with Heath. So instead, I said, "Guess who just won a golden ticket to Wonka's Cadaver Dissection Lab?"

IF YOU MAKE THE DECISION TO WILL YOUR BODY TO the university, you get two funerals: one when you die, and then a second after you've been dissected and used for research, when you're cremated and given a small ceremony by the students. This is what Simon Gan told me after he handed me a clip-on visitor's pass and provided a brief tour of the need-to-know areas of the anatomy lab and classrooms, which were clustered on the top floors of the same campus building where I'd originally met with Dr. Sheridan.

Lean and handsome, Simon had a quiet, smart-guy vibe. He was a local grad student from the Inner Richmond district, which is basically the real Chinatown—not the Grant Avenue Chinatown for tourists. He was kinder to me than he had to be, which took off some of the nervous edge. I wanted to ask him if he knew why Dr. Sheridan had changed her mind, but he was in a rush to get me settled and move on to his own work, so I just listened.

The actual lab with the bodies—the Operating Room, as Simon affectionately referred to it—was on the top floor, and it looked like a long, airy medical bay on a spaceship. Everything was white and gray, with vibrant submarine-yellow doors. Cameras snaked from the ceiling alongside bright lights on long, curved necks, and big LCD screens hung next to wipe boards and rolling medical monitors. Six life-size teaching skeletons—just like my own Lester, only these weren't missing their arms—stood sentry along the walls.

But the stars of the show were the bodies, which reclined on rolling gray metal tables, all of them covered by white plastic sheets. Just vague shapes. The effect was so sterile and cool there might've been anything under there—bricks, clothes, CPR dummies. But the faint odor of formaldehyde told me otherwise. Some of the bodies remained in the lab for an entire year—kind of crazy. But there was a state-of-the-art ventilation system, and the unpreserved bodies were kept in a refrigerated room nearby.

Simon briefly introduced me to his study group, who, like him, were all wearing blue hospital scrubs. I felt like a sore thumb in jeans and my glow-in-the-dark Mütter Museum T-shirt—that's the museum in Philadelphia that has all the preserved anatomical specimens, medical anomalies, and antique medical equipment—but Simon didn't seem to notice.

"We'll be working at the north end of the room," he said as he walked me to the other end of the lab. "So I thought maybe you could draw on the south end." He stopped in front of a white sheet in the last row of tables and pointed to one of several metal stands, the kind used to hold sheet music. "You can adjust this and use it for drawing on, if you need to. And here's a stool. The mirror can be angled, if you need to get a magnified view from above."

"Great."

"We're protective of our bodies—we get assigned one to study for months at a time. The one I picked out for you is assigned to my roommate, and I got his permission for you to use her. I opened everything up for you, and I'll take care of it when you leave." I had no idea what that meant, but I nodded. "With this in mind, I just ask you to be respectful and not touch or move anything on or near the body."

"Of course."

"Well, then. This"—he pulled back the sheet—"is Minnie."

I'd seen a lot of preserved specimens and even owned a few in small jars, but I'd never actually seen a dead human body.

It was more unsettling than I'd expected.

Minnie was stiff and nude, a white woman with brown hair, who, Simon informed me, was nineteen when she died. Her skin was thick, her face mottled and wrinkled like a pickled egg. Her torso was split down the center, skin and muscles splayed, ribs removed, heart visible. And her inner arm was sliced from wrist to elbow, buttery, fat-covered skin spread like angel wings around the muscles and veins.

I thought the dissected areas would be red and vibrant, but her insides looked more like ash-pale rotten meat, glistening under the surgical light.

"Mark sprayed her down before he left. They tend to dry out if they're exposed to air for too long, but you should be okay for a couple of hours. The chemical smell takes some getting used to. Sometimes it helps to take a break. Bathroom and soda machine is just outside those doors to the left. No food or drink inside here, obviously."

Was he freaking kidding? Who could eat in front of this?

"You okay?"

"Yeah," I said, playing it cool. "Thanks."

"Shout if you need anything. Whenever you're ready to leave, just give me a heads-up so I can wrap Minnie back up for the night."

He patted me on the shoulder before striding away toward his group, who were watching some surgery video on one of the monitors and comparing what they saw on-screen to the body in front of them.

I stared down at Minnie's gaping wounds, trying not to breathe.

This was no frog.

My mind tried to make sense of what lay in front of me. Why had she died? An accident? Disease? For all I knew, she had a happy life before this. Maybe she was someone's girlfriend. She might've been a star college student. Maybe she was a talented singer. Or an artist, like me.

And now she rested here, exposed. Enduring an immeasurable kind of humiliation, with her breasts cut away and her bushy pubic hair and her heavy thighs on display for everyone to judge. Just a body for students to cut up for practice. To be scrutinized. Studied.

Drawn.

It felt . . . *wrong*. Simon said he got his roommate's permission to "use" Minnie, like she was a possession. Did she know it was going to be like this when she signed herself over to the Willed Body Program? Did she figure she'd be doing her part to maybe one day save others' lives by helping to educate these future doctors? That one of the researchers here might run tests on her liver and discover a medical breakthrough?

And I wondered how I fit into this. Whether I was doing her more harm than good by being there. Or maybe it didn't even matter.

If it didn't, I wasn't sure why I was so upset.

But there I was, the girl obsessed with anatomy, on the verge of sobbing over the corpse of a woman I never knew.

If this was what I wanted to do with my life, this medical illustration, then I'd better get used to it. Because I'd have to take anatomy classes in grad school—maybe even in a lab similar to this one.

I did my best to disconnect and turn off my emotions, and then spent as long as I could setting up my drawing pad on the music stand, twisting and pinning up the braids at the back of my neck. And when it came time to sketch, I decided to stick to her dissected arm; it was easier than peering inside the hole in her chest.

The students at the other end of the room talked in the background, calling out Latin words, naming muscles. I hummed a stanza from one of the classical pieces that played on a loop in Alto Market, repeating it again and again as my pencil moved over the paper. I sketched loosely, then tightened my lines. Measured. Erased. Redrew.

I treated it like a punishment. Something to survive. And I did: no breaks, no running in the hall for clean air, no whining. If Minnie could endure my inspection, I could do my best work as quickly as possible.

When eight o'clock came, I closed my sketchpad and packed it up inside an oversize red bag. I set everything back where it was, and I waved to Simon, signaling him that I was leaving. He raised his arm, holding up a scalpel in one glistening rubber glove. I absolutely *could not* be anywhere near him.

So I rushed out the rear door.

The restroom was filled with chatty grad students, who were filing in from a another classroom down the hall. I quickly washed my hands, ignoring the numbness in my fingers and the growing buzzing in my ears, and I left.

By the time the elevator *ding*ed on the first floor, I was gasping for breath. Someone asked me if I was okay. I just put one foot in front the other and ran through the front door, into the approaching twilight that was trying to outrace the evening fog rolling in off the Bay.

My lungs were going to explode. They were going to burst inside my chest, and then I'd end up on one of those rolling stainless-steel tables, just like Minnie. And someone could dissect me and study my rotting tissue while they made plans to meet other students for crepes in Cole Valley after class.

I lunged off the sidewalk and barely made it to the safety of the building's shrubbery before I vomited.

My red bag slipped to my wrist as I braced one hand on the brick, head lolling, mind flipping through all the images of Minnie I'd been holding at a distance. They circled and penned me. Fell on me like football players piling up after a tackle.

Racing footfalls slapped against cement as someone approached, and before I could gather the strength to look up, a familiar voice lured me back to the present.

9

JACK PULLED ME AWAY FROM MY PILE OF MORTIFICATION and into the lengthening shadow of a nearby tree.

"Sit," he instructed, taking my red bag as my shoulders slid down the bark.

Pinpricks radiated through my hands and feet, and my head was still buzzing. He asked me a question, but I couldn't concentrate on the words. Was I crying, or were my eyes watering from throwing up? I wasn't sure.

The next thing I knew, Jack was squatting next to me and giving me instructions. "Slow breath in through your nose, long breath out of your mouth." He repeated it several times until I finally got the hang of it. "That's it. Keep it up."

Slowly, *slowly*, the buzzing finally stopped. The world inflated back to normal size, and right in the center of it blinked Jack's big brown eyes.

"You with me?" he asked in a voice edged with concern.

I nodded and wiped my face on my coat sleeve. My mouth. So gross.

He uncapped a half-filled plastic bottle of water he'd been

holding. "I don't have any exotic diseases, promise. Swish and spit, preferably over there."

I leaned as far away as I could and rinsed my mouth. A couple of students striding down the sidewalk gave me the stink eye. Great. Hope they weren't with Simon's group.

I rested awhile, eyes trained on the grass in front of me, until my stomach stopped cramping and I felt somewhat normal. He stared at me the entire time, but he didn't say anything. I was sort of thankful for that.

I finally gulped down more water and held up the bottle. "Guess this is mine now." My voice sounded scratchy. Throat hurt, too.

He shifted out of his squat and sat back in the grass, balancing his elbows on his bent knees, and handed me the cap.

"Thanks. Where'd you learn that breathing trick?"

"Years of meditation. Works, right?"

It really did. I tried a few more repetitions, just to be safe. "Why are you here?"

"If you keep posting vague hints about where you are, I'm going to look for you."

"Is that a threat?"

"Yes."

I pretended to be annoyed, but truth be told, I wanted him to find me.

Jack crossed his arms over his knees. He was wearing faded olive-drab jeans and the vintage black leather jacket. Just under the jacket's sleeve, carved wooden beads encircled his right wrist, along with a crisscrossed stack of braided-leather bracelets and cords. "You want to share what brought all this on?" he asked.

"Bad shellfish."

He squinted his disbelief. "Must've been really bad to make you cry like that."

"What do you want me to say? I'm a big coward, okay?" I sagged against the tree and sighed. "I'd never seen a dead body before. Not a human one, anyway. Unless you count mummies in the de Young Museum."

"Not the same."

I appreciated the reassurance, but the whole thing was humiliating. "Go on—tell me how I made fun of you for being squeamish about dissecting a fetal pig, and now here I am, falling apart."

"Are you kidding? My eighth-grade teacher died when I was fourteen—that was the first dead body I saw. I bawled my eyes out in front of the entire funeral home when I saw her in the coffin. Then I did exactly what you did in the bushes back there, only I did it all over one of the standing floral displays. All my classmates were there, and my ball-less display of emotion spread around school like wildfire. Took me a year to live that down."

"I think you're exaggerating to make me feel better."

"I'm not, but is it working?"

I took another swig of water. "Besides, it's different. This is what I thought I wanted to do with my life. And I can't illustrate how the lungs function if I can't even *look* at lungs. It's not like I can draw from other people's illustrations."

"Why not?"

"Do you think Albrecht Dürer copied other artists' work? No. And if I want to be great, I need to be able to draw directly from the source."

He didn't respond, but I was too frustrated with myself to elaborate any further. Besides, he was an artist, right? He had to understand. So why did he look so damn grave? Or maybe it was disappointment. Not sure what he had to be—

Oh.

"I'm such an idiot," I said. "I'm really sorry."

"Why?"

I gestured toward the anatomy lab. "Because you 'fixed' this for me. I don't know exactly what you did, but I'm thinking it couldn't have been easy."

He shrugged with one shoulder and waved it away with the flick of a wrist. "I'm more worried that everything I try to do for you turns to shit."

"It really does, doesn't it?" I was only joking, but he groaned, so I whapped him on the shin with the water bottle. "If you think a few tears and some upchucked pretzels are going to stop me from coming here twice a week, you don't know me."

He didn't smile, but his shoulders relaxed, and a few moments later he templed his fingers together, looking cheerfully devious. "Know what you need?"

"A stronger stomach?"

"Next best thing. Mint."

"Umm . . ."

He dug out his phone and tapped the screen a few times. "An inbound N train is ten blocks away. You feel okay to walk to the stop?"

"With you?"

"That was sort of the idea, yeah."

"How do I know you won't lead me into some creeptastic CSI situation?"

"Damn. There goes my plan to harvest your kidneys."

"Please, don't mention kidneys right now," I said, pressing the heel of my hand against my stomach.

He shuddered. "Now you're making *me* queasy. Look, it's a busy spot in the Castro. We only have to make one transfer. Fifteen minutes to get there, tops. Just text someone," he suggested. "Make sure someone knows where you are."

I thought for a moment. "Give me your wallet."

"Excuse me?"

I held out my hand. "If you want to take me somewhere, give me your wallet."

He didn't even hesitate, just dug it out of his back pocket and handed it over.

The black leather was warm and worn around the edges. "I thought you were vegetarian," I said as I cracked it open.

"A bad one, remember? Please don't dig around too much in there."

I wiggled out his driver's license. "Afraid I'll find condoms or your My Little Pony club card?"

"It's called a Brony card, *thankyouverymuch*. Oh, Jesus—don't look at the photo."

How could I not? It was ten times worse than the one on my state ID, and I wasn't sure, but he seemed to have a ton of acne, which made me feel a lot better about his stunning good looks now. "Let's see, Jackson Vincent *is* your real name, and not some fanfic

Fast and Furious character you made up—surprise, surprise. And your birthday is in December, so that makes me, what, five months older than you?"

"Told you I liked older women."

I held back a smile. "Five eleven? You seem taller." And closer. His cheek was only a few inches away from mine.

"Six one. I got the card a year and a half ago."

"Where's this address?"

"Ashbury Heights."

"Huh. Do you go to Urban Academy?"

"Checking up on me?" He puffed up, more than a little pleased about this.

"Well, do you?"

"Would that magically make me safer in your eyes?" he asked.

"Probably not."

"Good, because plenty of asshats go to that school, believe me."

"If your family's rich, I'm not impressed."

"That makes two of us. What are you doing?"

Mom thought I was working, and since she was just starting a twelve-hour shift a few buildings away, I figured I'd flown under the radar. But Heath expected me home. I snapped a photo of Jack's license with my phone and sent it to Heath with a text: Going out to the Castro. If I'm not home by midnight, this guy kidnapped me. Then I replaced the ID—seriously, was that the edge of a condom wrapper?—and stuck the wallet in my jacket pocket, along with my phone. "I'll give it back to you when you deliver me home with both kidneys intact."

If I hadn't been sitting down already, his grin would've knocked me flat on my ass. "Any more arguments? Because we need to leave if we're going to catch that train." He held out an upturned palm.

Most people who offer to help you stand just end up giving you a weak hand, but Jack tugged me off the ground with a surprising amount of force. This earned him a few extra points in my mind. I like people who follow through on promises.

10

TRUE TO HIS WORD, AFTER A TRAIN RIDE THROUGH Sunset Tunnel and a painless bus transfer, Jack led me across a street lined with parked cars to a corner shop nestled on the border between Castro and Mission. He was taking me to a tea lounge that served (wait for it) tea and small plates of food. It was one of those casual-swank places that probably charged an arm and a leg and attracted a weird mix of theatergoers and hipsters. Heath would love it; Mom would turn up her nose. And my heart was racing too fast to have an opinion.

Warm light glowed from soaring windows. It wasn't superbusy—probably because it was eight thirty on a weeknight. We left the chilly air and stepped inside a warm and steamy room that smelled intoxicating, all spicy and herbal and citrus. Despite the high ceiling, the lounge felt cozy and had a sort of eclectic Eastern exotic vibe, with lots of cinnamony orange paint, expensive wood, and bonsai trees.

In other words, it was everything the anatomy lab was not, and I couldn't have been more grateful.

A tea bar stretched along one wall, tables to the left, but instead of taking a seat, Jack asked for someone—a cheerful girl named Star, who looked to be a few years older than us. They hugged. When Jack introduced me as "my friend Beatrix," she shook my hand and winked.

"Can we get the table in the tatami alcove?" Jack pleaded. "It's empty."

"You're lucky it's late and I'm in a good mood. Come on."

Along the back wall, the table in question sat on a raised platform covered with a bamboo mat. It seated ten people on floor cushions—some kind of Japanese deal. A sheer gold curtain divided us from the rest of the room and provided the illusion of privacy, but we could still hear and see everyone.

"You feel like eating?" Jack asked.

"Not sure if I want to tempt fate." I really wasn't sure, and there were no menus anywhere in sight, but that didn't stop Jack. He ordered "Moorish tea service with extra dates" and an additional pot of some kind of Japanese-sounding tea. I set my red bag down and took off my jacket while he shrugged out of his. Beneath it, he wore a heathery plaid shirt with short sleeves rolled up several inches above his elbows. And if I'd thought his hands were beautiful, his arms were stunning. Nothing but muscle. Not beefy varsity football player mass, but lean and ropey. And covering that muscle was brightly colored ink that started right above his elbows and disappeared under his shirtsleeves.

The handful of tattoos I'd spotted on seniors in my school were boring or dumb—fake tribal crap and band logos. Or hand-me-down flash art they'd picked from grimy sheets in tattoo shops ten minutes before they got inked. But just below Jack's sleeves, a graceful vermilion fishtail swam in a sea of teal water on one arm, and a richly textured Japanese-style flower wrapped around the other. They looked like paintings come to life, vibrant and detailed and beautiful.

Do not stare. . . .

He was listening to Star call out a question about the order, so I gestured toward the door across the hall and darted inside the ladies' room to wash my hands and rinse my mouth out again. After wishing I'd brought along lip gloss, I took a deep breath and rejoined him. He was standing, waiting for me, and seemed to be relieved when I came back, like he expected me to bolt or something. Too late for that.

We sat cross-legged on the floor cushions and leaned back on pillows against the wall. For a few moments, it was awkward and silent. In my defense, I was out of my element, but I wasn't sure what his excuse was—or why he was wiping his hands on his jeans. He seemed too cocky to be nervous. But one of us had to say something, so I took the short straw.

"This is crazy," I said, looking out over the lounge through the gauzy curtain. "Sort of puts most coffeehouses to shame."

"Right? I love it here. The Zen Center has better matcha, but I'm there all the time, so it's not as special."

I had no idea what matcha was, but I'd heard of the Zen Center. "What do you do there? I mean, I'm guessing you don't sing hymns and listen to sermons."

He shook his head. "I usually go to a weekly zazen session—that's seated meditation."

"The breathing thing."

"Well, it's more than just that, but yes. And they offer a lot of classes, so sometimes I sign up for ones that interest me. Oh, and I volunteer at the City Center Bookstore a couple of days a week."

"Volunteer? As in no paycheck?"

He shrugged. "I don't mind. It was worse during school, because I had to work Saturday mornings. But for the summer, I'm only there a few hours in the afternoon on Wednesdays and Fridays. I usually work with my friend Andy. We're doing a graphic novel together. He's the artist. I write and do the lettering."

"Cool. You do it all by hand?"

"Mostly, though some of the captions I do digitally, but I design all the fonts."

Ooh. Now all the Golden Apple graffiti words made more sense. I guess he saw the realization on my face, because he gave me a sheepish smile.

"It's what I do," he said. "Just words. I'm good at layout and design, but unlike you, I'm total shit at drawing people."

He had an art thing. I had an art thing. I smiled, ridiculously happy about this.

"Did you design your tattoos?"

He ran his hand over the fish, pulling his sleeve up for a better view. The bright ink covered every inch of his biceps and stopped just above his shoulder. Half sleeves. Not a haphazard amalgamation of little tattoos inked one at a time, but an entire painting. "No. A local tattoo artist."

"It's stunning work." And had probably cost him a small fortune. Not to mention that he wasn't eighteen yet, so it wasn't exactly legal. "A koi?"

"Siamese fighting fish," he said with a shy smile. "That's a fancy name for a betta. I love fish. Oh, and that's a Buddhist prayer wheel turning the water. And here on the other arm is a lotus design."

He twisted to show me, and I leaned closer to smell him—I mean, to get a better look—okay, *and* to smell him, because *holy cow.* His scent and body and the pink lotus blooming in a spring-green spray of stalks were all . . . intoxicating.

"It's so beautiful," I murmured. I heard his breathing change and suddenly realized I'd been leaning over him a little too long. I awkwardly withdrew and felt my cheeks heating.

"I'm terrible at design," I said quickly, fumbling to focus on anything but how embarrassed I was. "And I'm not creative—I mean, not in a cool way. I used to paint, but color overwhelms me now. Maybe my tastes have changed over the last couple of years—I don't know. It's easier when I leave emotion out of it and just focus on line and shadow. I like things to be . . ." I used my hands to make a box shape on the table.

"Structured?"

"Yeah. I guess I'm a color-inside-the-lines girl. Worse, really—I'd rather shade inside the lines with a nice, light 4H pencil. Something dark like a 5B or 6B? That's me going nuts."

He laughed, stretching out his long legs beneath the squat table. When he did, his thigh bumped against my knee and then stayed there, sending a chain of warm chills through my nervous system that short-circuited my frontal lobe.

"Zen would tell me to embrace the middle pencil," he said.

"Ah, the HB pencil," I agreed, nodding.

"So boring, that HB."

"You're no HB. You're like ten Prismacolors all at once." Did I really just say that? Maybe if I just slid all the way under the table, no one would notice.

"You'd be surprised how tame I really am."

I seriously doubted that. He tugged on the small black cord that hung from one side of the bracelet I'd noticed earlier. "Is that a religious thing?"

"Mala beads," he said, offering me a closer look. The strand of irregular dark beads wound around his wrist three times. "Bodhi seeds. I use it to count a mantra. I twist each bead as I count, like this."

I ran my fingertips over the smooth surface of one strand, just for a moment; it seemed too personal to be pawed. "Like a rosary? To count penance or sins or whatever?"

"Sort of. Buddhists don't believe in sin—at least, not in a punished-by-an-angry-god way."

"So you can do whatever you want?"

"We follow a 'do no harm' moral code—basic stuff like don't kill, don't steal, don't criticize others."

"Don't destroy property?"

One side of his mouth twitched. "I haven't done anything that can't be cleaned up. I'm not knocking the heads off statues or setting fire to anything."

"But—"

"*But* I'm aware that what I've done affects others, and sometimes that might be in a negative way. And that's not cool. But I do my best to keep the harm to a minimum."

A couple of girls passed by our table on their way to the restroom, so I didn't push Jack about the vandalism, just in case we might be overheard. "How long have you been a Buddhist?"

"Two years. And before you ask, my family isn't religious. My mom's family is Episcopalian, so my parents make appearances at Grace Cathedral. But it's just for show. My dad sort of worships himself."

"My dad ran off with a strip-club owner a few years ago." I was surprised the words came out of my mouth, because I only talked about Dad with Heath, never with my friends, and never, *ever* with Mom.

"Yikes. Classy."

"Right? I have zero contact with him, so don't ask me to get you free passes," I joked. Of course, right after I said it, I realized that this wasn't exactly true anymore—the zero-contact thing. That carved artist's mannequin was currently stuffed in the bottom of my Ikea wardrobe under some shoeboxes. I hadn't decided what I was going to do about it yet.

"I'm sorry," Jack said in a low voice that made me feel self-conscious.

"About what? He's an ass, but our lives went on without him. Half of all marriages end in divorce. Everyone expects me to be crying over the fact that I don't have a father figure in my life, like I should be screwed up over it or something. But I never even really think about him."

I shrugged as Star and another server climbed the stairs to our platform carrying two pots of tea: one made of black ceramic, and the other glass. With those came a long tray overflowing with hummus and roasted eggplant and olives and plump dates filled with feta and garnished with flower blossoms—flowers!

"I'm suddenly starving," I murmured.

"I could eat all this by my lonesome, so we'd better get something else. Cheese or sweets?"

"Hmm, tough choice."

"Bring both," he told Star.

"Just so we're clear, I'm not paying for any of this, rich boy."

"That might be a problem since you have my wallet," he reminded me as he poured steaming cups of the most amazing-smelling mint tea I'd ever inhaled.

"In that case, drinks are on me."

Everything tasted amazing, even the tea. And the flowers were edible. They tasted like nothing, but still. As we stuffed ourselves with finger food, I stretched out my legs beneath the table alongside Jack's. It took only two bites of a honey-drizzled date stuffed with feta for me to end up pressed against him from hip to ankle. He was warm and thrillingly solid, and maybe it was because I was small and he was tall, or maybe it was the fact that I had his wallet in my pocket, but I couldn't remember ever feeling so . . . well, *safe* was the wrong word, because I was still nervous around him. I don't know. Maybe I was content—who knows? Could've just been that I was relieved to have some food in my stomach after what had happened at the anatomy lab.

We laughed at each other's stupid jokes and discovered we had a few things in common: We were both born in the city; we both had been to Alcatraz on school field trips and hated it; and at

Amoeba Music, we liked browsing the movies and retro rock posters more than the actual music.

Once I was sure no one was listening to our conversation, I said in a low voice, "Since I'm the only one knows your secret identity, I think I need to know why."

"Why I haven't told anyone else?" he asked.

"Why you're doing it."

His brows lowered, and for a moment his eyes were shadowed so deeply by his dark lashes that they disappeared, and he was a faceless ghoul with empty, dark sockets. Then he turned his head and pretended to smile. "It's not important."

"Just something you do for kicks?"

"No, not that."

"Daddy issues?"

Jack snorted. "If he ever finds out, I'll have some issues, all right, because he'll disown me." His upswept hair was wilting in the steam rising from our teacups. He pushed a lock of it out of his eyes. "My dad lives for work. Family comes—well, not even second. My mom's pretty high up there, but I'm probably tenth. And if I ever publicly embarrassed him, he'd send me away somewhere before I could open my mouth to apologize. Military school or Russia, probably. Not even kidding."

"To be fair, the stuff you're doing would probably land you in jail, so you wouldn't have to worry about being sent away."

"Good point. If I get busted, will you smuggle a sharpened HB inside a cake for me?"

"Maybe if you'd stop vandalizing, you wouldn't have to shiv your way out of San Quentin with a pencil."

He rubbed his cheek against his shoulder, and his face came close enough to mine that I could smell his lemony hair wax and the mint of the tea on his breath. I barely heard his whispered reply beneath the sound of footsteps racing toward our table.

"I can't."

Before I could ask him why, the table exploded.

11

PLATES AND DISHES SLID, HUMMUS SPLATTERED, AND Jack's pot of Japanese green tea tipped over and splashed across my face and his shirt. It wasn't hot anymore, but that didn't stop me from crying out in shock as if I'd been scalded. With soccer-mom swiftness, Jack's arm shot out in front of me like a shield, but the damage was already done.

"Oh, God! I'm so sorry!"

I wiped tea off my face and looked up to see a girl squatting beside me to help straighten the table. She was thin and small, but not as short as me, and she had asymmetrically cut hair that was black on the short side and streaked with purple and pink on the fringed, longer side.

"My toe caught on the reed mat," she explained in a tiny, high voice that didn't match her wild hair. "I'm such a klutz."

"It's okay," Jack said in strained voice, using his shielding arm to push our plates back from the edge of the table before they dumped in our laps.

"My cousin Trevor lives on the next block—you know, the one in college? Anyway, I saw your hair through the window when I was walking past. I couldn't believe it was you, but it was and—excuse me."

She leaned over me to hug Jack's neck.

"Uh, Beatrix," he said, clearing his throat. "This is my friend Sierra."

"Hi there," she said to me, putting her hand on my shoulder to steady herself as she sat back on her heels. Was she drunk or something? She smelled funny. "He's being modest. We're more than friends." She bit her bottom lip and grinned at Jack.

A positively horrified look crossed his face. He moved his mouth as if he were going to say something but couldn't force the words out.

"Hey, it's cool," she said. "We're not together or anything. Jackson doesn't do the couple thing, as I'm sure you know. Do you go to his school or something?"

"No."

Someone tapped on the window. A silhouette of a man.

"Shoot, I've got to go. Hey, you guys wanna come hang with us? We're going to a party in Rincon Hill."

"No, thanks," Jack said testily.

She shrugged and stood. "Give me a ring sometime. Maybe you and Andy and I can hang at his mom's place. God! I almost tripped again—you guys need to do something about this mat," she said to the waitress who had rushed up the stairs with kitchen towels to clean our table. "See ya, Jackson!"

WE HELPED STAR CLEAN UP THE TABLE. JACK APOLOgized to her and later to me on the way back to the Inner Sunset.

Our connecting bus was crazy full, and we had to stand. But once we'd gotten a seat together on the N train, we talked a little.

"Thanks for being cool about Sierra," he said quietly.

"One freak-out a day is my limit, and I'd already used it up at the anatomy lab."

"Oh, good."

"But while we're on the subject, are you and Sierra . . . ?"

He looked me in the eyes and said very seriously, "Absolutely not. Sierra and I are just friends. That's all we ever really were. Well . . ." He shook his head and glanced out the darkened window. "It's complicated. Or it was. But now it's simple, and we're friends."

"Okay."

"Okay?" he repeated, brows drawn together.

I pulled a wet tea leaf out of his hair and smiled weakly. "Okay."

After I returned his wallet, we exchanged phone numbers and email addresses and work schedules. I thanked him for not making fun of me outside the anatomy lab. He thanked me again for not freaking out about getting splashed with tea. When we got to my stop, I wouldn't let him walk me home. I can take care of myself, first of all. And second, no one had ever walked me home. Not even Howard Hooper. (And that's not some veiled reference to sex, because Howard and I had plenty of that—well, maybe not *plenty*, exactly, but *some*. And anyway, it was 100 percent in his car . . . and 100 percent disappointing.)

Besides all this, I wasn't sure I wanted to chance running into my mom on another unplanned shift break at home, mainly because I'd have to lie when I explained that, no, Jack had nothing to do with graffiti in the museum, and gee, I'm not sure why I failed to mention that I'd met him on the Owl bus in the middle of the night when I was sneaking off to do something *I was specifically warned not to do.*

I don't like disappointing her, so I disappointed Jack instead. Not that I was conceited enough to assume he'd planned to throw me down on my front steps and kiss me like there was no tomorrow. But it was pretty obvious that I'd hurt his feelings when I wouldn't let him walk me the measly block and a half from the Muni stop.

"It's not because I don't trust you," I told him before I left, but I don't think he believed me. And that made me feel kind of rotten, especially when I turned around at the bottom of the street and saw his silhouette standing below the fog at the stop, watching me. I waved, but he didn't wave back, and my rotten feeling slipped into a general all-purpose melancholy.

When I made it back home, I discovered that Heath was out with Noah. Good thing I didn't need him to utilize Jack's driver's license, because not only would it be hours before he even noticed I was gone, but the photo I texted him was so out of focus, I couldn't read half the information on it. Still, I remembered Jack's street name and searched for it online. It was on the western side of Buena Vista Park, and the houses there ranged in price from five hundred thousand to several million.

I wondered which one was his.

We used to live in a nicer place in Cole Valley, back before my dad took off. He was VP of academic affairs at the university hospital. That's how my parents met. So, yeah, he made a crap-ton of money and couldn't be bothered to pay child support. Heath and I pushed Mom to take him to court, but she went ballistic and screamed at us about how she didn't need a handout from a cheater and a liar. Hey. No need to tell us twice. We never brought it up again, not even on the occasions when both Heath and I had to pitch in our own money to pay an extra-high electricity bill, or whatever. It wasn't often—maybe a couple of times a year. And the three of us are all living here together, using the electricity, united in our stance against taking handouts from liars and cheats. So I didn't complain.

I just wasn't quite ready to look at Minnie again, so after stashing my sketchpad, I stripped out of my clothes and dug out the artist's mannequin. Dad might or might not be a bigwig VP anymore, but this thing wasn't cheap. I turned it over in my hands and thought of everything Heath had told me about the card he found in the trash. Heath couldn't remember the Berkeley address, but it was surreal to think that after not seeing my dad for years, he might be an hour away, just across the Bay.

I flipped over the hanging tag. Telegraph Wood Studio. A quick Internet search pulled up the contact information, including an email address for inquiries. I doubted artist mannequins sold like hotcakes, and surely whoever carved it would remember the name of the client. The studio might even have an address on file. What harm could it do to ask?

Before I lost my nerve, I sent a quick email.

There. Either Dad had sent it, or he hadn't. And if he had? Well, I'd cross that bridge later.

IT WAS PAST MIDNIGHT WHEN I CLIMBED INTO BED, mulling over everything that had happened that day. My session in the anatomy lab. The aftermath. The calm and patient way Jack had coached me to breathe. How warm his leg had felt pressed next to mine . . .

My phone buzzed with an incoming text message. Jack. Already? I halfway expected him to follow the usual pattern—that is, I wouldn't hear back from him for days.

Msg from Jack Vincent, received 12:33AM: *taps mic* Is this thing on?

Me: Maybe.

Jack: Just wanted to make sure you got home okay.

Me: Safe and sound. You?

Jack: Safe but not sound. Still sorry about earlier.

Me: If you apologize again, I'm going to have to shiv you with a pencil.

Jack: Yes, ma'am. Hey, Bex?

Me: Yeah?

Jack: Despite the vomit and face full of tea, was still the best night I've had in a long, long time.

I pressed a grin into my pillow before typing an answer:

Me: I'll be back at the anatomy lab on Thurs. Bring bottled water?

Jack: Okay, but this time I get to keep YOUR wallet.

Me: Deal. Good night, Jack.

Jack: Good night, Bex.

HE DIDN'T TEXT ME AGAIN THAT NIGHT, OR ON WEDNESday. By the time Thursday afternoon rolled around, my brain was once again conjuring crazy reasons why. Like, maybe when he said he couldn't stop doing the Golden Apple graffiti, it was because he was being forced by the notorious local Westmob gang to spray-paint inspirational words around the city to antagonize their rivals, Big Block.

Or maybe that Sierra chick really *was* the girl he was visiting in the hospital. And even though *he* said they were "just" friends, now I couldn't stop thinking about her "more than" correction and what exactly that might mean. I had a vivid imagination, and the more vivid it got, the more jealous I became.

On the train ride to the anatomy lab, I texted him the building number and the time of my drawing session. But he didn't respond. Not then, and not after I got off the train and headed along the same pathway we'd walked two nights earlier. But halfway down the path, I spotted his lithe frame striding down a sidewalk that crossed mine.

"Jack," I called out to his back. When he didn't stop, I jogged closer and called him again.

He turned his head in both directions. He looked dazed.

"Hey," I said, stopping in front of him. "I texted you a little while ago."

"Bex." His voice was shot to hell and back. Crap, his eyes were red, too. Either he'd developed a very un-Buddhist-like drug habit or he'd been up all night. "My phone died yesterday, and I haven't been home to recharge it."

"What's the matter?"

He shook his head back and forth several times and scrubbed the crown of his head, mussing his hair worse than it already was.

That's when I noticed how wrinkled his clothes were, and that he had the faint shadow of unshaved whiskers darkening his jaw and chin.

"Jesus, Jack. What's going on?"

"It's going to be . . . I think the worst is . . . I don't know. I haven't slept, and I need a shower. I wanted to call you, but no one needs this level of heaviness in their life and—"

"Why don't you let me be the judge of that? Tell me what happened."

"I—"

A deep voice bellowed behind me. "Jackson."

I swung around to see a middle-aged man in a slate overcoat approaching. He might've been handsome, but it was hard to be sure with the dark sunglasses and black baseball cap pulled low and tight. The only thing I knew for sure was that his clothes cost more than everything I had in my rickety wardrobe.

"The car's waiting," the man said, giving me the briefest of glances. Brief enough to let me know that I was inconsequential.

"Dad—"

"Now." He put a hand on Jack's shoulder and urged him along.

"Jack!" I said.

"I'll call you," he answered over his shoulder, giving me a pained look. A few seconds later, they were yards away, heading toward the drop-off area near the parking garage.

What in the world had happened?

12

SKETCHING MINNIE WAS A MILLION TIMES WORSE that night, partly because I knew what to expect, and partly because I was worried about Jack. But I didn't try to hero-up this time: I excused myself halfway through the drawing session to walk around and breathe, using the same in-and-out pattern Jack had shown me. It helped. I managed not to get sick all over the bushes again.

When I didn't hear back from Jack that night, I told myself that whatever he was going through, it was clearly serious. And if he really hadn't slept in that long, I hoped that's what he was doing.

The next day, I sent a text telling him to talk to me as soon as he could, no pressure. He texted back immediately:

Msg from Jack Vincent, Received 1:30PM: I'm not ignoring you. Promise.

Me: Are you okay?

Jack: Better. But I have to go back to the hospital in a few minutes.

Me: Is there anything I can do?

Jack: No. I just wish things were different. I'd like to say this is unusual, but it's just my screwed-up life.

Me: I'm here if you need to talk. But I can't help if you don't tell me what's going on.

Jack: I have to go now. I'll prob be out of commission for a while. Believe me, it's better this way.

I'M NOT SURE WHY I THOUGHT THAT MEANT HOURS, or even a day, but after a week passed, I couldn't take it anymore. It's not like I spent the entire time moping or anything. I dutifully sneaked off to my drawing sessions with Minnie. I worked four shifts at Alto Market. I checked my email to see if the wood-carving shop in Berkeley that made the artist's mannequin had responded. And I did my best not to worry about Jack.

Until ENDURE popped up.

Maiden Lane is this alley in Union Square. It used to be filled with sleazy brothels before the 1906 earthquake leveled it—which is sort of funny, because now it's a fancy-schmancy street filled with high-end boutiques and restaurants. It's also a pedestrian-only deal in the daytime. There are these gates that close to block off traffic until 5:00 p.m., when they open up to allow cars through at night.

However, *somebody* closed the gates late last night after the shops closed, and while the street was blocked off, that somebody painted the word ENDURE in fifteen-foot-tall gold letters down the middle of Maiden Lane. The letters were designed to look like an old-timey Western saloon sign.

My heart squeezed when I saw the word glittering across our TV screen on the morning news. A reporter interviewed the owner of a café whose tables were set up around the gigantic *E*. Using it as a chance to advertise, he said he "rather liked" the graffiti and encouraged the public to come check it out in person and buy a latte.

ENDURE. Did it mean anything? Was he expressing something about whatever he was going through? Was it a sign that he was ready to communicate again?

Later that afternoon, while Mom was taking a shower and getting ready for her shift, I heard footsteps bounding down the basement stairwell, and I made the instant decision to get some unbiased advice. So I tugged on fluffy socks and headed downstairs to Laundry Lair.

A door to the right led to the garage. The one on the left led to Heath, and it was closing as I called out, "Hey!"

Heath's head popped around the doorframe. "Yo."

"How was work?"

"Umm, fine. What's wrong?"

"Nothing."

"Okay, then why are you asking about my day like some 1950s housewife?"

"I need your advice about something before Mom gets out of the shower."

He held the door open and waved me inside. "That'll be in thirty seconds, so you'd better talk fast."

I strolled into the room as he closed the door behind us. Huh. Laundry Lair was . . . surprisingly clean. His single bed was pushed up against a wall, and it was unmade, sure. But normally the floor was covered with clothes (which was ironic, since the washing machine and dryer were *literally* four steps away from his bed), and his curtained-off clothes rack was filled with empty hangers. Today, however, everything was put away, and the stuffed chair in the corner wasn't piled with books and video-game cases. I curled up on it while he changed shirts.

"What happened to the brimstone wall?" That's what we called the painted cinderblock above the laundry-folding ledge, where a thousand metal slash punk slash indie band and bar stickers formed a giant collage of fiery, hellish logos. At least, they'd been there a few days earlier. Not anymore.

"I gave it a funeral. Mom was right. Everything was peeling, and all the sticker residue was covered in dust. It was sort of disgusting."

"O-*kay*. Since when did you start caring about being neat?" Because he was the messiest guy I knew.

"Are you here to give me a hard time? Because I thought you wanted my advice."

I sighed. "So, let's just say I met this guy on the Owl bus one night when I was coming home from the hospital, and we hit it off, but I found out he was on his way to commit a crime."

"He sounds like a winner."

"Hush, it was a really minor crime."

"Minor like scoring an ounce of weed, or minor like illegal parking?"

"Somewhere in between?"

Heath pulled a T-shirt over his head and stared at me, mouth open. "Stealing a car?"

"What?" I practically choked. "That's ten times worse than buying drugs."

Heath snickered. "Okay, what, then? He was robbing a gas station, but it was because his grandmother needed the money for surgery? Or was it just something stupid, like egging someone's house?" When I didn't answer right away, his eyes widened. "Hold on. Not egging, but something like it? TPing? Oh, shit! *No way.* Are you kidding? The thing at the museum?"

The blood drained from my face.

"Holy freaking . . ." he murmured. "It really *was* for you?"

"Heath—"

He pointed an accusing finger. "That text you sent of the blurry driver's license—that's him? You're seeing the Golden Apple street artist guy?"

"That's insane," I said weakly. "It was the egging thing."

"You are the worst liar in the world."

"Oh, crap," I whispered, covering my face with my hands. "You have to promise me not to tell Mom. Swear on your life, Heath."

"I swear. Jeez, Bex. When you do something, you really go for it. One minute you're holed up in your room being all existential and throwing out your paints, all 'I'm done with color,' and the next you're running wild with notorious street artists."

I glared at him over my bent knees. "Do you want to hear, or are you just going to guess the entire story?"

"Fine, go on and tell me your revolutionary story, Patty Hearst." He glanced up at a pipe squeaking in the ceiling. "But talk fast. The shower's off, so we've only got fifteen minutes of blow-drying and makeup."

He could hear everything down here.

In a rush of jumbled words, I told him the whole story. Well, half of it. I left out the parts about me swooning and lusting over Jack, and I didn't admit anything else about the Golden Apple stuff, because I felt guilty enough as it was that I'd failed as secret keeper. But I did tell Heath about Sierra bursting into the tea lounge and about Panhandler Will saying Jack had a lady friend at the hospital. And about the last time I saw Jack, when he was with his father.

"So now I have no idea what's going on," I finished.

"He told you his dad's some rich corporate guy who doesn't give a damn about his family, but why was he at the hospital with your boy?"

"I don't know."

"Maybe something happened to the mother."

Crap. Jack did say that his mother was "pretty high up there" in his dad's priorities—it was only Jack who wasn't. "What if his mom has cancer or something?"

"The university's cancer treatment center is across town at Mount Zion," Heath reminded me. "But it could be something else. Maybe she was seeing a doctor at Parnassus for regular appointments, and that's why Hobo Bill saw your boy all the time."

"Panhandler Will," I corrected sourly. Heath had talked to Will just as much as I had over the years; you'd think he'd know his name by now. Regardless, Heath might be onto something about Jack. It was the only thing that made sense. "If Jack's relationship with his dad isn't great, his mother's probably the only person in the family he can depend on. It would definitely explain why he was so frazzled when I saw him."

"Well, you've got *that* in common, at least. Shitty fathers, strong maternal figures hanging out at the hospital. There's hours of conversation right there. You're like two peas."

"Look," I said, sitting next to him on the edge of his bed, "these are the last texts Jack sent me. Don't scroll up past here."

"Why? Are you sending each other dirty photos?"

"We're not all you, Heath." And no, that self-portrait on *Body-O-Rama* didn't count.

He read the texts and handed my phone back. "Sounds bad."

"I know, so what do I do? 'Believe me, it's better this way.' What does that mean?"

"Sounds like he doesn't want to drag you into his messy family life. That's how I'd feel if it was Noah, especially if it was my fault that a cop showed up at his door."

Heath hadn't been going out to clubs this week. He hadn't been going out, period. "Are you and Noah—"

"We aren't talking about me and Noah. But if we were, I'd be telling you he's coming for family dinner tomorrow night."

I smiled. "We finally get to meet Saint Noah? That's a bigger sign of the apocalypse than the fall of the brimstone wall."

"It's no big deal," his mouth said while the anxious foot rocking over his crossed legs shouted *Biggest Deal Ever!* "Anyway, back to your crisis. By the way, I hope this Jack looks better in person than he does in that photo on the ID."

"He does, and you're an ass."

"Lighten up, silly rabbit."

Ugh. He used to call me that when we were kids, because of the Trix breakfast-cereal TV commercials. That's about the time I decided I *never* wanted to be called Trix or Trixie (but if I ever decided to ask Dad for a job at his new wife's strip club, at least I had a backup name).

I fell onto the bed with a groan and threw one arm over my face to block out light from the fluorescent workshop lamp hanging from the ceiling. "If you were struggling with something or going through a bad time, and you told Noah to stay away, would he?"

"Are you kidding? Noah's a better person than both of us put together. If he thought I needed help, he'd just show up. And even if I didn't realize it, not only would he know what was wrong but he'd just"—Heath spread his hands like a stage magician—"make everything better."

I lifted my elbow for a moment to peek up at him. "Oh, *really*?"

"Hypothetically."

"Mmm-hmm. You're a lucky guy."

"I am, indeed. But as far as your little vandal boy, I don't know what to tell you. He's in some serious trouble if he gets busted, Bex. And God only knows what's going on with him now. Do you really want to put yourself in the middle of all his garbage? I know I tease you a lot about being bad, but this guy sounds like trouble you don't need. Maybe it's better for both of you if you just back away and let him go."

Mom says you should never ask for advice you aren't willing to take. I wasn't sure I agreed. Having an unbiased pair of eyes point out a sensible solution was helpful. But the sensible thing and the right thing weren't always the same choice, and no one but you could truly understand the difference.

13

THE ZEN CENTER IS AN OLD BRICK BUILDING IN HAYES Valley. I'd probably passed it a million times and never really paid much attention to it. A week and a half after I ran into Jack and his father, I went in search of both the building and Jack.

To the left of the main entrance and up a wheelchair ramp, a hand-painted sign quietly announced the bookstore. I gathered my courage and marched up the ramp in a pair of gladiator sandals that wrapped around my toes and crisscrossed up my ankles. I'd even painted my toenails. It was practically an event.

Doubts flipped through my head like last-minute flash cards before an exam: *You should've followed Heath's advice. You should've texted first. You should've called the bookstore beforehand to see whether he was still working the same schedule. You should've, should've, should've . . .*

But I didn't. And it was too late to chicken out now. When had the weather gotten so warm? It might've been all that walking or the fact that it was way sunnier here than it was in my neighborhood, but this absolutely wasn't nervous sweat. I wasn't nervous. Why should I be nervous, for the love of Pete? I shrugged out of my jacket and hung it on top of my purse. Wiped my hands on my jeans. Then I took a calming breath and walked inside.

The bookstore looked pretty much how I'd imagined, cozy and quiet and very, very tidy. A couple of people browsed wooden bookshelves lined with rows of titles about dharma and Buddha and Dogen and mindfulness. A few mats and cushions—presumably for meditation—were for sale, as well as a lot of Buddha statues and bells. The whole place smelled faintly of smoky spice, which I assumed was the handmade incense for sale.

Apart from the traditional Japanese music playing, it was just *so quiet*. I lost my nerve and decided to blend in with everyone else and pretend like I was browsing. Could anyone tell I didn't belong here? Did my aura have a big sooty X on it that marked me as OTHER? Could they sense I wasn't on the Middle Path?

I looked around for Jack but didn't spy anyone who appeared to work there—no bald monks dressed in long robes, no one with a name badge. Since there was only so long I could stare at book spines, I meandered to a display of mala beads, like the ones around Jack's wrist, all different styles and lengths. I fingered a long strand that was meant to be worn as a necklace.

"Those are gorgeous, aren't they?" a soft voice said behind me.

I turned around to find a cute Chinese guy with tousled black hair and a labret piercing right below the center of his bottom lip. He pointed to the beads and then crossed his arms over his chest. "Yak bone from Nepal."

"Oh, yeah. They're pretty sweet." Probably not the right thing to say about religious jewelry (sorry, *philosophical* jewelry, as Jack would say). And great—Mr. Yak Bone Expert was checking out my boobs.

What was I thinking, wearing this top? Mom called it my Roman orgy shirt because it was white and the short sleeves were split up to the shoulders while the rest of it was loose. But it was also pretty sheer, and if you looked closely, you could see my bra right through it; in the right light, you didn't even have to look all that closely.

"The bone is inset with coral and the beads are supposed to promote good blood. . . ." He squinted at me for a second—my face, this time, not my boobs. "That is, circulation. Good blood circulation."

"Rolling any kind of bead between your fingers would briefly improve circulation," I pointed out.

He chuckled. "Probably Nepalese superstition, but it sounds nice."

"Do they all have special qualities?" I asked, touching a black strand. Why was he staring at me so hard? Did I have something on my face? And was this guy just an overly friendly customer or someone who worked at the bookstore?

"Some. Those agates are supposed to repel negative energy, and this may sound like an odd question, but your name wouldn't happen to be Beatrix, would it?"

Whoa. That was a mouthful of words. "Umm . . ."

"Hell." He ducked his head and glanced around the store, but no one was nearby. "I mean, it's you, right? The braids. I recognized you by your braids."

My hand crept up the looping plaits I'd piled on the crown of my head.

"And you look like your portrait online." He covered half his face with one hand. "Well, minus the gory muscles on one side."

Of course. Duh. "You're . . . Andy? Is that right? The guy who draws the comic with Jack?"

He grinned. "That's me. Andy Wong."

"No name tag," I pointed out.

"Buddhists don't wear name tags."

"Uh—"

"That was a joke. I just left mine behind the counter."

"Oh, that wacky Zen humor," I said nervously.

"Your stuff is, like, *whoosh*." His motioned over his head.

"Huh?"

"Your art. Out-of-this-world good. Very cool and retro with the gray-pencil vibe. Jack said you never do color."

"Oh, thanks. And no—no color."

He nodded his head several times, as if struggling for something else to talk about. "I didn't expect you to be so *wee*. You're like a tiny, gruesome pixie." His eyes widened. He shook his hands and backtracked. "No, no. I mean your *art* is gruesome. Not you. Definitely not you."

I pretended to smile, but what I was really thinking was:

Jack told him about me.

Jack told him about me, and he showed him my artwork.

Jack told him about me, showed him my artwork, and told him about my braids.

And perhaps because of all of those deep academic thoughts bouncing around in my brain, I interrupted Andy's apologies and blurted out, "Is Jack here?"

"He's—" Andy glanced behind me and smiled. My muscles froze, but it wasn't Jack. Just a customer wanting to pay for some books. Andy excused himself and rang the man up while I craned my neck in every direction, seeking a safe place to settle my nervous gaze. When the customer finally left, I looked for Andy, but he was heading to a door in the corner.

"Hold on just a second," he said. "I'll be right back."

But he wasn't. I waited forever. Okay, probably just five minutes, but it sure felt like forever, and it was long enough for another customer to walk up to the register. I shrugged at her like "Yeah, I don't know where he is, either." And just when I thought the lady might be upset enough to walk out (apparently Buddhism doesn't automatically grant a person saintlike patience), the back door swung open and Andy walked into the store, breathless.

He wasn't alone.

My heart springboarded into my throat.

Dressed in loose, old jeans, a black T-shirt, and a thin, ash-gray cardigan, Jack walked up to me and stopped, looking me over without saying anything. I knew he could probably see my bra through my shirt, too, but I was too busy studying him to care. I'd forgotten everything—how haunting his kohl-dark double eyelashes were, and the way his cheeks hollowed beneath his cheekbones. How his clothes smelled like name-brand fabric softener, not the cheap stuff my mom used.

"You cut your hair," I said dumbly.

He ran his fingers through the pomp part of the pompadour, which was slightly less unruly. The sides and back had also been buzzed closer. "My mom said it was looking more old Elvis than young Johnny Cash, so I got a couple of inches whacked."

"You look better than the last time I saw you. Rested, I mean."

"That was a bad day. Things are better now."

I nodded, waiting for more that never came. I finally said, "You *endured*."

He was momentarily confused. "Oh, uh, yeah," he said, lowering his voice. "You saw that, huh?"

"One of your best pieces."

"Thanks." He cleared his throat and stuffed his hands into his pockets. "How's Minnie?"

"We're getting along better."

He smiled softly. "That's good."

"I've looked for you when I've gone into the lab," I said.

"It's . . . been hectic."

We stared at each other's feet a few seconds. If this was all he was going to give, then maybe I *had* made a mistake in coming. I'd had deeper conversations with customers in my checkout line at the market. A weird mix of frustration and hurt made my chest feel tight.

"Okay, well then," I said, vaguely moving my shoulders up and down in a gesture that wasn't quite a shrug. "I'll let you get back to whatever it was you were doing. See you around."

I strode toward the door, more than aware of Andy watching me from behind the counter. An old man with a limp hobbled around a bookcase just as I was rounding it. I nearly bowled him over and had to make an awkward lunge to avoid him. As I did, a warm hand grabbed my elbow.

"Pardon me," Jack said to the limping man as he danced around him to get to me. "Bex, wait. Please. I—" He pulled me over to one of the windows facing the street. "I'm not doing anything. I mean, you said 'whatever it is' I was doing, but it's slow in here today. I was just doing some meditation."

"Don't let me stop you."

"You already did."

"Yeah, I went out of my way to see you because I like you, Jack. And I'm pretty sure you like me, too."

"You have no idea how much."

"Is there someone else?"

"No. Jesus. Definitely not."

"Then stop shutting me out, and tell me what the hell happened at the hospital last week. I'm not going to sit around waiting for you to throw me a crumb. All of me or none of me—that's what I'm offering." I realized when I said this how much it sounded like something I'd overheard my mom say before my dad left. Which wasn't totally fair, but I was trying to make a strong point.

"You're right," he said after a moment.

Well, yeah. I was. But I needed more than that from him, so I waited.

His head dropped. He leaned closer. I stared at the silvery pearl button on his cardigan as his breath rustled the stray wisp of fine hair around my temple that wouldn't behave and stay put in my braids, no matter how I tried to tame it.

"I've missed you," he murmured.

I had no idea how badly I'd wanted to hear that until he said it. Those small, barely-there words erased gravity and made my feet rise off the bookstore carpet. I truly would not have been surprised if my head hit the ceiling.

I wanted to say something meaningful and honest in return. Something like "I've missed you, too" or "I thought I was going to die if I didn't see you again." But because I was overwhelmed, I settled on "Your button's chipped."

As he ducked his head to inspect it, I fit the edge of my fingernail into the triangular notch.

"Damage inflicted by a flying piece of board," he said, extending a finger next to mine. "Andy was convinced he could karate chop a wooden piece of shelving that broke off beneath the counter, but"—his fingertip traced the edge of mine, slowly moving down and around my knuckle, a whisper of a touch that sent a rush of goose bumps over my arm—"the board didn't break. It did, however, chip my button, and the corner nearly neutered me. But I was dumb enough to hold the damn thing, so I guess I deserved it."

I snorted a laugh, meaning to be quiet but failing miserably. Embarrassed, I pulled my hand away. "Ugh, it's like a library in here," I complained.

"Shh," he scolded, ten times louder than my laugh.

I glanced at the cash register. Andy was smiling. Yep, definitely watching us.

"You know, I was just checking the afternoon temp before you came," Jack said. "It's, like, sixty-seven degrees out there."

Which meant it was probably foggy and a good five degrees colder back at home, but that didn't matter much, since I wasn't there. "Too bad you're stuck in here meditating," I said.

"Someone already interrupted me. Besides, it's always better to meditate closer to nature. I know a perfect place. Do you have to work tonight?"

I shook my head.

"Trust me?"

"You ready to give me a reason to?"

"Did I mention the perfect place I had in mind was away from listening ears?" He flicked a glance at Andy and then added, "Far away."

"All right," I finally said, like I'd actually considered turning him down.

Jack smiled and held up both hands, walking backward. "Give me five minutes."

14

JACK'S FIVE MINUTES WAS MORE LIKE TWO, AND THEN he was whisking me through the bookstore door and we were out in the sunshine. He looped the handles of a bulky canvas bag around my wrist as we headed down the sidewalk. "Hold this for a second."

He stripped out of his cardigan, giving me a peek at the brightly colored fish and lotus tattoos beneath the short sleeves of his T-shirt. "What's inside the bag?" I asked.

"Vegetarian bacon."

I made a face. He laughed and took back the bag to stuff his sweater inside it.

"What Muni line are we taking?" I asked as we passed a stop.

"The *me* line." He pulled a set of keys from his pocket and stopped in front of a shiny black car that was parked in an impossibly tight space near the curb. It was an old two-seater sports coupe—all curvy and beautiful and compact, with a convertible black top and white scalloped insets in the door that looked like one side of an opened paperclip.

"This is Ghost," Jack said with unabashed pride.

"Ghost?"

"A 1958 Corvette." He unlocked the passenger door, which was covered with dings and scratches in an otherwise mirror-shiny paint job. "She was stolen last fall and taken for a joyride, which is why she's a little beat-up on the outside. I decided to keep her that way for now so she wouldn't look so showy. Plus it pisses my dad off, and that's always a good thing."

The door squeaked when he opened it. I peered inside at dark red leather seats. A chrome steering wheel jutted from a space-age dash, every bit of it restored. "Holy smokes, Jack. This is gorgeous."

"She doesn't have air-conditioning, and the convertible top leaks when it rains."

If he was trying to convince me that this wasn't the coolest car I'd ever seen, he'd need to try harder. "Why do you even ride mass transit?"

"You ever try parking in this city?"

I shook my head. "I don't drive."

"Do you ride?" That sounded sort of dirty, and the way he looked at me felt sort of dirty, too. No one ever looked at me like that.

"Why 'Ghost'?" I asked.

Grasping the top of the car door, he leaned over it and spoke in a dramatic, foreboding voice. "Because she's so fast she disappears down the streets at night."

"That sounds dangerous."

His dimple appeared. "The best things in life are. Hop in, Beatrix Adams."

I feigned difficulty getting inside the tiny bucket seat. He was right about one thing: It smelled a little mildewy. But apart from that, everything inside the crowded interior was polished and beautiful. I clicked the seat belt around my waist and exhaled nervously.

After shoving the canvas bag into the tiny trunk, he somehow folded his long legs inside and fired up the rumbling engine. We rolled our windows down to let in a pleasant cross breeze. "You look pale," he said as he plucked a pair of sunglasses off his visor. "You okay?"

"Not much cushion between our flesh and another car's bumper if you wreck."

He buckled up and put the car in reverse, a smile on his lips and dark shades covering his eyes. "Then I guess I'd better not."

It had been so long since I'd been in a car other than the paddy wagon or Howard Hooper's shit-mobile, and I'd never been in anything quite like this. He wasn't kidding about the fast thing: The fancy muscle car zipped up and down steep inclines as if the tires and asphalt were an old married couple. But Jack was a good driver, and I felt a little silly that I'd been nervous.

I propped my bare elbow on the window frame, enjoying the warm breeze that fluttered the split in my short sleeve while the city sailed by. It was exhilarating, being so close to him again—almost as close as we were in the tea lounge, and more alone. I sneaked a few glances at his face and a few more at his half-tattooed arm as he shifted gears. When he caught me looking and smiled, I wasn't as much embarrassed as thrilled.

Despite one minor traffic jam that detoured us through the edge of Duboce Triangle, the drive wasn't long. When he finally slowed down to find a parking space, it took me a minute to realize we'd been steadily going uphill, and that hill was Buena Vista Park.

"You live around here, right?"

"Don't you have a photo of my address?" he teased as he stalked a couple in running shorts heading toward a parked BMW.

"It was blurry," I said. "Couldn't read the house number, just the street."

"I live a few blocks away."

"Ah. Wait—didn't someone get set on fire in this park?"

"Someone gets set on fire in *every* park, Bex," he joked. "Sure, it's got a few park punks that squat in certain areas at night, but the police sweep through and kick them out. I come here all the time, especially when I just want to get out of the house and think. And you'll probably only see Benz-driving families in the day, if that makes you feel better. Which it shouldn't. Hello, parking space. It's our lucky day."

Maybe it really was.

After some tight maneuvering, Ghost was parked and we were strolling up a wide walkway into the park. Apparently, we weren't the only people with the bright idea to commune with nature, because it was pretty crowded: moms with strollers, dads with picnic baskets, teens walking dogs. But a perfect June day was a hard thing to come by in San Francisco, and the best way to enjoy it was a mass pilgrimage to one of the parks to soak up the sun.

But much like everything else worth doing in the city, the hike to the top of the park put a strain on my calves. Just when I was ready to ask Jack to slow his roll, he grabbed my hand and pulled me off the paved path and into the woods.

"Hurry before someone catches us," he said, tugging me behind some trees.

My little legs pumped at double time to keep up with his, and as we dashed through the trees, my head was a balloon, inflating with the singular fact that *Jack was holding my hand!* His fingers swallowed mine, and his palm was hot and a little sweaty, but so was mine.

One tug beneath a low-hanging branch and we burst out onto a shallow clearing of grass that clung to the side of the hill. I teetered on my tiptoes as Jack threw an arm around my waist to stop me from falling over the side.

"Oh . . ." I said, breathless.

The city lay at our feet, a dizzying labyrinth of rooftops and white buildings, spread out like a giant patchwork quilt. The Golden Gate Bridge stood in the distance, and the wrinkled coastal bluffs behind it.

"Right?" he said a few seconds later, as if he could read my mind.

"How did you find this?"

"Exploring, when I was, like, ten."

I heard people talking from somewhere behind the thick shrubbery that lined the clearing, but they were too far away for me to make out what they were saying.

"It's just a few yards away from some steps that go to the top," Jack noted as I glanced around. "So it's extra-cool, because it's private, more or less. I used to hide out here and feel like a total rebel, until one day I found a middle-aged couple out here. I was crushed."

I laughed. "Well, if they come back today, we were here first."

"Exactly. Now, help me with this." He extracted two rolled-up padded black mats from the canvas bag that looked an awful like the ones for sale in the bookstore. I spread out one of the mats, and he butted the second one right next to it. They were square, and only big enough to sit down on, but I wasn't complaining. "I'm just borrowing them. Not burgling them."

"I swear that's not a real word, but I haven't been educated at your fancy-pants private school, so I could be wrong."

"Be glad. There are a mere fifty people in my graduating class."

"I've only been going to Lincoln for a couple of years—since we moved to the Inner Sunset. But my class is over seven hundred."

He pulled off his gray Chuck Taylors and socks, and I took off my sandals, and we sat side by side on the mats and stretched out our legs in the warm grass, wiggling our toes.

"I know some people at Lincoln," he said, passing me a bottle of water from the bag. He named a few names I didn't recognize. Then he handed me a piece of mottled red fruit I didn't recognize, either.

"What is this?"

"Pluot."

"Plu what?"

"Plum crossed with an apricot. You've never had one?"

"I've never said it, much less had it."

"Vegetarian bacon," he said, squinting at me with merry eyes. He polished one on the hem of his shirt, lifting it up enough to give me a peek at A) a shiny silver belt buckle that was probably vintage and definitely stamped with the words 4-H CLUB and B) the bottom half of a shockingly well-muscled stomach and an enticing trail of dark hair arrowing into his jeans.

My pluot dropped out of my hand and nearly rolled off the cliff. Jack and his speedy arm caught it.

"Thanks," I said, concentrating superhard on cleaning off my alien piece of fruit, and concentrating even harder when I bit into the flesh. It was sweet and plum-y and tart. "Not bad," I said, trying not to think about the 4-H belt buckle (which made me want to giggle) or the trail of dark hair (which made me want to stick my hands down the front of his jeans to see where it led).

"The Zen Center has a lot of fruit trees in Marin County," he explained while I flushed all the dirty thoughts out of my wandering mind. *Fruit trees. Concentrate, Beatrix.*

"So you burgled these, too?" I asked.

"No, these are from my lunch. I hoarded them. That's completely different."

We grinned at each other, and his dimpled smile made me beyond glad I'd gone to the Zen Center.

Chatting mindlessly, we polished off the fruit and pitched the pits over the side of the cliff as Jack said, "Make a wish!" and then, "What did you wish for?"

"Not to nail someone on the head," I said with a grin.

"See? You're already walking the Middle Path." He scooted forward until he had enough room for his head on the mat, then settled on his back, using one thrown-back arm for a pillow. After a few moments I joined him, lying down with my shoulder against his. I didn't say anything. He didn't either. We just warmed in the sun and gazed up at the sky. Strangers chattered on the path beyond the trees.

Silent minutes passed. I closed my eyes. It was so warm I nearly dozed off. His voice pulled me back to the present.

"Have you ever heard of word salad?" he asked.

My heart thudded, but I didn't open my eyes. "It sounds familiar, but I'm not sure."

"It's when your words get all screwed up, and you try to say one thing, but it comes out as gibberish. Like, instead of saying 'I saw a man walking a dog on a leash in the park,' it might come out as 'I saw a man with a collar and claws walking a tightrope under the trees.'"

"Okay." Where was he going with this?

"People with schizophrenia do it. Especially disorganized schizophrenia, which is one of the worst types. They aren't as delusional as people with paranoid schizophrenia, but their reality is distorted, and they have major problems with disorganized thought and speech. Their thoughts get jumbled, and they have a tendency to blurt out weird things and laugh at inappropriate times. And the longer the disease goes on, the worse their speech gets, and the harder it is for them to communicate, and they can't do simple things like, I don't know, take a shower. Stress builds up; they get frustrated and lash out. Sometimes they try to hurt themselves or other people."

Oh.

The day I'd gone down to talk to Heath, we'd tried to puzzle out what had happened with Jack at the hospital. We settled on it having something to do with Jack's mother and wondered if she—maybe?—had cancer, but I realized now that we'd made the wrong diagnosis.

"The person you've been visiting is in the psych ward," I said softly.

"For the last year and half. She was sick before that and hospitalized once, just for twenty-four hours. But eighteen months ago, she crossed the line."

He didn't volunteer what that line was, so I asked, "Family?"

"Yeah. My so-called 'lady friend.'"

We'd been right about that, at least. It *was* Jack's mother. "Is she . . . okay?"

"The meds help with the hallucinations and the panic disorder. Without them, she gets stressed and confused, and starts to hear voices, and all of it will eventually build until she's completely agitated and has a violent episode. When she's coming down from that, she's emotionless. Like, just staring at the walls, completely flat."

"Sounds bipolar or something."

"They thought she was at first. Then the voices started." He shook his head, as if he could erase the thought of it. "But anyway, she'd been doing okay recently. They experimented with a new antipsychotic, and she had a bad seizure. That was when I saw you at the hospital. She almost died."

"Oh, Jack."

"She's all right now. Things are under control. She's got good doctors, and there's not really much we can do but trust them. She does. She feels better staying there. The routine and boundaries help. And the people working there care, you know? They aren't just doing a job."

I thought of my mom and all the worrying she did for some of her patients. Their families, too. She brought them food. Listened to them. Sometimes even went to funerals.

"How often you do see her?" I asked.

"Family therapy is once a week. And she has a private room, so the orderlies have been letting me see her a couple days a week after visiting hours because she sometimes paces at night. I hang out with her while the other patients are asleep. Keeps her occupied. My dad gives massive amounts of money to the hospital, so they're lenient with us."

"That's how you 'fixed' things for me in the anatomy lab."

He nodded. "Would be much better if you'd continue to think I'm just that cool, and that it wasn't the influence of my family's money and name."

I gave him a soft smile. "I still think you're just that cool—don't worry."

"Do you?"

I couldn't see his eyes behind the sunglasses, so I just kept staring up at the sky and reached between us to curl my pinkie around his. His chest deflated as he blew out a long, slow breath through his mouth.

He threaded his fingers through mine and murmured, "I'm sorry I didn't tell you earlier. Part of me wanted to. I almost dialed your number a hundred times. But it's a black cloud hanging over our family. My dad has to keep up appearances, so I'm forbidden to talk about it to strangers. Not that you're a stranger, and not that I give a damn about what my dad would say if I told you. It's just . . . I don't know. I was worried you might cut your losses and bail if you found out. You wouldn't be the first."

"Do I need to shiv someone with a pencil? I might be small, but I'm sneaky."

His laughter rippled down his body. He sat up on one elbow

and pushed his sunglasses on top of his head to peer down at me. "How do you that?"

"What?"

He lifted my bent arm and untangled our fingers to press his big flattened palm against my small one. "I've spent the last three days at the Zen Center trying to get back on my feet, and you just pull me up like it's nothing."

I stared at our hands, unable to think of a witty comeback.

As he folded the tips of his fingers over mine, the sun burnished tiny hairs on his forearm. For two people who'd mostly spent time together after dark, seeing him now, stretched out alongside me in warm daylight, was a luxury. Here, I could freely inspect all the small things, like the white half-moons at the base of his thumbnails, and the freckle on his elbow at the bottom of his lotus tattoo. And maybe the sun shone on other things I didn't really know were there, like the fierce knot inside my chest that had been tightening since the last time I saw him. But as I lay there with him in the grass, it unwound and relaxed, and the sun lightened all the heavy things he'd just revealed.

"I'm so glad you came looking for me," he murmured.

I remembered what he'd told me in Alto Market. "If you leave vague hints about where you are, I *will* find you."

"Did I really say that?"

"You did," I confirmed.

He groaned. "You should've punched me."

"It's not too late."

His gaze roamed over my Roman orgy shirt and lit on my mouth. Everything inside me fluttered. Was he going to kiss me?

Was he still staring at my lips? I couldn't tell, because I was staring at his, and they were parted, and he was breathing heavily, and I could feel his leg against mine, and *mother of God,* this was happening. This was definitely happening, and I could hear—

Scandinavian black metal.

Jack arched away from my hip as my phone buzzed inside my pocket.

Ugh. It was Heath. He'd changed my ringtone to play something that sounded like a screaming subway accident whenever his number came up. "Sorry," I mumbled, sitting up and frantically fishing out my blaring cell, which everyone and their brother could probably hear through the trees. So much for our private hideaway. I finally managed to mute the phone, but not before my pulse cranked up to a zillion beats per minute.

"Wow. I'd never pictured you as an angry-shrieking-vocals kind of music fan," Jack said with a bemused look on his face.

"It's my jackass brother."

A text popped up from Heath: Where the hell R U?

"Something wrong?" Jack asked.

"It's already five? How did that happen?"

"I thought you didn't have to work."

"I don't. It's worse than that. It's"—I lowered my eyebrows—"family dinner night."

"Oh," he said, pulling his hand away from mine. Was he disappointed our near-kiss moment was kaput? I certainly was. "Do I need to drop you off?" he asked.

I didn't want to leave, not when I'd already spent more than a week away from him, and not when I'd just learned all this stuff

15

JACK PULLED GHOST NEXT TO THE CURB IN A PRIME spot almost directly in front of my house.

"You can change your mind," I said.

He stowed his sunglasses on the visor and stared at our front steps like a monster might come storming down them at any second. "And turn down a free meal? Never."

"You say that now, but you haven't met my family yet."

As traffic sped behind us, we headed up to the front door. On the other side of it, a trio of laughs floated from the kitchen on a fragrant cloud of tomato and melted cheese. It smelled freaking delightful. And Mom was in a superior mood, laughing it up and practically singing her curiosity when I called from the park to find out if I could bring Jack along. Now, if she just wouldn't put two and two together about the graffiti in the museum, and if Heath would keep his mouth shut about everything I'd told him about Jack, this might not turn disastrous.

I signaled Jack to follow me through the living room toward the chatter. Our kitchen wasn't fancy, having last been updated in an ugly 1990s shade of pale mauve, complete with fake butcher-block countertops. But it was pretty big for a city kitchen, with a long peninsula counter that separated a round four-chair breakfast table from the rest of the room. Mom was standing on the other side of that peninsula, and Heath was lounging at the table. And right as I walked under the archway from the living room, an African-American man as big as a professional wrestler stepped in front of me.

And when I say wrestler, I mean bulging muscle—beefy and corn-fed, with a few extra pounds of cushion, and tattoos snaking up both arms. He was dressed in a T-shirt with a fiery metal logo, and he had one of those wallet chains looping from the back pocket of his black jeans. To go along with all that, he had a full-on badass beard, like one of the big S&M dudes who walk around with nothing but a bullwhip and leather chaps at the Folsom Street Fair.

The whole package announced *You do not want to screw with me,* but the beautiful smile curving his lips was all sunshine.

"Beatrix?" he guessed.

"Noah?" I guessed back.

His rumbly laugh echoed around the kitchen as he scooped me up into a hug. "Damn, you're a little thing like your mama, aren't you?"

"And you're apparently made of mountain. Are you sure you're an engineer and not a lumberjack?"

"Last I checked."

When he pulled out a chair, I widened my eyes at Heath, who was beaming so much he nearly blinded me.

"Well, I'm glad to finally meet you," I said, moving into the kitchen to make room. "And while we're on introductions . . ." Jack stepped under the arch. "Jack, this is my family. This is Saint Noah, my brother's boyfriend. And that's my brother, Heath, and over there is my mom, Nurse Katherine the Great. Everyone, this is Jack." I refrained from adding *the Vandal*.

Jack extended his hand to Noah, and then to my brother, who looked Jack over like he was a piece of cake as he purred "Hello, Jack" in a voice an evil cartoon cat would use on a doomed mouse. "I've heard *all* about you."

Ugh. Kill me now.

"But I haven't," Mom said, wiping her hands on a kitchen towel. "Come closer and let me get a better look at the person my daughter's been hiding under a bushel."

Uh-oh. She was strangely cheerful and teasing, but it didn't stop my neck muscles from clenching. And poor Jack had no idea what he was walking into, but he strolled around the counter and shook my mom's hand, too.

"Thank you for having me. Hope it's not an inconvenience."

She made a sweeping gesture toward two pans of lasagna cooling on trivets. "If we can eat all this, we should get some kind of prize. It's no inconvenience whatsoever. Do you go to school with Beatrix?"

"Your daughter and I met on the N line a few weeks ago," he said. Which was pretty much true. "And I've seen her at Alto Market." Also true, just not quite *the Truth*.

"What's your last name?" she asked.

"Vincent."

"Jack Vincent," Mom said, leaning back against the counter to peer up at him. "Why does that name sound familiar? Oh, Mayor Vincent."

"Yes," he said, looking uncomfortable. "That's my father."

His father . . . What?

A chorus of "oohs" swirled around the kitchen. Except from me, because *his father was the freaking mayor of San Francisco and he didn't tell me.* Sweat pricked my scalp under my looping braids. Jack coughed into his hand and sneaked a fear-filled glance my way. I did my best to keep my face blank.

"Well, well, well," Mom chirped. She grabbed his chin and angled it for her inspection as though he were a patient; sometimes Mom forgets normal physical boundaries. "I knew you looked familiar. Handsome like your daddy, huh?"

Jack chuckled nervously.

"First a saint, now a prince," Mom said, letting go of Jack's chin to grin at Noah across the counter. "God's finally listening to my prayers."

"I don't know about that," I mumbled. "Jack's a Buddhist."

"O-oh," Mom said, like it was the coolest thing she'd ever heard.

I suddenly felt like I were in a David Lynch movie and there was some bizzaro, surreal plot I didn't really understand unfolding all around me. I quietly had a heart attack while Mom and Jack and Heath and Noah all chatted about Buddhism and about how funny it was that Jack had shown up for dinner, because Mom had made meatless lasagna to appease Noah, who was apparently a pescatarian—which just meant he was a vegetarian who cheated and ate fish. And they talked about Jack's superstar father, who was serving his second term as one of the youngest mayors in the city's history, not to mention one of the most popular, but, no, Jack had no idea if the rumors were true that Mayor Vincent might be entering California governor's race in the near future. Blah, blah, blah.

For the love of Pete, how flipping stupid was I? To be honest, I always tuned Mom and Heath out when they started talking politics. Yet I'd known his last name sounded familiar. I couldn't believe I hadn't connected the dots when I saw his dad, but if I tried to picture him without the dark shades and the baseball cap, yeah, I supposed it was him, all right.

Everything made more sense now, like how Jack said his dad lived for his job. And the mayor was notoriously private about his family life, which was probably why I couldn't dig up much about Jack online. No doubt they lived in one of those six-million-dollar houses near Buena Vista Park—*not* the six-hundred-thousand-dollar ones. And the car that was waiting for Jack and his dad at the hospital that night? That was the freaking *mayor's car*. No wonder the man had been cooler than ice with me. He was the king of the city.

Which was why he'd forbidden Jack to talk about the schizophrenia. I vaguely remembered seeing pictures of the mayor and his wife together, but maybe I hadn't seen any recently because, you know, she was in the hospital. Keep up appearances, Jack had said. His father was worried it might hurt his political career. Pretty crappy attitude, if you ask me.

"You feeling all right, babe?" Mom asked, rubbing my back.

"Oh, I'm one big bag of sunshine and puppies."

She squinted suspiciously at me and then spoke to Jack. "How are you at grating cheese, Prince Vincent?"

"My cheese-grating skills are second to none. I'm a fully licensed grate master."

"Excellent. I'll need enough Parm grated to cover those baguettes. Bex will show you where the grater is. And, babe," she said, talking to me, "do the garlic butter thing you did last time. Noah, I need your height to get an extra chair down from the hall closet. It's stuck sideways on the top shelf, thanks to your boytoy's inability to follow simple instructions."

"Thanks, Mom," Heath said drily. "You're a real hoot."

The three of them chatted their way into the hall. I pulled out a block of Parmesan and some butter from the fridge. Jack stepped behind me as I unwrapped it on the counter.

"You pissed?" he said near the side of my head.

"Surprised. And feeling more than a little dumb. But in my defense, I'm used to seeing him in a suit behind a podium. And, you know, you might've mentioned it."

"I wasn't thinking clearly when you saw us together at the hospital. I should've introduced you. It's just that everywhere I go, I'm always Mayor Vincent's son. I know, boo-fucking-hoo, right? But that's all I am to people at school, the neighbors, the hospital doctors. . . . Even one of the masters at the Zen Center has hinted that having my dad show up at one of the charity events would help raise awareness. I get so damn tired of it. And for once I just wanted . . ." He paused, searching for words. "I wanted you to see me and not my family—not the politician or the psych patient. Just me."

I opened a bottom cabinet and rummaged until I found our ancient metal box grater. "To be honest, I hate politics. If you never mention anything remotely mayoral ever again, it won't hurt my feelings. Now, the schizophrenia? You can talk about that all you want, anytime. However, none of it changes the way I think about you."

He didn't reply, so I figured the matter was settled. I tapped on the grater. "Now, I should warn you that Mom is a total freak about wasting food, so if you grate more cheese than we need, I'll be eating Parmesan on cereal for the next week. Just so we're clear, don't do that."

I stepped out of his way and grabbed a bulb of garlic from a bowl near the stove. On the other side of the kitchen wall, a loud *boom!* was followed by laughter. Guess Noah got the chair down.

"Hey, Bex?" Jack said as he grated. "Just so we're clear, if we were alone, I'd probably kiss you right now."

I gave him a swift glance as the hallway laughter made its way back to the kitchen. "Just so we're clear, I'd probably let you."

DINNER WAS ODDLY PLEASANT. THERE WAS BARELY room for all five us around the kitchen table, but it was nice to be squished next to Jack, and we played elbow wars every time we bumped into each other.

And if Mom had detected any weirdness between us earlier, it was long forgotten—partly because Jack and I were fine now, and partly because Mom was too busy flirting it up with him and Noah. (Who knew all it took was a couple extra guys praising her cooking to turn Katherine the Great into a gooey pile of strumpet? It was almost embarrassing.)

And the pleasantness turned to joy for my mom when Heath

announced he was moving in with Noah at the end of the summer. And the joy turned to outright glee when Noah announced he was going to help Heath figure out a way to go back to school. Not for nursing, but to become a vet tech. "We were looking at a veterinary program in San Leandro. He'd have to commute across the Bay on BART—"

"But a few of my nursing credits will transfer," Heath said excitedly. "I'm too late for fall, but I might be able to get in this winter. January, hopefully, if I don't get turned down for financial aid."

It took all of ten seconds for Mom to raise two victory fists in the air, and then she was hugging Noah like he really were a saint. Maybe he was.

So why wasn't I over the moon about all this? I was happy for Heath, sure. But it was only a couple of weeks ago that he was out partying. And it was only a couple of months ago that the two of them were on "a break." And it was only *six* months ago that Heath was ditching a community-college nursing program. Again.

But despite his long list of screwups, he was still my brother, and I guess I was sad he'd be breaking up Team Adams and leaving Mom and me behind.

"You can have Laundry Lair," Heath said after dinner, leaning across the counter toward me while Jack and I rinsed off plates and filed them in the dishwasher. Now I knew why Heath had cleaned off the brimstone wall; he'd already been planning on moving out.

"I dunno," I said. "On one hand, more privacy. On the other, it smells like car exhaust and mold down there." I didn't mention it was half the size of the dining room—a sticking point between us since we'd moved in here.

Heath smirked at me. "And once you get your stuff down there, it'll smell like formaldehyde and pencil lead."

"Where *is* your room?" Jack asked me.

"Not exactly the mayor's mansion here," Heath said. "Rooms are where you can find space to fit a bed."

I threw a kitchen towel at my brother. "You can handle the glasses." They never got clean in the dishwasher, so we had to do them by hand. I left Heath to it and walked Jack to my X-ray doors, explaining the whole dining-room-origin story, while, at the other end of the living room, Mom and Noah conspired over coffee to plan my brother's future. I left one door cracked so it wouldn't look like I was luring Jack into my web to have my wicked way with him.

"This is amazing," Jack said, peering into the mission china cabinet at my strange assortment of anatomy tchotchkes. "It's . . . so you."

"Go on and say it. It's weird, I know."

"It's very weird. And I love weird, so you're in luck. Whoa—is this vintage?"

I showed him my Visible Woman (which he went bananas over) and introduced him to Lester the Skeleton (which creeped him out). I almost pulled out the artist mannequin that my dad had (possibly) sent—the wood-carving shop in Berkeley *still* hadn't answered my email—but I was too worried Mom might stroll in and ask about it. And while I was busy freaking over the fact that *Jack was in my room*, he flipped through a couple of sketchbooks—random drawings I hadn't posted online. Some were from art class at school. He stopped on a still life and chuckled.

"What?" I said, sitting next to him. *On my bed.* Some primitive part of my brain was already running through potential seduction fantasies, like accidentally spilling something on his shirt so that he was forced to take it off, and then I'd have to rub down his bare chest with my bedspread.

The primitive part of my brain wasn't particularly bright.

"Still Life with Fruit," Jack said in a faux-cultured voice. "I can practically feel the resentment in your crosshatching. Definitely not your favorite subject matter."

"You're not wrong. Guess you had me pegged from the get-go. Keep flipping through that and you might find some angry logo design, too."

"Where's"—he lowered his voice—"Minnie? Can I see her?"

"I'm not finished or anything," I said, suddenly self-conscious.

"When's the deadline for the art contest?"

"I've already signed up, but I have to turn in my piece three days before the exhibition. Which means I have to finish by July twentieth. I can show you what I've done so far. I haven't quite decided how I'm going to put it all together, but if you want . . ."

"I want. Believe me, *I want.*"

Wait—what did he want? Not Minnie, that's for sure. Dark eyelashes blinked at me as his knee rested against mine, and suddenly it was that first night on the bus all over again, staring at each other with flames shooting between us. I quickly decided my fantasy with the spill on the shirt was far too tame—I needed to spill something down the front of his jeans.

"What are you thinking?" he murmured.

"I'm thinking about your 4-H belt buckle," I murmured back.

Well. That shocked him. Guess my future *bon vivant* college self had officially chosen Jack over the ex-swimmer college professor.

"I was thinking about how hot your bra looks beneath that see-through toga shirt, so I guess we're even." He leaned closer and whispered, "Show me Minnie before I embarrass myself in front of Nurse Katherine the Great."

Guh. Okay, now he'd shocked me. But God as my witness, I would see that belt buckle again in the near future or die trying.

I wiped my sweaty palms on my jeans and blew out a long breath as I stepped across the room to my drafting table. The sketchbook was stashed among a couple of others between the table and the wall. Not that Mom would instantly know I'd been at the lab if she saw the sketches. I copied a lot of "internals," as I liked to call the inner-organ diagrams, from old textbooks.

Jack hovered near my right arm, watching me flip open the sketchbook. If anything could put a damper on rampant sexual frustration, it was looking at cadaver drawings. I skipped over my preliminary sketches and went for the one I'd been working on the last two sessions: a view of Minnie's full torso, including the dissected arm. It was pretty disturbing and, frankly, I'd been having a hard time looking at my sketches after I left the lab. This one was extra-bad because I'd included her face and hair. But I really felt I needed to because it humanized her—made her less of a "thing" and more of a real person.

Maybe a little too real . . .

“Think I’m going to pass out,” Jack mumbled at my side in a funny voice.

I started to apologize, but the words never left my mouth. His legs folded, and he dropped like someone had shot him. He was pranking me, surely. That’s what I thought for all of one second.

He wasn’t getting up.

16

I FELL ON MY KNEES BY HIS SIDE AND TOUCHED HIS face. He wasn't dead. He groaned and tried to lift his head off the floor, but his eyes weren't opening.

"Mom!" I yelled, but she was already racing into my room with Noah and Heath.

"What happened?"

"He was looking at one of my drawings and said he was passing out, and he just collapsed."

Mom went into nurse mode. "Honey, can you hear me? Jack?"

"M'okay," he slurred. His eyes fluttered open.

Her hands moved in quick succession over his neck, forehead, wrist. "Listen to my voice. Are you diabetic?"

"No." He tried to shift his legs.

She quickly repositioned them. "Are you on any meds?"

"No." He swallowed thickly and opened his eyes. "God, I'm dizzy."

"Bex, hand me the pillows off your bed."

When I brought them to her, she was unbuckling his 4-H belt buckle. I nearly flipped until I realized what was going on: restrictive clothing. She loosened it, wiggling open the top button of his jeans before checking his neck again. He was wearing that black T-shirt, which wasn't tight. "Under his feet. They need to be higher than his heart," she instructed. "Has this happened before, Jack? Have you fainted before?"

"Fuck," he said. Then, "I didn't mean to say that, sorry."

"Don't be. I'm sure Buddha will forgive you."

He tried to laugh. "I can't believe . . . I've never . . ."

Mom went through a series of questions. Could he breathe okay? Did his chest hurt? Numbness? She took his pulse again and inspected his head.

"I'm okay, really," he said, pushing himself up.

"Oh, no you don't," Mom answered, pushing him back down. "Heath, go fetch a glass of water and find that stash of Easter candy in the pantry. Noah, you help him." After the boys trotted off to the kitchen, she said, "Okay, so tell me what was happening. No judgment here, and I mean that."

"Did you . . . ?" His hands felt around his open belt buckle.

"Nurse Katherine's a perv," I said.

"Bex," my mother scolded.

"Look, the whole thing's my fault," I told her. "I was showing him gruesome sketches."

"No, no. I haven't had a lot of sleep lately," he argued, buckling himself back up. "I'm probably just run-down. Either that, or I've got a Victorian woman living inside me. Jesus, this is embarrassing."

"Sweetie, nothing embarrasses me," Mom said. "The things I've seen and done in the ER this week alone would make Vin Diesel faint. I just want to make sure you're okay."

And he was, or he seemed to be—enough that he finally fought off Mom's ministrations and stood with no problem. He made self-deprecating remarks in front of Heath and Noah, and after it was determined that Jack was back to normal, he said he had to get home and promised Mom twenty times he could drive himself.

"If you don't make it back safe, your dad will sue me," Mom argued.

"I can drive his car, and Heath can follow on my Harley," Noah suggested.

Jack shook his head. "I appreciate your good intentions, but I'm trying to impress a girl and not look like a total putz, so I'm leaving now. Thank you for dinner. It was excellent, and I mean that."

"It was probably food poisoning that did it," Heath joked. "Jack's just the canary in the coal mine. The rest of us will be on the floor before the night's over."

Mom smacked him in the arm as we all headed outside, and because Heath was staying over at Noah's, they were leaving, too. So I had to walk Jack back to Ghost under my family's watchful eyes.

"I know you're tired of answering this, but are you really okay?" I asked. "I'm so sorry about Minnie."

"Not your fault. Seriously, I'm just tired."

Some tiny voice in my head whispered that he wasn't exactly telling the truth, but I decided not to hammer him on it. "Despite the bad ending, I'm glad you came."

"I'm glad you hunted me down at the Zen Center."

"It was only fair. You hunted me down at Alto Market." I crossed my arms and shivered in the night air as he unlocked his car door.

"What are you doing for the Fourth?" Jack asked. "You scheduled to work?"

"I don't think so. It's already here?"

"Day after tomorrow. My dad will be showing his face at Pier Thirty-Nine for fireworks over the Bay, which, as you know, might be a moving patriotic display or a muddled cloud of pink fog, depending on the weather."

"We used to hunt a spot to watch them, but it's not worth the hassle."

"Then, how about a movie at my place? Andy and a few other people are coming. It's been an Independence Day tradition over the last couple of summers, since I always have the house to myself."

"Sounds fun."

"Okay, well, since Nurse Katherine is watching us, I'm going to leave now with half my male pride intact."

"We should advertise: Lose your machismo at the Adams family home. We're like the opposite of that skeevy roll-on underarm testosterone treatment."

"Even having lost my machismo, I can promise it's not enough to keep me away," he said as he slipped into Ghost and rolled down a window. "Good night, Bex."

"Good night, Jack."

I watched him drive off and waved at Heath, who looked ridiculous on the back of Noah's motorcycle. Then I headed back up to Mom. It took her all of one minute to end up in my room, perched on my bed where Jack had sat earlier.

"Okay, what *really* happened?" she said.

"I don't know. Like I said already, I was showing him my art—"

"Dammit, Bex. Normal people don't want to look at that stuff. It's grisly."

"I know."

"You used to be so creative. Why don't you paint anymore?"

"I like doing this, and it's practical. I'm thinking about my future, which is what you've always drilled into me. And it's not that different from what you do at work—or what you're all jumping up and down about Heath going back to school to learn. My art could help save lives one day."

She grabbed my shoulders and forced me to look at her. "Heath and I aren't blessed with a gift. If I had your talent, I wouldn't be stressed out, working graveyard and missing out on my kids' lives."

"But—"

"Art shouldn't be practical. It should be emotional and expressive. There are other ways to save people's lives than drawing teaching diagrams for med students. You could do something bigger. Something that makes people happy—and that makes *you* happy."

I pushed free from her grip. "I'm not unhappy. I've told you that a thousand times. Why don't you believe me?"

"Because you're the most stubborn person I know."

"Tenacious," I corrected. "It's a gift."

She sighed dramatically. We both looked anywhere but at each other until she finally said, "People don't faint for no reason. Could be an indication of something more serious going on with Jack's health, or could've been emotionally triggered. Anything he's stressed about at home?"

Besides his mom's seizure and having the mayor of San

Francisco for a father? Gee, I didn't know. "He's definitely going through some serious stuff right now with his mom." I couldn't tell her any details about Jack's mother—not even the little I knew—because what if Mom said something at work? It might spread all over the ER and get back to the Vincents or someone in the press. I already spilled Jack's vandalizing secret to Heath, which was bad enough.

"His mother?" she mused. "Oh, that's right. There was that break-in."

"What break-in?"

Mom shrugged absently. "A couple of years ago. It was in the news. Someone broke into the mayor's house. His wife went to the hospital—injured by the burglar. Maybe Jack was traumatized. Some people can't handle seeing blood after witnessing something shocking. Acute stress disorder, it's called. Over time, it can develop into PTSD."

First of all, I thought PTSD mainly affected soldiers. And second, I sort of remembered hearing about the break-in, but seeing how Jack's status as the mayor's son was only a couple of hours old to me, I hadn't really had time to think about it.

Mom sighed. "Why didn't you tell me about him? Jesus, Bex—the mayor's kid?"

"I know." Or, rather, I *didn't*, but no way was I admitting that now.

"How serious are you two?"

"The smallest amount of serious you can imagine—like, not even a teaspoon. We haven't even kissed. You've gotten further with him than I have, unbuckling his belt. Or he could be more into

Heath than me for all I know." Okay, that definitely wasn't true, but minimizing my mother's curiosity about my romantic life was of the utmost importance to me at that moment.

"Oh, sweetie," Mom said. "He's completely into you. He couldn't keep his eyes off you during dinner."

"All hail the power of the Roman orgy shirt," I said with a smile.

She closed her eyes. "God help me make it through the summer."

You and me both, Mom.

THE NEXT MORNING, A DAY BEFORE JACK'S MOVIE party, I got ready to work a full nine-hour shift at the market—a rare thing for me. Nothing like last-minute holiday grocery shopping. As I was preparing myself to clean up corn silk and heft organic seedless watermelons across the scanner, I checked my email and stilled when the words *Telegraph Wood Studio* appeared in my inbox.

> Dear Miss Adams,
>
> Thank you for your email inquiry. Your artist's mannequin was made in house by one of our master wood-carvers, Ben. He greatly enjoyed working on the project, which was, indeed, commissioned. Unfortunately, we do not give out clients' names over email. But if you could make time to visit our shop in Berkeley, I think you'd find Ben a rather talkative conversationalist, and perhaps you'd be able to get answers

to your questions. Let me know what date and time would be best for you, and I'll gladly arrange an appointment. Perhaps next week after the holiday?

Happy 4th,
Mary Spencer

I reread the email several times. I should've expected this. Anything connected to my father is always complicated. If I wanted to know more, I guessed I'd have to make an effort. Taking a BART train to Berkeley wasn't a huge deal, but it would eat up an entire afternoon, and I'd have to lie to Mom. And was it worth it? Did I really want to pick open a wound that had already healed and been forgotten? I honestly wasn't sure. I'd have to think about it.

And I had more important things to worry about, like Jack.

After he left our house, I went online and skimmed a few news articles about the break-in Mom mentioned. They were all vague, mentioning only that Mrs. Vincent was injured and treated at the hospital and that no one else in the household was hurt. All the articles included the same handful of quotes from the mayor: that his wife was doing fine, that she'd returned home in good spirits. He requested that the press respect his family's privacy.

Nothing was particularly interesting . . . until I clicked on a local blog run by the opposing political party, which not only theorized that there was something more to the break-in that the mayor's office was trying to keep quiet, but also mentioned that the mayor's teenage daughter had been sent overseas to boarding school in Europe.

Jack had a sister.

Why hadn't he mentioned her? I wondered if they were close or if he ever saw her. But if I asked him about it, then he'd know I'd been stalking him online. Not cool.

I started poking around in the comments section to see if there was any mention of either the sister or his mom's schizophrenia, but reading the first few nasty remarks not only pissed me off, it also made me feel guilty for snooping into his family's life. Like they were disposable celebrities and not real people. So I decided that if I was going to learn anything more about the break-in and Jack's mom and his faraway sister, I'd avoid the toxic gossip online and just wait to hear it from Jack himself.

The next afternoon, Mom left for her holiday-pay shift at the hospital, and for once I didn't have to concoct some elaborate story about where I'd be. She was completely fine with my going to Jack's house, and even said, "Maybe you'll make friends with some of the other youths." *Youths.* Like it was some sort of church group.

It definitely wasn't.

Jack had offered to pick me up at seven, but Mom was still getting ready for work, and I didn't want her to give him the third degree about the fainting thing. Besides, just because he had a car didn't mean he was obligated to chauffeur me around town. That's what I told him, but after standing for the better part of an hour on a packed train, I regretted it. Holidays plus mass transit equals disaster.

Jack texted me directions to his house. It wasn't a long walk from the Muni stop, but I was already an hour late, it was all uphill, and I'd stupidly worn my tall gray boots over my jeans in an attempt to fake coolness for his rich friends. Huge mistake. Blisters would haunt me later. But after several minutes of schlepping past million-dollar homes, I finally spotted Ghost. The vintage Corvette was parked in front of a three-story wood-shingled house tucked away on a side street.

Like everything else on the block, the house was jammed right up next to its neighbors and at first glance didn't have much curb appeal, with nothing to show but a two-car garage and a fancy copper street number. Lilac vines dripped like frosting over the garage, where a semiprivate entrance hinted at the wealth within. To get there, you had to enter an arched redwood gate and go up a steep flight of steps. You also had to pass under two Big Brother security cameras. Did his dad have Secret Service around here, too? Or was that only for DC politicians? I really had no clue, but the cameras weirded me out.

I texted Jack: Do I need clearance to enter this place or what?

A few seconds later, rubber soles slapped against stone, the gate swung open, and there he stood, filling up the redwood arch: pompadour, black boots, black snap-front shirt with silver koi over the front pockets, and, heaven help me, that 4-H belt buckle.

His slow gaze swept from my boots (the blisters were a small price to pay) all the way up my tasteful (yet boob-flattering) shirt to my face. "Happy Fourth," he finally said. "Or is that 'Merry Fourth'? What's the standard Independence Day greeting?"

"I think you're supposed to salute the flag while imitating the mournful call of a bald eagle."

"Is that like using a turkey whistle at Thanksgiving?"

"Exactly the same."

He stepped closer. "I can't believe you're actually here."

"You're not going to faint on me again, are you?"

"Am I ever going to live that down?"

I shook my head.

"I figured as much," he said with a smile. "You're in color."

"I am?"

"Red," he said, pointing to my head.

Breaking my long-running cycle of grayscale fashion, I'd tied a red bandanna around my head à la Rosie the Riveter ("We Can Do It!") and gone with one loose fishtail braid that I'd wound up and pinned underneath. "Holidays bring out my daring side."

"Good to know," he said with a teasing smile. "Come on. We're back here."

17

AS I WALKED UNDER THE ARCH, I GLANCED UP AT THE camera and felt his fingers slide around mine. "Hi," he said in a softer voice. God, he smelled nice, all woodsy and clean.

Someone yelled out from behind the house. "Keep your pants on," he called back. Up-tempo guitar-and-drum music grew louder as we walked side by side down a stone path between his house and a crazy high wooden privacy fence. Tree branches from the neighbor's yard curved over the fence to create a shaded green canopy, and the farther back we went, the darker and more heavily wooded it became.

There were zero trees on my block. In fact, about two yards of dirt and broken cement patio sat between the back of my house and the one behind it.

But not the Vincents'.

Within the castled defense of their soaring privacy wall, a series of terraced decks rose from the wooded property, separating Jack's house from those of the surrounding neighbors. We stood on the most expansive deck, which started at the back door and fanned out to other, smaller decks—one behind a waist-high stone wall and another that sat behind a small guesthouse in the corner. Modern stairs zigzagged to a fourth, loftlike deck above us, where a bridge led to a door on the second story.

"Is M. C. Escher your architect?" I asked.

"My dad built all this when he won the first election."

"Are there cameras back here, too?"

"Only over the back door," he said. "But the house is off-limits tonight. Surprise—my dad doesn't want unsupervised party guests trampling his polished wood floors. Though I don't spend a ton of time in the house anymore. I moved into the guesthouse last year." He gestured toward the small building in the corner of the yard. "My parents used to have people stay over a lot, but not anymore."

Before the conversation got too sad, I said, "The guesthouse is private, which is cool. And now I see how you're sneaking out for your midnight expeditions. Except for the cameras."

"Willy taught me some tricks with those."

"Panhandler Will?"

Jack grinned. "He's sharper than you'd think."

We strolled beneath the stairs. A dozen or so people were lounging around the main deck. A couple of towheaded boys out of an Abercrombie & Fitch ad appeared to be divvying up the contents of a flask into several plastic cups on a long table crammed with food and soda. A guy with a Mohawk was hanging up a white sheet on the wall of the guesthouse, and another was setting up a digital projector.

There were only three other girls. One of them was piggybacking on Jack's friend Andy. He rushed toward us and tilted back to drop her onto her feet. She landed with a breathless laugh.

"Hi, again," Andy said, grinning as the girl he'd been carrying ducked into the crook of his arm. A very familiar girl with asymmetrically cut hair streaked purple and pink.

Sierra.

"Oh, wait. I know you. It's *her*?" she said to Jack. And because of the fairylike pitch of her voice, I couldn't tell if her words were condescending. But what I could tell was that Jack was uncomfortable, because he was squeezing my hand harder and drawing me ever so slightly away from Sierra.

With his arm slung around Sierra's shoulder, Andy said, "You two have met?"

"A couple of weeks ago," I said.

"I accidentally dumped tea all over her," she told Andy with a little laugh.

So funny. Yuk, yuk. Before she could elaborate, I asked, "How do all of you know each other?"

She leaned into Andy. "I met Jackson when I was staying at the Zen Center. I was going through some stuff at home, and they gave me a place to sleep and fed me in the student quarters for a few weeks until I got my shit together. I'm back at home now." Then she added, "He helped me, so I helped him." I had no idea what this meant, but from the way she was biting her lower lip, it was 100 percent salacious. "And now I'm helping Andy."

Andy looked mildly horrified by this statement, but she just laughed it off.

Super. Just when I'd abandoned my nightmare vision of Jack getting it on with some hospital candy striper, I could now replace it with the image of Sierra the Runaway sleeping in some sort of weird cultlike housing, where she met Jack and exchanged sexual favors for enlightenment and pluots.

If Sierra was clueless to the unease radiating off me, Andy sure wasn't. From the inside of his mouth, he wiggled his labret stud around with his tongue. "The extension cord isn't long enough for the projector," he told Jack.

"I'll find a new one in a minute." Jack steered me around Andy and Sierra and apologized under his breath as soon as we were out of earshot. "I didn't know he was bringing her tonight. I guess she called him after she saw us in the tea lounge."

"Are they seeing each other?"

"Sierra's . . . a free spirit."

Loving her more and more.

"Let's go meet everyone else," he said.

He herded me around the decks, and as dusk began falling and small golden lights lit up the tiered backyard, he introduced me to the partygoers. They included his rich friends from school, his poor friends from the Zen Center, his quirky friends from judo class (news to me that he knew judo, but maybe it explained all those muscles), and some nerdy kid who lived down the block, David, who was painfully shy and had busied himself with setting up the projector. And it was the pressing matter of the too-short extension cord, along with the request from—get this—catering-service people for Jack to sign off on their work order so they could leave, that left me standing alone in the middle of these motley strangers.

At the far end of the main deck, facing the white sheet, a gas fireplace built into a stone wall was roaring, and around it was an L-shaped bank of bench seating. Sierra stood in the middle, removing all the cushions from the seating and tossing them in a pile on the deck. She saw me watching her and smiled. "Those benches are super-uncomfortable. We can all stretch out on the floor."

I sat down on the cushionless bench. She wasn't wrong. A girl I'd met earlier sat down next to me, untucking a long, dark brown ponytail from the back of a sweater she was pulling on. "It's getting chilly. Someone needs to turn on the heat lamps."

I glanced to where she was pointing and spotted a couple of standing lamps that looked like the ones on restaurant patios, just nicer.

"Lala," she said when it was clear I didn't remember her name.

"Sorry," I replied.

"No worries. I wouldn't remember them all, either."

But I did remember her story: a girl originally from Brazil who went to school with Jack. She was willowy, pretty, and friendly, and she was dating one of the Abercrombie & Fitch blonds. She lifted her plastic cup of alcoholic fruitiness.

"No, thanks," I said, waving it away.

"Hunter tried to get a mini keg from his brother, but no go. We did, however, score two bottles of Fernet. He's running to the store to get ginger ale."

I had no idea what Fernet was.

"Tastes like old-timey medicine," Sierra said, making a face. "You have to chase it with ginger ale, or it'll come right back up. All the local bartenders drink it."

Whoop-de-freaking-do. Heath was the drinker in my family,

and I'd hit my once-a-year vomit limit that first day at the anatomy lab, so I'd be passing, thank you.

"How long have you and Jack been dating?" Lala asked.

I didn't know how to answer that question. Sure, he'd vandalized a museum for my birthday, but dating? Dates were things you planned. You asked someone out. You didn't just say, "Hey, it's sunny and you're standing here, so let's go to the park." But even if I knew in my heart there was something more between Jack and me, it wasn't definable—not in the way this girl was asking. So I answered, "We're just friends."

"That's not what I heard," Sierra said. "Andy told me Jackson's in *luuurve*."

My cheeks warmed. Had Jack told Andy that, or had Andy just said it? You couldn't be in love with someone you'd never even kissed . . . could you?

"Um, I don't know about that," I said. "But you guys dated?"

Sierra pointed at herself. "Me and Jack? Is that what he said?"

"No, that's what *you* said at the tea lounge."

"You told her about *that*?" Lala said.

Sierra gave us both a dismissive wave. "You make it sound like we banged each other's brains out. Jackson was going through a rough time, and I provided some cheer."

"You can keep your cheer away from Hunter," Lala warned.

I truly did not know what to say to any of this.

The last of the three other girls at the party appeared from nowhere and plopped down in the middle of Sierra's island of cushions. "I'm not finished, Nicole," Sierra complained.

"Work around me. I'm too buzzed to stand." Nicole threw her arms back and stretched like a cat, long auburn hair fanning around her head like a pinwheel. She had a natural, girl-next-door kind of vibe, and I would've pegged Nicole for one of Jack's Zen friends, but he'd said she went to school with him. "Who are you guys talking about?"

Lala slurped her drink. "Sierra's bragging about giving Jack a blow job. In front of his new girlfriend."

Wait—what? *This* was her idea of "cheer"? All my insides twisted into knots.

"Ugh, Sierra. Shut the hell up," Nicole said, closing her eyes.

"I wasn't bragging," Sierra argued. "But while we're on the subject, lemme just say, damn. That boy is packing, *amIright*?"

She was seriously saying this to me? "Um, we're just friends," I repeated.

"Really? I'm sorry. You mean, you guys haven't—"

"Jesus, Sierra," Nicole said. "No one wants to hear about your stupid erotic adventures with the entire population of San Francisco. Don't listen to her—" Nicole looked up at me from the cushions, her face upside down. "What's your name again?"

"Beatrix."

"Don't listen to her, Beatrix. Her grandmother was a Haight hippie, and she thinks this gives her some kind of free-love club card."

"At least I'm not all hung up on sex," Sierra argued. "We're all just bodies. It's not a big deal. And if you want my opinion, I think it's weirder he's going around telling everyone he's tripping over someone he's just *friends* with," she said.

Um . . . what?

Nicole shooed her away. "Why don't you go bounce on Andy and leave us the hell alone."

"Whatever. This is why I don't hang out with girls anymore. You're all bitches." Sierra threw down a cushion and stomped away.

Nicole groaned. "Oh my god, she drives me nuts."

"Give her a break. She's had a bad home life," Lala said, gesturing with her cup. "Her mom kicked her out of the house for, like, three months. Can't you see how screwed up she is? It's sad."

Nicole propped herself up on one elbow and watched Sierra merrily jumping on Andy's back. "I'll play a tiny violin for her as long as she stops flashing her tits at every guy I'm interested in."

"It takes two to tango," Lala said before glancing at me. "Don't worry about Sierra. Jack's a good guy. He's just a little screwed up, thanks to Jillian."

My body tensed. Jillian must be the sister in Europe. Was digging up firsthand gossip from his friends any better than snooping around for secondhand info about Jack's family online? I didn't know, but I was too curious to let it pass, so I feigned innocence and said, "Who's Jillian?"

Nicole and Lala glanced at each other. "Jillian is the Vincent family's dirty little secret," Lala said.

I didn't have time to ask for clarification before Nicole elaborated.

"Wouldn't we all be a little screwed up if we'd been through what he has? I sure as hell would. So, big deal, he's never had a steady girlfriend." She raised her chin at me. "I think you're lucky, being his first. Just look at him. He's gorgeous and funny, and he's got that cool retro-rockabilly thing going on. And he's just plain sweet."

"And *those eyes*," Lala said.

"So unfair," Nicole agreed. "Who cares if he's a man-whore. I mean *was*, not present tense. Sorry, Beatrix."

Lala laughed. "He's not a whore, Nicole. Where'd ya hear that?"

"Well, Sierra, for one."

Lala shook her head. "Sierra never went all the way with him. That's what I was saying about Jillian—she really screwed him up. Sierra said Andy told her Jack's a—"

A what? A WHAT?

Part of me knew that listening to all this wasn't as bad as reading gossip about Jack's family online; it was way, *way* worse. So why wasn't I getting up and walking away?

Lala's ice sloshed against the rim of the plastic cup. Nicole sank lower into the cushions. I glanced up to see what they were staring at and spotted Jack at the edge of the fireplace nook. He'd heard. I could tell by the anguished look on his face. And at that moment, I wanted to die.

18

THE GIRLS SCATTERED LIKE DANDELION SEEDS, DISAP-pearing into the crowd that was now gathering around Hunter, who had apparently lived up to his name and successfully hunted down ginger ale.

"They're just drunk," I assured Jack when everyone was out of earshot. I wanted to tell him that none of it mattered to me, all the things they were saying that I only half understood. I felt guilty for listening to all of it. Doubly guilty that he'd overhead—exactly how much, I didn't know.

"Do you want to go home?" he asked in a low voice.

"No," I answered over the thickness in my throat. "Do you want me to leave?"

"No!" Then more softly, "No."

Loud laughter billowed from the drink-mixing table. Jack glanced back at them. "Let's . . ." He scratched the back of his neck. "Let's talk. Not here."

I followed him over the smallest deck and into the guesthouse. As he closed the door, muffling the drunken laughter outside, I looked around. It wasn't much bigger than my dining room, but he had room for a double bed and a sofa at the foot of it that sat in front of a TV screen and several game consoles. Everything was tidy. His bed was made. (Mine wasn't.) A shelf held a small green ceramic Buddha and a few other trinkets—an altar of sorts—and I recognized the meditation cushions from the Zen bookstore. Being here felt as if I'd opened a door on the side of Jack's head that led into his brain.

Looking around, I noticed a door to a bathroom, next to which several odd portraits hung on the wall. They looked almost childish and were brightly colored. One of them was an alien woman. "Your work?" I asked.

He shook his head but didn't say anything else, so I continued my surveying, passing by a desk with an expensive computer and stopping at his drafting table, where a built-in shelf on the wall above it held a small fish tank. Beneath the white glow of its hood lamp, a single intensely blue betta with lacy fins rippled through a miniature town of tiki huts sitting among a forest of live aquatic plants. A school of tiny gray fish was the betta's only company.

"He looks a little like your tattoo," I said.

"Mmm."

Well. He was certainly in a black mood. Couldn't say I blamed him. I wanted to ask him about everything—his sister, Sierra, what the girls outside were all gossiping about. But I didn't know where to start.

My gaze slid over sketches pinned to an oversized corkboard. Alphabets. Dozens of them. All drawn by hand with pen and ink and markers, the occasional telltale pencil lines showing behind some of the letters. "You did these? They're incredible."

"Thanks."

"Is this a page from your comic?" It looked like a storyboard, illustrated with what I assumed were Andy's drawings and Jack's lettering. The hero seemed to be some sort of martial arts expert slash mechanic. "What's the story about?"

"I'm a virgin."

I froze. "Excuse me?"

"What they were saying is true. I am."

"Oh." How in the world was I supposed to respond? High five? "So, blow jobs don't count, then, I suppose?"

He closed his eyes. "That was one time and, no, I don't think it counts."

I disagreed, but then, I wasn't a blow job expert.

He sighed heavily. "And, no, I haven't really had a girlfriend. A couple of girls came and went before the incident." The break-in? Or his sister being shipped off to Europe? I wanted to ask for details, but he kept talking. "There was one other girl. I guess we started seeing each other around Christmas. She's the one I sort of mentioned to you in the park. Pretty early on, she found out about my family's so-called dirty little secret, as Lala put it, and got freaked out."

"And Sierra," I reminded him.

"Sierra was a mistake."

"Not to hear her talk about it," I said, toying with a comic inking pen on his desk.

"I'm not saying it wasn't fun—"

I glanced up at his face.

"Wrong word," he muttered. "And it was the absolute wrong person."

"Oh." But what I meant was "good."

After a long moment, he said, "It's not like I'm saving myself or anything."

"It's not a Zen thing?"

"No. The only rule about sex is not to misuse it, which basically means that you shouldn't do something that will harm yourself or someone else—like, literally, of course, but emotionally, too. It's pretty broad, and you're supposed to figure out what works for you. But that doesn't mean . . . it's not because—"

"Look, you don't have to explain."

"I just don't want you to look at me like you did out there."

"Like how?"

"Like you pitied me."

I stared at his inked alphabets for a long moment, not knowing what to say. It's not like I cared one way or the other about his experience or lack thereof, and he could've just lied and I never would've guessed differently; he certainly *seemed* much more experienced than I was. But he didn't lie. He told me the truth, and I had to think it took a lot of guts for him to admit it, which made me like him even more. It also made me want to be up-front in return. "I'm not, you know—a virgin, I mean. Is that weird for you?"

"How many?" he asked in a low voice.

"Four."

"Four guys?"

"Four *times*! One guy. Well, one and one-half guys, if you count Lauren's anti-prom party, but we didn't actually, uh, you know, and"—I shook my head, secretly wishing lightning would strike me down—"it really wasn't anything." Definitely not a blow job, but I didn't say that.

"Oh." He looked greatly relieved.

"Would it have been an issue if it was four guys?" After all, I'd known plenty of guys our age who'd slept with twice as many girls. Double standards were the worst.

"Intimidating, maybe. But, no, it wouldn't matter. Were things serious? With the one guy—not the half guy," he clarified, one side of his mouth quirking up.

"With Howard Hooper? God, no. I didn't even like him toward the end. He was kind of an ass. And the sex was disappointing, if you want to know the truth. At least, it was for me. He seemed to enjoy it, and that really pissed me off." Talking too much again. What was wrong with me? Was I trying to out-honest him with the embarrassing confessions? "Anyway, I overheard him calling Heath a fag, which was a deal breaker."

"I hate this Howard Hooper already."

I laughed a little. Things got quiet again.

"I'm not screwed up," he insisted.

"I've never thought that."

More silence.

"I'm not a monk, either," he said. "And I don't just want to be friends with you."

Well then.

"What *do* you want?" My voice sounded strange. I wished my heart would slow down. It was hard to breathe through my nostrils.

"What do I want?" His fingers brushed over loose strands of hair near my temple. "I want to call you every five minutes. I want to text you good night every night. I want to make you laugh. And I want you to look at me like you did that first night on the bus."

Oh.

My pulse was out of control. I was so overwhelmed, I couldn't meet his eyes. Couldn't even respond. His head dropped until our cheeks were touching. I turned my face to his, and his mouth hovered over mine—just for a moment. Long enough for me to feel his arm circle my waist, and one warm hand slide up my back. Long enough for chills to bloom across my forearms.

And then he kissed me. Slowly, softly. He tasted like he smelled, sunny and warm, but the sweetness lasted all of five seconds.

My hands snaked around his back, and he pulled me closer. And then he was kissing me like we were both on fire and he was trying to put the flames out, and I kissed him back like an arsonist with a pocketful of matches.

We were both frantic and fevered, and it was the first kiss I'd ever had that felt like a fight. And the way he made my body ache made me think I'd been doing it all wrong until now.

We broke apart for air, but our hands didn't stop moving.

"Jack," I whispered against his lips. I wasn't sure whether I was thanking him or begging. But before I could figure it out, my back was against the door, and I could feel every hard line of his body pressing into me, including what pressed against my stomach. When I pushed back, he picked me up until my toes left the floor and he didn't have to bend to fit his mouth to mine. And then my legs were around his hips and he was pulling me against him in exactly the right spot.

Maybe he was trying to prove something—I wasn't sure. And frankly, I didn't care, because it was the best kiss I'd ever had in my life. And the way he looked at me when he broke away for air, with his eyelids all heavy and those double lashes fanning... damn. It almost made me moan.

And I might've done exactly that if someone hadn't pounded against my shoulder blades. "Yo, Vincent. Let me in, man," a muffled male voice complained from the other side of the door. "Nature's calling. And it's time for the movie."

"Dammit," Jack mumbled against my neck before letting me slowly slide between the door and his hard body until my tiptoes reached the ground. I tried to pull away, but he wouldn't let me. Not until he'd dropped another kiss on my lips and a couple more on my eyelids. And this just made me want to start up all over again.

More pounding. "Vincent! You hear me in there?"

"I hear you," he answered in a rough voice. "Give me a sec."

He held me at arm's length, fingers gripping my shoulders, and he blew out a long, dramatic breath.

"Are you sure you are?" I whispered. Because, virgin or not, hell's bells, that was *good*.

He grinned. "Pretty sure."

Could've fooled me.

WHEN WE WALKED OUTSIDE, RINKY-DINK BACKYARD fireworks were popping and whistling around the neighborhood. Most of the party had gathered on the main deck to watch the movie, and as Jack made some final adjustments to the projector, I ignored the stares and found a space at the back of Sierra's cushion mountain. I leaned one striped pillow against the stone bench seating and watched a couple of the boys light an entire box of sparklers at once. I was pretty sure Jack and I were the only sober people there, but I couldn't have cared less.

I don't think he cared, either, because he was all smiles as he announced "one of the greatest cinema treasures of all time"—a martial arts flick from 1973, *Enter the Dragon*, which I'd never heard of, starring Bruce Lee, whom I had. But when the deck lights were turned off and the movie raced across the white sheet, I couldn't tell you a single thing about the plot. I was too busy being ridiculously happy inside the circle of Jack's arm, which curled over my shoulders, and too busy memorizing how his chest felt under my cheek. And every time I tried to steal a glance at the movie's white glow reflected in his face, he was smiling down at me.

But after the movie was over, instead of our retreating into his room—which is what I was hoping for, in all honestly—the party came to an abrupt end.

"Car out front!" Andy called out. "Hide everything!"

Everyone scurried around the decks, tossing drinks overboard, putting out cigarettes, and hiding the last bottle of Fernet inside the grill. As the madness subsided, the side gate creaked, and a couple walked around the side of the house.

"Might as well get this over with," Jack mumbled, taking my hand.

"This" turned out to be one person I vaguely recognized: Mayor Vincent, who looked a lot less in a hurry than the first time I'd seen him, at the hospital. And walking at his side was a dark-haired woman in a lavender summer dress.

"You're home early," Jack said.

"And on first sight, nothing appears to be on fire," the woman said, elbowing the mayor.

"Well, not *now*," Jack said. "An hour ago, this place was a raging inferno."

The mayor, who was a touch shorter than his son and wearing khakis and a button-up shirt one shade darker than the woman's lavender dress, peered hard at Jack's face. "You been drinking?"

"Tonight?"

"Jackson—"

"Kidding!" Jack said. "Jeez. Lighten up."

The mayor did not care for this suggestion, like, at all. "I'll lighten up when one of your friends wrecks his car and says he got drunk at our house. How's that going to look in front of a judge, huh?"

"No one's driving, Dad. You can relax. Your reputation remains sterling."

"We'll talk about this later. In the meantime, why don't you make sure everyone gets to the Muni stop without waking the whole damn neighborhood."

Yikes. His father was kind of scary—definitely not the smooth and friendly Mayor McDreamy I knew from the news. Not like I'd ever really paid much attention to him before Jack walked into my life. But still. Kind of a jackass, just like he was when I first saw him that afternoon at the hospital. And he had barely even looked my way, unlike the woman at his side, who was studying every stitch in my clothing. Who was this? Did the mayor have a girlfriend? Some sort of escort while his wife was institutionalized? When the woman's gaze met mine, I expected to see the same kind of dismissive vibe the mayor was giving off. Instead, she smiled like she knew me.

"Hi," she said, one oddly familiar dimple making an appearance as she extended a hand. "You must be Beatrix. I'm Marlena Vincent, Jackson's mother."

I shook her hand robotically, suddenly seeing how much more Jack looked like his mother than like the mayor. But if this was Jack's mother, and Jack's sister was overseas, who was in the hospital?

19

TWO NIGHTS LATER, I GOT THE ANSWER TO THAT question when I walked outside the anatomy lab. Jack was leaning against a tree, one foot up, hands in pockets. My heart leaped. I hadn't seen him since he dropped me off at my house after the party, after which he apologized for his father's lack of charisma and his mother's surplus of it. She was excessively nice. She knew not only my name but my age and what school I went to, and that my mom was a nurse at the hospital. She'd even seen some of my drawings online, and she was "so very glad" Jack had found a "friend" with whom he had something in common.

I didn't bother correcting that we were no longer "just friends," since he'd all but melted my panties off when he pushed me against the door of his bedroom. And she was so polite, it was difficult to do anything much but be polite right back, especially when King Mayor was there, lording over everyone.

"Hey," Jack said, pushing off the tree.

"Hi." I stopped in front of him, feeling a little awkward. He'd kissed me good night when he dropped me off after the party, but it was a tiny, tender kiss, and that had been two days ago. And even though we'd texted and talked on the phone since, both of us had been busy, and now it felt a little like the morning after. What were we supposed to do? Were we together? Could I just jump him right here in front of the premed students strolling up and down the sidewalk? Because I wanted to, but at the same time I was also nervous to touch him. And it didn't help that he'd called yesterday, sounding all mysterious and saying he wanted to show me something after my drawing session.

"How did it go?" His hands were still in his pockets, which made me feel guarded.

"Fine." Drawing Minnie was never *really* fine, but I certainly wasn't going to provide gruesome details or whip out my sketches. Ever again. "So, what's on tonight's agenda?"

"Walk with me?" he asked, extending his hand.

I took it, and he twined his fingers around mine, which instantly made me feel more relaxed. Him too, I guess, because he leaned down and quickly kissed my forehead in front of some professors. And that made my stomach flutter.

After a brisk walk in the twilight, we ended up at a four-story building. The psychiatric hospital. Jack didn't say anything, just looked down at me like he was asking for approval. And when I nodded, he opened the door and ushered me inside.

The person at the desk recognized him. "I called Dr. Kapoor and got approval for a guest," Jack said.

After a couple of phone calls, a muscle-bound orderly in green scrubs met us at a locked door, and we headed up in an elevator with him to the third floor. After Jack made introductions, Rupert told him, "Gotta be quick. Don't want to get her wound up this late, and you know how she is about new people."

"She might get overly excited," Jack explained as we walked into a well-lit corridor on a surprisingly modern, pleasantly designed floor. Bright artwork filled the walls, and plants stretched in front of long windows. "Or she might withdraw. Don't be offended, either way. It's not personal."

She, she, she. Who was this *she?* He hadn't said a word about the gossip he'd overheard on the night of the party, and I'd been too embarrassed to admit that the person I'd oh-so-wrongly assumed to be his mother was, clearly, not. I greatly regretted my earlier cowardice and wished I'd just asked him. Too late now.

"Does she know I'm coming?" I asked, a slow panic brewing in my stomach.

"Yes. But she gets confused about time, so she might not be expecting you."

"She's expecting," Rupert said. "She's been talking nonstop about it since dinner. You tell her all the rules?" he said, motioning his head toward me.

"What rules?" I asked.

"Don't give her anything," Jack said. "And don't let her take anything, either. No cords, no electronics, no shoelaces, no metal or glass."

"Anything can be a weapon," Rupert said. A weapon she'd use on me? Shoelaces? Would she try to strangle me?

"And don't try to shake her hand or anything," Jack added. "She sometimes gets freaked about touching."

We passed a set of double doors marked DAY ROOM ONE and

headed to a patient wing, passing a couple of nurses along the way. Other than that, it was quiet, which seemed bizarre—no screaming and wailing like the psych wards on TV. Midway down the corridor, a door cracked open and a head poked out, just for a moment. And all my slow panic speeded up significantly.

"Fifteen minutes," Rupert said. "I'll be at the end of the hall when you're ready."

Jack took a deep breath and knocked on the door before opening it. "It's just me."

No reply came. I followed him into a small private room that smelled of cigarette smoke. A darkened bathroom sat to the left of the entrance, and further in, the rest matched my mental image of a college dorm room: white walls, tiled floor, chunky wooden table, and some built-in shelves. A single bed sat under a window, and on the bed was a chubby girl who had short, dark hair and wore pink pajamas.

"Yo, Jillie," Jack said. "I brought someone to meet you, just like I promised."

Jillie. Jillian.

His sister was definitely not at a European boarding school.

The girl appeared to be our age. She looked relatively normal. No crazy eyes. Well, at least not that I could tell, because she wouldn't look at me directly. She blinked a lot and tugged on a curling lock of hair at the back of her neck.

"Jillie, this is my friend Beatrix. Bex, this is Jillian, my twin sister."

Twins.

I didn't know what to say, but she still wasn't looking at me, and things were getting uncomfortable. So I just said, "Hi there."

It was enough to warm her up. She flicked a couple of furtive glances my way. Then she surprised me. "Jack told me about you. It's your birthday."

"*Was* her birthday," Jack corrected. "A few weeks ago."

"Oh, that's right. I'm allergic to dairy, so I can't have cake," she said, picking up a pack of cigarettes hidden beneath a stuffed frog on her windowsill.

"You got your lighter back?" Jack asked.

"Out of pity," she said. "Dr. Kapoor will eventually take it away. He always does."

The window opened only partially, allowing a few inches of fresh air before a set of chains went taut. With shaking hands, Jillian lit up a cigarette and blew smoke through the cracked window. "They don't want you to jump," she said, catching me staring at the chains. "On the fifth floor, you can't even open the windows."

"The fifth floor blows," Jack said, pulling out a chair from her table and gesturing for me to sit. He then perched on the bed next to Jillian. "You okay today?"

She drew her knees up to her chest. "Not really. Well, I guess I am. Pretty good. Yeah. Sort of." She floundered as if she truly wasn't sure how to answer, and took a long drag off her cigarette. "It's not a bad day."

"Excellent. I'm glad to hear it."

"You're really tiny," Jillian said to me. "What's your shoe size?"

I thought about the shoestring warning. Was she angling for my shoes? I fought the urge to hide my feet behind my sketchbook satchel. "Uh, five?"

"That's small. I miss buying shoes. We only get the slip-ons," she said, nodding toward a pair of Vans that were decorated with painted zigzags on the flaps. Then she tapped Jack on the shoulder. "Remember those purple heels Mom told me I couldn't have? She said they looked like porn star shoes."

"I remember," Jack said.

"They had the bows on the straps. I loved those bows. Why do bows make everything cuter? If you have a shitty present you want to give someone, you can slap on bow on it, and then it's okay. Doesn't really matter what's inside. If it's wrapped nicely, no one is going to complain. And really, anyone who complains about a present is a dick. Unless it's an inten—" She grimaced, sucking in a sharp breath, then tried again. "An in-ten-tionally bad present. Like, maybe if you hate someone, but you're forced to give them a gift in one of those white elephant tiger safari exchanges."

"Like at Christmas," Jack supplied. "White elephant."

"White elephant," she repeated. "But not us. You already know what I'm getting you for Christmas. Another lame portrait."

My gaze jumped to the wall at the foot of her bed. A collection of things was taped there: a green felt-tip marker, a packet of sugar, a rubber duck, and six paintings of faces. One was an alien man who matched the alien woman in Jack's room.

"Shut up. I love your portraits," he said.

Jillian ducked her head and beamed. "*You* shut up," she said affectionately, squinting at him from the crook of her arm. Not crazy eyes, no. But there was something different about them, a weird, glassy look, as if she were drunk or high. The trembling hands and chain-smoking didn't help.

"I remember seeing the"—crap. What if it wasn't an alien?—"uh, the green one hanging on your brother's wall."

"You've been to his room?" She said this like it was an accusation.

I looked at Jack. *Help me out here.*

"That's right, she has," he said smoothly. "Not my old room. The guesthouse."

"I remember," she said irritably, flicking her cigarette butt out the window and lighting up another. The girl was a machine.

"Rupert said you need to go to sleep soon. Maybe you should make that one the last of the night."

She ignored him and spoke to me. "I see why Jack likes you."

"Oh?"

"You're a lake."

"A lake," I repeated.

"What do you mean?" Jack said.

She tugged the curl at her neck. "Calm like a lake. Still water."

If only she knew how crazy my life actually was under the surface, what with my sneaking around behind my mom's back to draw dead bodies, being questioned by the police for romantic crimes committed by my felonious boyfriend, and having my cheating, gift-giving father trying to woo his way back into my heart.

"He's got enough craziness in his life, so you're the opposite," she said, fanning smoke away. "And by craziness, yeah, I mean me. Did he tell you why I'm here?"

"Jillie," he cautioned.

"It's better to talk about it openly—that's what Dr. Kapoor says. And it's not like I'm here because I'm on vacation. I'm schizoid. I hear voices in my head. Sometimes I see things that make me feel like I'm dreaming while I'm awake. And I'm not dreaming. I'm just screwed up, and they can't fix me."

"They can, and they are," Jack said.

"Okay, maybe I'm a little better."

"A lot," Jack said.

"Yeah, a lot," she said dreamily. "Sometimes I'm a lot better. I really thought I was going to come home this summer until they nearly killed me with meds."

"But they straightened it out."

She laughed loudly and then spoke in a low, singsong voice. "'Doctor, she hasn't tried to kill herself lately. Better fill her full of poison to stay on track.'" She made a gurgling sound effect and pantomimed swallowing a bottleful of pills.

"Not funny," Jack said, pulling down her arm.

"I didn't say it was." She sniffled and wiped her nose on her sleeve. "But it's all good now, because these old meds are the best. They make me feel pro . . . um, pro-duc-tive, and the doctors had to up my dose, so now I get a little buzz off them."

"Jillie—"

"You want to know what it's like," she said to me in a flat voice. She was looking in my direction, but I wasn't sure if she really saw me. "Everyone wants to know. It's better to talk about it when I can, because sometimes I can't, so I'll tell you. It's like when someone offers you candy, and you think, 'I want that,' but then another part of you says, 'Sugar is bad for you.' And for a moment you're torn, because you're not sure if you should eat the candy, and a little war goes on inside your brain. That's what happens to me all day long. A little war in my head. And it stresses me out. And the more I get stressed out, the more soldiers join the war, and sometimes a few of those soldiers will start talking to me. Then it's like a running commentary playing in the background, judging every move I make."

"That sounds frustrating," I said.

"That's a nice way of putting it." She made a grunting noise and closed her eyes. "What was I saying? God. The rambling. It's enough to drive me crazy." She gave me a quick smile before turning to Jack and smacking herself on the forehead. "Oh, yeah! Hey, I have a new puzzle for you. Can I show it? I know it's our secret, but she's been inside your room, so she can see it, right?"

"Yes," Jack said, smiling at me from the bed. "She's a good secret keeper."

Jillian mumbled something to herself and furtively glanced over both her shoulders before tossing the second cigarette out the window. Then she ducked her head below the bed and whipped out a manila folder overflowing with wrinkled papers. "I lost the new one. . . . Oh, wait. Here it is."

Jack bent over it with her, studying whatever was written on the paper. And I did some studying of my own, using the opportunity to really look at Jillian. She was pretty. Heartbreakingly so. And though she didn't have Jack's dark double lashes, she shared his terrific bones and height.

But when I looked closer, what stood out the most wasn't genetic: Thick, shiny scars ran up both her inner forearms and across one side of her neck. The scars were shocking, and once I'd noticed them, I couldn't see anything else. A dozen questions raced through my head. It took everything I had not to gawk.

"This is a tough one," Jack said. "I'm not sure if I can use any of these."

"I thought there were a couple. 'Screw' is always good."

"I'm not using 'screw,' Jillian."

"Okay, okay. What about this one."

Jack twisted the page and smiled. "Yeah. That'll work great. Here, let's see if Beatrix can find it."

"It's a test," Jillian said excitedly while handing the paper to Jack, who handed it to me; I guessed she really didn't like touching.

When I took the wrinkled page, I caught a glimpse of the other "puzzles." They were all basically the same: homemade word searches. A grid of letters, most of them legible, some not so much. I sat back down and studied the one in my hand.

I wasn't sure what I was supposed to find. Nothing had been circled, but one word was bolded in the center of the grid: "Charlie." It looked like she'd started with that and built words off it. And seeing how quite a few of those words were things like *kissing* and *licker* and the previously discussed *screw*, I didn't really want to get into exactly who Charlie was, but she told me anyway.

"Charlie's one of the orderlies. It was just a joke because he's too mean."

"He's tough, not mean," Jack said.

"No, I meant he's straight, or, um . . . what's the word?"

"Stoic."

"Yeah, yeah." She pointed at Jack and nodded. "Stoic."

I studied the puzzle, searching for the word they'd found. The marker she'd used wasn't the same metallic gold that Jack used for his pieces. But it could definitely be called golden. And at the bottom of the grid, I spotted four letters that shook something loose in my brain. I could already envision it written in glittering spray paint.

"*Rise*?" I guessed.

Brother and sister shot me dueling grins.

And that was the exact moment I fell in love with Jack Vincent.

20

I'VE NEVER REALLY MINDED THE SCENT OF HOSPITALS. Maybe it's because my mom's a nurse. It's familiar. Comfortable. Sure, I understand why some people might associate the scent with bad things, like tears and pain and death. But it should be associated with good things, too, like healing and hope and second chances.

And as I exited the psych building with Jack, I associated the scent with other positive things, like admiration. Understanding. And a strange sort of tenderness that melted the right ventricle of my heart.

"You're painting all the words for her," I said, looping the handles of my sketch bag over my shoulders and clamping it between my elbow and ribs. Chilly night air gusted through my open jacket.

"She feels trapped. She loves the city, but she's been terrified of it ever since she got sick. Too much noise, too many people. And you saw her on a good night—a really good one. Some days, she shuts down completely and won't talk. She's lost all her friends, and she hasn't been out in public doing normal things for so long. I just wanted to show her that the walls aren't closing in and that there's something out there. Something that's hers."

"Something to give her a reason to keep going."

"Yeah."

We strolled down the sidewalk, both quiet, until we ended up at a bench near the back parking garage entrance. Jack stopped and sat me down. "I need to tell you the rest before I lose my nerve."

"Tell me."

A long breath gusted from his lips. Legs spread, he leaned forward and rested his forearms on his knees, cracking his knuckles. "It happened at Thanksgiving, when we were sophomores. Things had slowly been going downhill for her for months. She dropped out of all her extracurricular stuff at school and started staying at home more. Her grades fell. Her friends stopped coming over. One teacher called my parents in, all concerned about the way she stared in class, like a zombie. The teachers all thought it was drugs."

"But it wasn't."

"No. But I thought it might be, too, for a while. She went from being homecoming princess to someone who stopped wearing makeup and dressed like a slob. My parents got her on an antidepressant, which helped for a little while. But after a few months, she started saying strange things and complaining about hearing voices. She seemed agitated and tweaky. And that's when she started secretly smoking. She said it calmed her nerves. We later found out that something like eighty percent of people with schizophrenia smoke. The researchers don't know why, exactly—there's a ton of theories they can't agree on. But for Jillie to smoke? It was just so out of character."

He shook his head and waited for a couple of students to walk past before continuing. "Anyway, early that October, she went into a rage at school. It was our old school, before I transferred to the one I go to now, and we were in the same class, so I saw it happen. She couldn't answer a history question about the colonies, and Mr. Davis snapped and mocked her. The next thing I knew, she'd dumped over her desk and was screaming crazy stuff, running erratically, knocking things over. She grabbed a stapler and lobbed it at Mr. Davis. It hit him in the face. Hard. He had a black eye for a couple of weeks. And Jillian got an overnight stay in a psych facility across town."

"Not here?" I asked.

"No, and they said she was bipolar. Gave her meds. My dad made good with the teacher and the school. And a week later, she was back in class. No report filed with the police, nothing on her school record. It was as if it had never happened. But by the middle of November, she started skipping school. Ran away for two nights. One of our neighbors found her in the ravine behind our house—she'd been camping out in his shed."

"Jesus."

"She'd gone off her meds. Not that they were the right ones. But that's when I first noticed the cycle thing. She gets agitated, withdraws, gets agitated, withdraws. . . . And by the time Thanksgiving weekend rolled around, she was agitated. Talking to herself. Constantly startled and on edge. Making a lot of weird gestures. Stopping in the middle of sentences.

"We were having family over that afternoon," he continued in a lower voice. "And I was in the kitchen, arguing with my parents about her. My dad didn't want my grandmother to see Jillian like that. He was talking about checking her back into the hospital for the holiday, and my mom was defending her, and I was arguing with both of them. And Jillian walked in on it."

He cracked his knuckles and looked away toward the slowing traffic, so I couldn't see his face. But the tension stiffening his arms was telling.

"It all happened so fast," he said. "Everyone was yelling, and then I saw the knife glint in the kitchen light, and Mom was bleeding through her shirt. Dad wrestled Jillian away, and she wasn't Jillie—not in her eyes. She was someone else. But there wasn't time to . . . do anything about it. Mom was bleeding out on the floor, and Jillie had gone catatonic. Dad told me to lock her in the basement. He thought she might run again. Maybe try to hurt someone else."

He didn't say anything for a while, so I pressed. "What happened to your mom?"

"Dad and I followed the ambulance. They had her in surgery for an hour. The knife didn't puncture anything important. Mostly muscle damage around her shoulder. That's why if you ever see her at political events with my dad, she waves funny—she still can't lift her left arm all the way."

I recalled seeing a couple of ignorant comments about that online before I stopped snooping around for stuff about the Vincents, but I didn't say this, and he continued his story.

"Once we found out Mom was okay, I went back home to check on Jillie. Dad told me not to unlock the basement until he got back. But she wouldn't answer, and I couldn't hear her moving around."

He slowly shook his head several times, reliving it all in his mind, I supposed. When he spoke again, his voice was so gravelly I could barely hear him. "I walked downstairs, calling for her. I couldn't find her at first. When I flipped on the light in the game room, all I could see was blood. On the carpet, her clothes . . . I couldn't tell where it was all coming from. I found the neck wound, and she was still breathing, so I called 911 and tried to stop the bleeding. But it was coming from her wrists, too. I thought she was dying in my arms, and I didn't know what to do."

Several things clicked into place: Jillian's scars; my drawing of Minnie, dead, with her forearm dissected in exactly the same place; Jack fainting at the sight of it.

Now I was breathing too fast. I wanted to touch him—console him somehow. But was that what he needed? What was I supposed to say? I didn't know. But I tried to picture the girl I'd just seen—chatty, nervous, and almost shy—doing everything Jack had just told me. I couldn't.

"There was never any break-in," I said.

He shook his head. "That was to keep the press out of it. My dad's opponents would go nuts if they knew it was really Jillian who'd stabbed my mom. They still found out that she'd been hospitalized, but the 'official' reason was stress and trauma due to the supposed break-in, and my dad's staff then came up with the cover story about Jillian going away to boarding school in Europe. The press bought it, and everyone forgot about her."

I didn't say anything, but after a few moments Jack dropped his head and mumbled, "How did no one see the knife? We still can't figure out how that happened. Dad knocked it out of her hand. I saw it for a second. If it hadn't been so chaotic . . . I just . . ."

I took a deep breath, hugged my stomach, and leaned forward to get closer to him. "If it hadn't been so chaotic, she might've found another way. If not that day, then another. You seriously cannot be blaming yourself for this—you don't, do you?"

"No. I mean, I know better. Logically. We all go to family counseling every week. So believe me, I've looked at it from every angle. Our therapist says it's survivor guilt—I got the good genes, and she got the screwed-up ones. It's worse because we're twins."

"But you can't change that. And she's better, yeah?"

"Better, but she'll never be okay. She won't have a normal life. She won't ever go to school again, and she won't get married or have kids. And even though I saved her once, I can't always be there. I think about going to college, and I don't know how that will work. What will she do if I can't see her for an entire semester?"

"You could go somewhere local. See her on the weekends."

"Maybe. But if my dad runs another campaign, my parents will be out of the picture. Campaigning is nonstop stress for both of them. Long hours. Trips. And if he wins? Governor of California? We'd have to move, and I can't even fathom the drama."

"I don't think it's your job to worry about that."

"Kind of hard *not* to when it's my life. Now do you see what you've gotten yourself into? Do you understand why I didn't call you after her seizure?"

"I understand," I said, tapping my knee against his leg. "But don't ever do that again. If anything happens, no matter what, you call me. Okay?"

He tilted his head to look at me and nodded. "Okay."

"Promise me, Jack."

"I promise."

A friendly voice called out from the parking garage entrance.

I spotted Panhandler Will walking toward us. "Sad Girl and Monk," he said cheerily. "You found each other."

"We did," I confirmed. "Thanks for your help."

"Anytime, anytime. No, man, I'm good," he said, waving away the money Jack had dug from his pocket. "I just wanted to say hi. I wasn't asking."

"Take it anyway," Jack said. "You should open a dating service for the hospital. Play matchmaker and get people together."

"You're teasing me," Will said, taking the offered bill.

"Yeah, I am," Jack said with a smile.

Will smiled back, almost shyly, before swiveling around to peer farther down the sidewalk. "Dammit. Rent-a-cops. Gotta go. Thanks, Monk. See you, Sad Girl."

After Will disappeared into the garage, Jack said, "You know he used to be a patient in Jillian's ward, right?"

"Seriously? I mean, I knew he wasn't . . . jeez. How long ago?"

"Like, seven years ago. One of the orderlies remembers him. He says they never diagnosed exactly what was wrong, but he's on a low-dose antipsychotic. They sneak him free medicine and try to check up on him. I guess he has no relatives and no place to crash."

"That sucks."

"Many things in life do, Bex."

I slid my hand into his. For several beats, his grip was almost tight enough to hurt, but I didn't let go. Not then, and not when he told me he had to get home because his parents were expecting him. Or when he insisted on riding the N-Judah back with me because it was "dangerous to ride public transportation at night."

(Oh, the irony.) And not when he walked me down the block-long hill to my house.

"What are you going to do about 'rise'?" I asked after we turned the corner and the pale yellow siding on my house came into view.

"Ah, yes. 'Rise.'" He cleared his throat. "I've been trying to match up the words to places Jillian likes. But it's a hard balance, finding a spot that's both significant and hidden enough that I can work. And security cameras are a problem. So it's like solving a secondary puzzle to figure out the perfect spot."

I stopped across the street from my house. "Could you use a getaway girl?"

"Absolutely not."

"Why?"

"First, you don't drive, so you'd make a terrible getaway girl. And second, you told me yourself—felony charges. I won't put you in a situation where you might get dragged down with me. Nurse Katherine the Great would never let me see you again."

"This is true. But I thought feeling alive is always worth the risk. At least, that's what someone once told me."

He smiled for the first time since we'd left the psych ward. "That person was an idiot."

"I don't know about that. Personally, I think he's pretty amazing."

"Amazing, huh? Tell me more about how great I am."

"Were we talking about you?" I asked, squinting up at him quizzically.

Smiling, he finally let go of my hand. "You really are a lake," he murmured. Then he slipped his arms around my back, and I curled my arms around him, boldly taking the liberty of going right under his scuffed leather jacket, like I'd been doing it for years. He smelled good. He felt good. And when he bent his head and kissed me—slowly, deeply . . . doing this lazy, rolling thing with his tongue that drove me wild—I forgot that we were standing in the middle of a city sidewalk. I forgot everything but the two of us. And nothing else mattered.

When he finally left, my kiss-weakened legs were barely able to climb our front steps. Two hours later, I got a text from him: Good night, Bex.

And the next morning, I got another: If you really want to be my getaway girl, be ready tomorrow at midnight. Dress in black.

21

JUST BEFORE OUR MEETING TIME, I DID JACK'S CONtrolled breathing trick to relax and padded down the hallway to my mom's room. Dressed in loungewear, she was stretched out beneath her bedcovers, a glass of wine on her bedside table.

"Hey," I said. "My shift kinda sucked and I'm supertired, so I'm just going to crash for the night."

Mom looked up from her e-reader. "You're working too much at Alto."

"But I'm putting a ton of money away in savings."

She gave me a sleepy smile. "Which is why you won't be living here when you're twenty, like your brother. Keep it up."

"You're not the least bit sad he's moving in with Noah?"

"Of course I'm sad. He's my baby. He always will be, even when he's fifty and has kids of his own."

I tried to picture Heath as a father. "Do they make studded leather diapers?"

"Imagine trying to clean those."

"Blech. I'd rather not."

"While we're on the subject, I brought something home from

the hospital for you." She pointed toward the opposite wall, where a stack of folded multicolored scrubs sat on a rocking chair. My gaze swept upward to the nearby chest of drawers. Hold on. What was that, sitting on top?

Oh. *Oh.*

A tower of condom boxes, all shrink-wrapped together.

I wanted to dissolve into vapor and hide under the floorboards.

"As much as I, myself, have fantasized about having Mayor Vincent's love child—"

I covered my ears. "Please, stop. Don't say anything else."

"—I don't want to raise a grandchild while you run off to college."

"There is zero chance of that happening at the moment, I promise."

"Moments change, and that boy is *awfully* charming. Besides, you're smiling a lot lately, and that's always a bad sign."

"Oh, God," I said, moaning. She knew how I felt about him. How did she do that? I hardly knew it myself. I wasn't even positive. Maybe I was just riding a wave of body chemicals and animal attraction. I mean, how well did I even know Jack? He could have some irritating habit I didn't know about—some hidden character flaw. I didn't realize Howard Hooper was homophobic until I'd had sex with him four times. (Then again, maybe I was the one with the character flaw because I was stupid enough to have sex with a jackass.)

Mom had never once pushed condoms on me. Sure, there were some in the bathroom drawer, and I'd had multiple safe-sex conversations with her over the years; she *is* a nurse. But why now?

"I can't take them back," Mom argued. "It's one thing to abscond with supplies and a whole other thing to sneak them back in."

"They're stolen? You're a terrible influence."

"The supply manager was rotating stock and was going to throw them away because they expire at the end of the year, which was ridiculous. At least five months of use left in them. Probably more."

"So, you're telling me these are leftover garbage condoms?"

"They haven't been used, Bex. You know I hate waste."

"Maybe you should hand them out on Halloween instead of candy."

"Don't be smart. They're perfectly fine. I bring them home for Heath all the time."

Too much information. I quickly steered the conversation back between the yellow lines. "If you're asleep when I wake up, I'll see you in the afternoon."

She rolled onto her side, with her back facing me, and curled up with her e-reader again. "Tomorrow I have to run an errand in the Mission at lunch. If you want to come with, we can get burritos at El Farolito. I have a coupon."

Of course she did. "Sounds good."

"Night." She kissed her fingers and wiggled them at me over her shoulder.

I stood there for a moment, grabbed the stack of condom boxes, and quickly made my way back to my room to stash it in the bottom of my wardrobe. Eight boxes. That was a lot of condoms. I could probably sell them at school in the fall and make some extra cash.

Or...

But I didn't have time to think about *or*. I had only fifteen minutes to dress in black—definitely not a problem, since I barely owned anything with color—and make my big escape. Arranging dummy humanoid shapes under the covers never worked for anyone in the history of the world, so I just left a note on my pillow that said: *I'm fine, don't worry. I'll be back before dawn. If you've busted me, please remember I'm the good kid. And if it's Heath reading this, cover for me. You owe me, big-time.*

It took me several minutes and snail-paced movements to close my X-ray doors behind me and sneak outside. I tiptoed down the front steps and watched the living room window for movement. Nothing. I'd made it!

"Psst!"

I spun around and spotted a dark figure behind the stairway to the top-floor unit.

Jack was wearing his old jewel-thief getup, with the black knit cap pulled down to his eyes and a backpack slung over one shoulder. I didn't have a cap, but I had a hoodie beneath my tight jacket, and my hair was wound up in a plaited chignon above my neck.

"Is that you?" I asked in a stage whisper, joy pinging inside my chest.

"Come here if you want to find out." Jack pulled me into the shadow and then against his chest, grinning as he kissed me quickly—first on the mouth and then, when I hugged him, on my neck, right below my jaw. And, *whoa*. Major shivers.

I held him tightly, as if I could absorb all his goodness. He felt safe and warm and exciting, and I had trouble letting go of him.

"Mmm." His low voice burred against my skin in the most

thrilling way. "This is already way more fun than usual. I should've hired a getaway girl a long time ago."

"Does that mean I'm getting paid?"

"Depends on what you'll take for payment."

I had some ideas, thanks to his shiver-inducing neck kisses. But when one of the women who lived in the neighboring teal-blue row house stepped outside with her terrier on a leash, I decided it was best to table all my lusty thoughts and get the heck out of there before we were spotted. "Let me get back to you on that."

Hand in hand, we rushed uphill to the bus stop. Jack never took Ghost on graffiti runs because she was crazy identifiable, so tonight we'd be slumming it on Muni with all the other late-night riders. It was almost like the night we met, only this time I was filled with excitement instead of dread.

"I can't believe I'm doing this," I said while Jack used his phone to find out exactly where the train was. There would be one or two more trains coming before the Owl took over the route.

"Second thoughts?"

"One or two," I said. "But no chance I'm bailing now."

"What about Nurse Katherine?"

I grunted. "She's drinking wine in bed, which means with any luck she'll be snoring in about an hour. Either that or she'll be pushing expired condoms off on Heath."

"Um, what?"

"She gave me a billion hospital condoms that expire at Christmas."

He gave me a sidelong glance, and I was instantly aware that this conversation was heading into untested waters. "Is this something she often does?" he asked carefully.

"You know how thrifty she is," I said with a forced shrug. "The hospital was throwing them away, I guess."

"Huh."

Ugh. Why had I even brought this up? "She says she gives them to Heath all the time. Not that I want to think about that. I don't know. She's just weird sometimes."

"A billion of them?"

"More like a hundred. What, do the ER patients need to get it on before they leave the building?" I laughed nervously.

"But they aren't expired yet?"

"December, apparently. That's what she said, anyway. I didn't look." More like I didn't want him to think I was studying the boxes in my room like a fiend.

"A hundred condoms by December. That's nearly one a day."

"Is it?"

"We could break your record with Howard Hooper in less than a week."

I nearly choked. We, as in *us*. Was that a suggestion, or was he teasing? "Quality over quantity," I managed to say over the erratic thump of my pulse.

"Why settle?"

I made a small noise. "You're awfully confident."

"You bring out the best in me."

To hide my smile, I pretended to watch a car passing. But it didn't matter, because the train was pulling up to the stop. I boarded ahead of Jack with a spring in my step. I even greeted the driver.

Yep. I was definitely a goner.

The train was mostly empty and fairly clean, and we settled together in a two-person seat. I assumed we'd be discussing the plan for his graffiti attack, but all he'd tell me was that we were headed for the Civic Center BART station on Market—where underground rapid-transit trains depart for the outlying counties beyond the city and across the Bay. "We'll have some time to waste when we get there, so we can stop for caffeine if you need it."

I wouldn't.

As the train picked up and dropped off other passengers, we spent the trip talking about this and that. Friends. School. The art contest and my plans for using the scholarship money if I won. I even told him more of the story about my parents' divorce, and about the mysterious artist's mannequin being delivered and my email response from the wood-carving shop in Berkeley. He offered to go with me if I decided to talk to the guy who'd made my mannequin and find out how to contact my dad. If I was going to make the trek out there—behind my mom's back, I might add—I'd definitely rather do it with Jack at my side.

Not surprisingly to either of us, toward the end of our conversation the train broke loose from the overhead cable near Duboce Park (this happens all the time), and we had to wait nearly half an hour for the driver to reconnect it. By the time it dropped us off near the Civic Center, the BART station was closed and locked up.

"Perfect," Jack said, slipping on thin leather gloves.

"It is?"

"Yep. Follow my lead. And let me know if you see any cops."

This area was dodgy at night, but it was mostly homeless people and nonthreatening street punks. I wasn't all that worried, since Jack was with me, though my nerves were bouncing with anticipation. What I didn't understand was why we were *here*, exactly. It was a major thoroughfare, and though it wasn't exactly bustling at one o'clock in the morning, it wasn't hidden, either—unlike most of the other places he'd hit.

At the end of the block, he watched for a moment before we retraced our steps.

"Where are we—"

He stopped at one of the subway entrances. It was a small one—like many others around the city, just a railed-off area of the sidewalk with a BART sign. Normally, there would be steps descending underground inside the railing, but on this night the entrance was covered by one of those temporary plywood construction enclosures with four walls and a roof. A makeshift door was boarded up, with a laminated sign attached: ENTRANCE OUT OF SERVICE UNTIL ___. The blank had been filled in with the next day's date, and the sign instructed riders to use an alternate entrance around the block.

"Tell me if anyone's coming and hold this," Jack said, and before I knew what was happening, he'd handed me a heavy flashlight and—*dear God!*—was prying open the door to the enclosure . . . like cars weren't rushing by, and like a couple of vagrants weren't huddled inside a closed store entrance half a block away.

He got the door open in a few seconds. "Flashlight," he said, as if he were a doctor requesting a scalpel. I handed it over. We waited for headlights to pass, and he cracked open the door and shined the flashlight inside. Satisfied, he gave one last glance around the area, rushed me through the door, and quickly closed it up behind us.

Trying not to inhale the unpleasant, dank smell, I surveyed the dark area with Jack while he beamed the flashlight around. We stood at the top of the subway entrance. A set of stairs on the right was marked for entering the station, and a nonworking escalator on the left was marked as the exit. Dull fluorescent light blanketed the bottom of the stairwell, glowing from behind locked scissor gates that blocked the station entrance.

"It reeks," I complained in a whisper.

"Have you never used this station?" he whispered back. "It's way better than usual. When it's not closed up, homeless people go down there to the bottom"—he beamed the flashlight over the station gates—"for some primo private restroom time. The BART workers have to clean up shit and piss every morning. If they don't, when they turn on the escalator, it gums up the works. That's why half the escalators in the stations are always broken."

"Vomit."

"Right? My dad told me about it. Instead of spending money to have gates built up here to block off the escalators when the station's closed, they just keep funneling nickels and dimes into repairing them. This one got so bad, they had to replace the entire escalator motor. That's why it's boarded up."

"And it reopens tomorrow."

"It's already tomorrow." He shined the flashlight under his chin, looking like an old-school monster-movie actor, with all his beautiful bones casting eerie shadows. "It opens in three hours, so let's get to it."

Jack had every detail planned: a small head-mounted camping flashlight that lit up the area directly in front of his face; a portable airbrush system preloaded with metallic gold paint; three cans of the fancy spray paint I'd spied the first night we met; a small plastic container filled with exactly five extra nozzles (because he had to occasionally swap out nozzles so the paint wouldn't clog, he kept track of the number he came with—couldn't leave any behind or the cops could trace the paint brand); folded-up hand-cut stencils and masking tape; and, lastly, two masks to filter out the paint fumes, which we each donned. We were ready.

He pulled his mask down to talk. "If anyone dangerous tries to get in here, jump the handrail and get behind me."

"Don't worry. I've got pepper spray."

"Terrific, but I'd rather defend you, if you don't mind. I have a modicum of male pride that needs feeding on occasion."

"Fine, but what about cops or people patrolling the station down there?"

"They don't patrol the station. They don't even monitor the security cameras—not in the budget. But if a cop comes from the street entrance, he'll likely have a gun. So just put your hands up, and I'll do all the talking. Hey, you okay?"

"I'm not built for a life a crime."

"You want to bail? Say the word. I won't be mad in the least. I'm serious, Bex."

"No way. Let's do this."

"Aye, aye, getaway girl. Mask on."

While I stood across from him on the stairs, holding his backpack and handing him supplies, he started painting at the top of the escalator. It was hard to see much at first, because he was mainly spraying the escalator steps solid gold. But as he switched back and forth between the cans and the airbrush, the grated silver tops of the steps became gilded, and on the vertical planes between the steps, in a contrasting flat gold, the top of an *R* took shape.

He moved down as he worked, step-by-step—because once he'd painted, he couldn't go back up and fix anything without smearing wet paint. And I followed his slow path on the stairs, handing him supplies on the way down. The farther we descended, the less we heard pedestrians and cars passing, and the more it felt like we were headed into a hellish pit, where the devil himself would appear behind the station gates.

Fear and excitement clashed inside my chest, churning up the same kind of distress I felt on amusement park rides—only, when I was riding the Grizzly roller coaster at Great America in Santa Clara, I didn't have to worry about getting arrested or being stabbed by a dangerous vagrant.

Nearly two hours passed. I spent most of that time memorizing the way Jack's long arms and fingers moved as he painted. How his eyes crinkled in the corners as he squinted at his work, and how he rolled his shoulders to stretch out the tension in his sleek body.

We could break your record with Howard Hooper in less than a week.

And that. I thought about him saying that. A lot.

By the time we got to the bottom, I had a headache from the

paint fumes, and Jack's fingers were cramping. But when we met by the gates, pulling off our masks, I beamed the flashlight up the escalator. It was something to see. RISE. Each letter was elongated and multiple steps high. The font looked glamorous and sleek, like the titles on a 1940s Hollywood movie, and he'd tweaked the perspective so that the *R* was smallest and the *E* was biggest, making the whole thing look even grander and more epic than it was. When the escalator was switched on, Jack explained, the word would float up the stairs, one letter at a time, like movie credits.

"It's beautiful," I whispered, taking it all in. His Golden Apple signature demurely sat to the right of the last letter.

He slung his arm over my shoulders and kissed me on the cheek, utterly pleased with himself, and rightfully so. "It went twice as fast with you helping. Oh, hold on. Photographic evidence. For Jillian." He stripped off one glove and navigated to the camera on his phone before snapping several photos.

"I wish we could see it when the escalator is on," I lamented. "Maybe we should come back tomor—"

Static crackled from inside the station.

We both froze.

It was a two-way radio, sputtering instructions. And footsteps. And voices that said, "*Blah blah* junction box *blah blah* escalator—"

BART guards patrolling the station? Was it already time for them to open it back up?

"Crap!" Jack snatched the backpack out of my hand, stuffing his head-mounted light and the rest of the supplies inside. He pushed me up the stairwell, and we took the stairs two at a time, racing to the top—

—only to hear the *beep-beep-beep* of a truck backing up to the curb right outside the temporary plywood walls that covered the street exit. And another two-way radio. And male voices talking about disassembly and barking directions to workers about where to barricade the sidewalk.

These were not BART guards. It was the freaking escalator repair company, coming to reopen the subway entrance and conduct final tests on the escalator before the station opened.

We couldn't go back down, and we couldn't leave the way we'd come in.

We were trapped.

Jack zipped his backpack and strapped it on. Then he pulled up my hoodie and whispered against my ear, "Get ready to run."

Was he serious?

Oh, hell—he was!

As voices approached the makeshift plywood door, Jack reared back, lunged, and slammed his shoulder into it. The door flew open, smashing into one of the workers. Shouts of surprise ballooned behind the door as Jack grabbed my hand and jerked me through the opening.

"Hey!" someone roared as we bolted along the sidewalk. "We got transients!"

I didn't even look at their faces. I just booked it as fast as I could go. Chilled air knifed through my lungs. The rubber soles of our shoes slapped against the sidewalk, the sharp sound echoing off the buildings and the cars rushing past.

"Hustle!" Jack shouted.

Stupid short legs. I was slowing Jack down, which made me a

lousy getaway girl. At the end of the block, Jack pulled me around a corner and straight into a covered alcove that harbored a café delivery door.

He held up a finger in warning and then stuck his head around the corner. My heart hammered. Images of being chained at the ankles in a female prison flashed in front of my eyes, along with my life.

Jack turned back around and grinned at me with breathless delight. "That was, I believe, what you'd call a close one."

We'd made it? They weren't going to chase us down with guns and crime-sniffing dogs? I peered around the corner to see it with my own eyes, and Jack was right. We were in the clear!

I stood on tiptoes, fisted the front of his coat, and pulled him down to kiss him—firmly, wildly, until our teeth clinked and I nearly bit my own lip. I didn't care. I was high on adrenaline and in love. I felt invincible. Like the entire city belonged to us. Every fog-ringed streetlight, every neon sign, every jagged crack in the sidewalk. All ours.

"Thank you," I whispered, smiling against his mouth.

"For turning you on to new criminal possibilities?"

"For making me feel alive."

"Alive is good," he said, offering me his hand. "But let's get you back home before they call the cops."

22

IT WAS A MIRACLE MOM DIDN'T CATCH ME SNEAKING in that night, because she was still up at 4:45 a.m.—which was when Jack left me in front of my house. I stayed up long enough for him to text me **Good morning** instead of "Good night." And then I slept like the dead until almost noon, when Mom woke me up for our lunch date.

Thankfully, her gift of condoms was not a topic of conversation. The graffiti on the BART escalator, however, *was*.

The escalator repair workers had apparently found Jack's graffiti after we ran off, and told the police that we were the Golden Apple vandals—*we* being two guys dressed in black, one tall, one short. I'd have been insulted if I wasn't busy freaking out.

The local radio station debated the incident while Mom drove us to the Mission. One DJ thought it was a "crying shame" that a brand-new escalator had been defaced. Her partner said it was "urban art" and "inspirational." And squirming in the passenger seat of the paddy wagon, I embodied both viewpoints, in turns horrified and giddy. In the middle of all this, Jack texted to tease me about my new status as "the short male suspect."

On top of that, Mom asked me a lot of questions that made me sweat. Like about the student art contest. She wanted to know what I was submitting; the deadline was quickly approaching. But a paranoid part of me was convinced she knew about Minnie, too, and was giving me a chance to confess that I'd blatantly disobeyed her in pursuing the cadaver drawing. It made me realize that I really needed to be more careful. She worked only a few buildings away from the Willed Body lab. All it would take was one ill-timed break on her part to see me with my portfolio, strolling into my next drawing session, and my entire summer's work would be ruined.

While she ran her errand—picking up some custom-size discounted blinds to replace the ones in our house that had fallen apart from old age—I made a rash decision that had nothing to do with Minnie or my new criminal standing. Maybe it was all the leftover adrenaline from the night before rotting my brain—I don't know. But I pulled out my phone to email the lady at the wood-carving shop in Berkeley. Yes, I actually *would* like to meet with the guy who carved my artist's mannequin, I wrote her. Why not? In a week, I'd be too busy getting ready for the art contest. Besides, if my dad thought he could start up a conversation with me on his terms, he could think again.

And while I polished off half an overstuffed carne asada Super Burrito with Mom, I got a speedy response from the shop in Berkeley: Could I come by at one the following afternoon? I texted Jack, and he said he'd gladly drive me.

"Sometimes I think you're full of secrets," Mom said wistfully, eyeing the leftover plastic cup of salsa verde on the table like she might ask for a to-go lid.

I balled up my napkin and stuffed it inside the cup so I wouldn't have to eat it on eggs the next morning. "None of them are all that interesting," I assured her.

THE NEXT DAY, JACK PICKED ME UP AT ELEVEN THIRTY in the morning. My whole body went haywire when I saw him in the doorway as I peered over my mom's shoulder. Chills. Warmth in my chest. Jackhammering heartbeat. I practically swooned. *Swooned!* This couldn't be good. Everything felt . . . intensified. Like, overnight. Magically. I quietly prayed he couldn't tell.

Or Mom.

If I were going to *his* house, and his mom had just presented *him* with a hundred condoms, I think I'd rather jab a screwdriver in my ear than face her. But Jack greeted Mom like they were best friends.

"Prince Vincent," she said before I could step around her. "Where are you two going on this fine foggy morning?"

His lie was smoother than smooth. "We're heading over to the East Bay for lunch. I wanted to check out a record store."

I'd pretty much told her same thing an hour before; how come it sounded so much more natural coming out of his mouth than mine? And Mom smiled at him like he was charm incarnate. "Just make sure she's back in time for work," she told him.

"I will. Don't worry."

"I'm taking my uniform with me," I added with forced casualness, patting the red bag I normally carried back and forth to the anatomy lab. "My shift starts at four."

This definitely mollified her. Because if I was going to work, I surely didn't have time to get into trouble or pull any "shenanigans," as she said when it was Heath doing something behind her back. Little did she know, I could cram a lot of shenanigans into a short span of time.

She watched us jog down the stairs. "Take care of my baby," she called out. If she knew I was headed into enemy territory, she probably wouldn't be so cheery.

But when she went back inside the house and we were safely out of her range, Jack reached for my hand, and I said, "I've missed you"—as if it had been a week, not a day, since I'd last seen him. And just like that, we fell on each other like rabid dogs, kissing against the passenger door of his car until someone passing by on the sidewalk made a rude comment.

"Yeah, maybe we will," Jack called to the pedestrian's back after she was too far away to hear him.

I smothered a laugh into his shoulder. He pretended to bite my ear and growled against my hair, which only made me laugh harder. I hugged him tighter and sighed into his neck.

"God, I'm crazy about you," he whispered. "If you don't stop me, I'll be begging to see you every day, because I can't stand being apart from you."

"Oh, good. I thought it was only me."

"Not just you," he said, kissing the side of my head.

I clung to him for a moment and then pried myself away, clearing my throat.

"Right," he said, blowing out a long breath. "Let's get on the road before we get arrested for public indecency."

"I believe that's the least of our potential charges."

"How does it feel to have aided a wanted felon?" he murmured as he unlocked the car door.

"Exhilarating," I whispered back.

Maybe I was better at being bad than I thought.

The drive to Berkeley took only a half hour, and we rolled down our windows when the sun chased away gray skies over the Bay Bridge. Jack had gone back to the scene of our crime and shot a one-minute video of the escalator in action. I'd already seen a couple of videos posted online, but it was so much more exciting watching it on his phone.

"A spokesperson from BART said they'll be closing it down for cleanup in a week," he told me as Ghost's motor rumbled through my seat. "I think that's the longest one of them has ever stayed up. And it's easy to clean metal. I'm betting foot traffic will wear the paint off the tops of the steps in a couple of days."

"Has Jillian seen it?"

"Yeah," he said, lips curving. "I showed her the video last night. She couldn't stop smiling. We used to go to the main city library across the street from that BART station, and Jillie always headed for that looping stair sculpture on the fifth floor. You know what I'm talking about?"

I hadn't been there in years, but I knew which one he meant. "The stairs that lead nowhere."

"Exactly. That's what she said when she saw the video, and that the stairs to nowhere matched up nicely with 'rise.' I hadn't even remembered how much she liked those stairs. I was only matching up the word to the escalator."

"A happy coincidence."

He shook his head. "Everything's connected, Bex. Whether we understand it or not." He drummed his thumbs against the steering wheel, tapping out a happy rhythm. "She asked about you."

"She did?"

"I told her you helped me. I was worried it might upset her—that she might get jealous, or whatever. Change stresses her out, and Dr. Kapoor has been monitoring her since your visit. No—don't be worried," he said when I groaned. "It wouldn't matter if it was you or someone else. Little things set her off, and she's been juggling meds since the seizure. But it's cool. She likes you."

"I'm glad," I said, and he grinned at me, squinting over the top of his sunglasses.

The address for the wood-carving shop was near the edge of UC Berkeley's campus. Jack parked Ghost on a side street just off Telegraph Avenue, a few blocks away, and since we still had forty-five minutes to waste, we strolled past bookstores and cafés and herb shops until we found a curry place that had a bunch of vegetarian dishes, where we ate a quick lunch (validating our lie). At exactly one o'clock, I strode by a blonde in a green Jaguar who stared at me so hard I gave her a dirty look, and marched through a glass door into Telegraph Wood Studio.

True to its name, it smelled strongly of wood shavings. The front of the shop was cluttered with totem poles and carved fireplace mantels. Sculptures of dancing women. A solid-wood globe. Even a mermaid figurehead dove out of a wall, looking as if a ship might crash through behind it at any second. A long counter separated the front from the workshop, where multiple tables stretched around carving equipment and large pieces of furniture.

"Whoa," Jack said in a low, reverent voice. "Check out the old cable-car replicas. They're gorgeous."

I looked at the handwritten price tag. "Fifteen hundred? That's one hell of a toy train set." And it wasn't half as detailed as my artist's mannequin, which lay at the bottom of my red bag. I didn't think the guy who'd made it would need a reminder, but just in case . . .

A woman's voice floated out from behind the counter. "Hello. Would you be Beatrix?"

Her gray hair was loosely clipped behind her head. Long strings of wooden beads dangled over a flowing caftan.

"Yes," I said. "Are you Mary?"

She nodded. "And I have someone here who wanted to see you. I really hope you don't mind the subterfuge too much."

Before I could unravel what that meant, she gestured to someone behind a carved Japanese screen, and out stepped the man who'd ruined my family.

My father had changed his hair. Grown it out from his old, boring VP crew cut so that silver-streaked locks of brown now curled around the collar of his expensive sport coat. His face was a lot tanner than I remembered, and crow's-feet now furrowed the outer corners of his eyes. But his wire-framed glasses were the same, and so was the way he stood: head high, chin up, back made of steel—and a look on his face like someone had just shoved a big, fat stick up his butt.

Yep. He'd looked at me exactly the same way the last time I'd seen him. When he'd told me that the separation had nothing to do with me, and that nothing would change between us.

The biggest lie of all.

"Beatrix," he said in a low voice.

I couldn't even answer him. I just turned and stormed out the door. "Please, take me home," I managed to say to Jack, who stuck to me like a shadow while I started down the sidewalk. That stupid blonde in the Jaguar was still staring at us from the curb.

"Beatrix!"

My father had followed us outside, and he was angry now. Big surprise. I swung around so fast he had to jerk himself backward not to run into me. "How dare you," I said to him.

"If she'd said I wanted to meet you, you wouldn't have come."

"No, probably not. But that's my decision, not yours."

"What could I do? Your mother wouldn't let me see you."

"So you sent me the artist's mannequin to lure me here, like some creepy old man in a white van?"

His face looked pinched. "No, I sent it because I wanted to give you something that would make you happy. I knew you would like it."

"Because you know me so well."

The depressing thing was, he'd gotten it right. He, not Mom, was the one who'd actually sparked my interest in anatomy. When I was a kid, he had these big pull-down diagram charts of the human body hanging on the wall in the home office of our old house. The brightly colored muscles and organs were endlessly fascinating to my ten-year-old brain, and after school he'd spend hours answering all my questions about bones and arteries and blood. Of course, he didn't know half of what Mom knew about anatomy, so when he didn't know the answer, he'd make something silly up.

He'd always had a knack for lying.

I started to walk away again, but he held his hands out as if to show me he wasn't armed.

"Please, just hear me out for one minute." His arms slowly dropped to his sides. "Let me look at you. My God, you're practically a woman. I haven't seen you—"

"In three years," I finished. "Been too busy banging your strip-club-owning wife to bother communicating with your own children until now?"

Jack made a small noise at my side, but he said nothing. Somewhere in the back of my mind, I knew I'd be sorry later that he'd witnessed this messiness, but right now I was too angry to care.

My father's nose wrinkled. "Strip club? What in the world are you talking about? Suzi owned a cabaret in Santa Monica."

"Cabaret?" What in the world was that?

"A piano bar," he elaborated. "Singers, not strippers."

That's not what Mom had told us. But who was I going to believe? The woman who worked her ass off to keep a roof over our heads, or the man who abandoned us for a newer model?

"Strip club." He said this like he was spitting out rancid food, shaking his head. It took me a second to realize he had darted a look toward the Jaguar. *That* was "Suzi"? No wonder Mom had gone ballistic. Suzi couldn't have been that much older than I was! And by then she was standing outside the Jag, arms crossed over her breasts. Wearing designer clothes, which my father had probably paid for.

I wanted to vomit.

My father just shook his head and pushed his glasses up the bridge of his nose. "And I haven't been too busy to see you. Your mother won't let me near you or Heath."

"Maybe that's because you're too *broke* to pay child support." I used finger quotes on "broke" and crossed my arms over my chest, mimicking his new wife's stance. "Guess those car payments are more important than our utility bill."

My father growled. "Oh, that's rich. Is that what she's telling you? She refused child support. It's in the divorce papers, Beatrix. Go look at them. She had her lawyer strike right over the payments. She said she wasn't taking a dime from me—that she'd rather the three of you live at the YMCA than accept a 'handout' from me." He, too, used finger quotes. And his Dutch accent began creeping out of his Stanford-educated crisp words.

"A likely story," I said. But if I was being honest with myself, it did sound a little like Mom. A *lot*, really. But, still, she wouldn't have lied to us about something that big. Maybe there was a misunderstanding about the so-called cabaret—maybe—but not this. Not when we lost the house in Cole Valley. Not when she struggled to work twelve-hour graveyard shifts that barely kept us in generic shampoo and those weird-tasting tubes of discount ground beef.

"Not a story," my father said firmly, hands on his waist, elbows pushing the tails of his sport coat back like angry wings. "Truth, Beatrix. It's the goddamn truth."

"Truth is action, not words. Mom helps me with my homework. Mom cooks me dinner. Mom takes care of me when I'm sick."

"I know she does."

"Do you know? Really? Did you know Mom received a Distinguished Nurse award from the chancellor in May?"

"That's wonderful."

"*She*'s wonderful. And she's there every day for us. But what have you done? Have you even tried to write me or Heath a single postcard?

"As a matter of fact—"

"Did you know I lost all my friends when we were forced to move and I had to change schools? Did you know I'm one of the poorest kids in my class, and I've had to work since I was sixteen to pay my own cell phone bill and Muni pass? Did you know I can't afford to go to the college I want, and that I'm spending my summer busting my ass for an art project because the only way I can go to any school at all is to win a stupid scholarship in a competition? Did you know Heath has dropped out of two colleges and gotten in all kinds of trouble? You wanna know why? Because *you fucking left us.*"

His face jerked back as if I'd slapped him, but the hurt left as quickly as it had appeared, and the calm and reasonable Vice President Van Asch got control over himself. "I can't apologize forever."

"Forever? Try once!"

"I'm sorry, Beatrix. I should've done better. Tried harder. But I want to now. It's one of the reasons I moved back—I took a provost position at Berkeley so I could be closer to you and Heath. Just let me try. Come have coffee with me. Meet Suzi—"

"Never."

He was livid. And for a second, I saw a familiar look on his face—the same one he'd given me when I spilled a bottle of drawing ink on his precious Moroccan rug. He wanted to take me by the shoulders and shake me. His hand twitched, and he reached out as if he might just do it.

My shadow stepped between us.

Jack towered over Dad by a good head. And at that moment, with his face tight and his dark brows lowered, he looked like more of a man than my father.

"You don't want to do that," Jack said in a deep, scarily calm voice.

Oh, my father *did not like this.* Not at all. And for a moment they were two bulls, one young, one middle-aged. One wrong word and they'd be going at it, *mano a mano.*

"Lars," a feminine voice called from behind him. His new wife, Suzi. It was a plea and a gentle warning. And it was enough to break up the pinballing tension.

"Let's go," I said to Jack.

Without hesitation, he curled his arm around my shoulders and pulled me away from my father.

"Beatrix," Dad said as we started to turn away from him. "Please contact me when you're ready. My university email address is on the campus website. We can talk on your terms."

I stopped long enough to dig the artist's mannequin from my bag. My father's face twisted with hurt, eyes quietly pleading, and that made my throat catch. Just for a second. I steeled my resolve and hurled the mannequin down on the sidewalk between us. The carved body cracked at his feet, splintering in half.

23

THE SKY DARKENED AS JACK AND I STRODE DOWN THE sidewalk. Like the heavy clouds above us, I held myself together until we got back to Ghost. Both the quiet side street and the cover provided by tree branches drooping over our parking space must've given my brain the illusion of shelter, because once I shut the Corvette's door against the sudden deluge of rain, I let go and broke down.

It wasn't pretty.

The older, cooler fantasy me was horrified to be ugly-crying in front of Jack. But the present me was hurting too much to care. And when his hand warmed the back of my neck, it felt like permission to sob even harder.

Before I knew what was happening, Jack had leaned his seat back and pulled me sideways into his lap. I buried my face in the collar of his vintage bowling shirt and cried a little longer while steady rain battered the convertible top.

His hands stroking down my back were soothing, and little by little, I pulled myself together.

"I'm sorry," I said, wiping my face.

His muscles flexed as he strained to reach across the seat. He retrieved a rumpled fast-food napkin from his glove box. "I don't know why," he said, handing it to me. "Nothing to be sorry for."

I turned my face away and blew my nose, then looked for a place to throw the napkin away.

"Go on," he encouraged, cracking the window. "Berkeley's too clean anyway."

I croaked out a chuckle and tossed the napkin outside. He started to roll the window back up, but I stopped him; the rain smelled good, and I didn't mind the occasional drop or three on the back of my neck when the wind blew. It felt nice.

His thumb swiped beneath one eye, then the other. "Makeup goo," he explained, cleaning up my running mascara. "Better?"

I nodded and let my head loll back against his shoulder. "I don't know why my father got to me that way. It's not like my family problems are anywhere near as epic as yours. You must think I'm a whiner."

"I think no such thing. You have every right to be upset. My family's been through a lot, but I can't imagine what it would be like if my dad left us. I love her, but my mom is no Katherine the Great. She's a cheerleader, not a provider."

"Your mom's fought her own battles," I reminded him.

He grunted his agreement.

"What if my father wasn't lying? Why would Mom turn down child support?"

"I don't know. Maybe she's too proud. Maybe it made her feel weak."

"If that's true, okay, but she lied to us. All this time, I thought he was this deadbeat dad. Why would she do that?"

"Because she's human, and she makes mistakes? Or maybe your father wasn't telling the truth, either. Maybe he's feeling guilty and saying whatever it takes to win you over. Confront your mom and ask her."

"I can't. Then she'll know I lied about coming out here. And she'll know I kept the artist's mannequin from her. And she'll feel betrayed."

"Don't *you?*"

I thought about that for a second. "I'm not sure what I feel. All I know is that I'm tired of being the innocent bystander who gets punched in the gut. It's their fight—Mom and Dad's. But how come Heath and I are the ones who end up bruised?"

He rearranged one of my braids and wound the loose tail around the tip of his index finger. "Because everything we do in life affects someone else. Buddhists say that inside and outside are basically the same thing. It's like we're all trapped together in a small room. If someone pisses in the corner, we all have to worry about it trickling across the floor and getting our shoes wet."

I chuckled again. "Or clogging up the escalator."

He smiled against my forehead. "Or someone painting a message on the escalator you don't understand."

"I don't want my mistakes to affect everyone else in the room," I said after a moment. "I want to keep to myself and do as little damage as possible."

"That's one way of living, sure. But it's lonely, and doing nothing can cause as much damage as doing something. We're part of a machine, whether we like it or not. If one piston stops working, the engine will run poorly. And I for one would much rather that you piss on my shoe than that I watch you withdraw into the corner."

"Gross."

"What? It's how you get rid of jellyfish stings."

"That's an old wives' tale. If you ever pee on me, I'll hurt you."

"So violent." His splayed fingers danced over my back like a spider.

I squealed as he attacked my side, tickling me with gusto. I couldn't pry his fingers away from my ribs. "St-top!" I protested in the middle of a fit of laughter.

"Say the magic word."

"Uncle!"

"That's not it."

I changed tactics and tickled him back. He jumped, lifting us both off the seat. "All right, girl," he purred roughly. "You're asking for it now."

"Oh yeah? What are you going to do about it?"

He cradled the back of my head with his hand and reeled me closer. His mouth covered mine, strong and confident. I laughed against his lips, just for a second, and then gave in.

The kiss deepened, and his hand drifted down my neck to my side, tracing the curve of my waist, over my hip, and back up. Like he was trying to imagine what I looked like beneath my clothes. That thought thrilled me almost as much as his roaming hand . . . until he boldly cupped my breast.

Breathing heavily, he broke the kiss—barely—and said against my lips, "Okay?"

I put my hand over his to hold it in place.

"You feel fantastic," he murmured, his breath teasing my neck.

"You sound surprised."

"I've fantasized about you in every possible way, but the real thing... God, Bex. You're so soft. And—oh. Well."

I gasped. I couldn't help it.

"Does that feel good?" he asked, running his thumb over my nipple.

I didn't answer; he was too full of himself, sounding all pleased with his discovery. A field of goose bumps bloomed across my arms and warmed me from his hot mouth, down my chest, my stomach... and lower. I knew that heat followed the same path in him, because he stiffened against my hip, which excited me even more.

As rain drummed against the car, he slouched lower in the seat and silently urged me to straddle his lap. I didn't care that the steering wheel poked my back when I got carried away. We kissed forever, leisurely, until his big hands palmed my butt, greedily tugging me against him. The bump in my jeans where the seams converged between my legs was wedged between the softness of me and the hardness of him.

"You're killing me," he murmured huskily against my ear.

I closed my eyes and grinned. "Am I?"

"I want you."

"I know."

His low laugh sent chills down my neck. "I did warn you I wasn't a monk."

"Definitely not if we keep this up."

Exhaling heavily, he pulled back and cupped my cheeks in his hands. "We should probably cool it anyway. I promised Katherine the Great I'd get you to work on time, and the rain will gum up traffic on the Bay Bridge. Plus, it's going to take me a couple of minutes to . . . calm down."

I cleared my throat and tried not to smile. "I don't think I could stand up right now if I tried. Just hold me a little while longer, okay?"

"Okay," he said, and gathered me closer. I rested my head on his shoulder and breathed in the scent of his old leather jacket while our breathing slowed and synced. Everything that had happened with my father felt a million miles away. Like it had happened to me in another lifetime. Jack made me feel safe and strong and good and calm.

Maybe he was my lake, too.

24

TWO DAYS LATER, I COVERED FOR ANOTHER GIRL AT Alto Market and worked a ten-hour shift. By hour number eight, I was completely exhausted. How did Mom work twelve hours like it was nothing? I didn't understand, but as I scanned my kajillionth block of imported cheese, I wondered just how much I understood about my mom in general.

I googled cabarets in Santa Monica and found the Freckled Rose, a cabaret slash piano bar formerly owned by one Suzi Cameron. Guess Dad was right, because it really didn't look like a strip club. Most of its performers were older than my parents, and they were all wearing (awful) clothes. I *so* wanted to call Mom out on this, but I just couldn't bring myself to tell her how I found out. So I told Heath instead.

"Sometimes people exaggerate when they're upset" was all he said.

Exaggerate? Exaggerating was saying you ate a whole sleeve of Girl Scout cookies when you really ate only half. But I couldn't get into it with Heath, because he asked me how I'd tracked it down. Because of the way he was grilling me about it, I didn't feel like revealing my meeting with Dad. So I just said I was poking around and found it online.

"Just drop it, Bex," Heath told me. "Even if Mom exaggerated about the cabaret, Dad cheated on her and left all of us. We don't have a father. Big deal. It's just life."

He was probably right.

Ms. Lopez checked in on me after our last rush of customers for the night. "Hanging in there? Feet sore?"

"I should've bought some of those inserts you told me about," I said, stretching my neck side to side.

"No, you should've told Mary to stop dumping her shifts on you." She clicked the top of a ladybug pen and clipped it to her apron. "Did you miss your anatomy drawing session tonight? How is that going?"

"I missed it, but it's okay. I'm almost finished. The one good thing about doing a million sketches before I decided on the right angle is that I've got it down perfect now. One more session for the final details and I'll be done."

"Just in time for the art contest?"

"A week to spare," I said with a smile. I was feeling a lot better about it, especially after my last drawing session, during which a group of med students came over to my end of the lab to check out my illustrations of Minnie. They acted impressed. Like, *really* impressed.

I was going to win that damn contest. That scholarship money was mine. As long as I kept my head down and didn't let any emotional family weirdness distract me. Which wasn't easy.

"Hey," I said. "Can I ask you something about Joy?" She was Ms. Lopez's daughter.

"Sure."

"Would you ever lie to her about something big? Like if, let's say, your mother stole money from you—"

"My mother? She's deeply religious. She would never steal."

"Let's just say she did, and let's say you were hurt by it and worried that she might be a bad influence on Joy. Would you lie to Joy and tell her that her grandmother was worse than she really was, just to discourage Joy from having anything to do with her?"

"Did you steal staples from the storeroom? I thought it was someone from the new janitorial service."

I groaned. "No, I didn't take any staples. Why would I need—" I shook my head in frustration. "It doesn't have to be stealing. Maybe your mother's got a violent temper—"

Ms. Lopez made a little anguished noise.

"I'm just trying to say, is there any reason you'd tell Joy a lie or an exaggeration about someone in your family because you thought it was the right thing for your daughter?"

Ms. Lopez stared down at me through narrowed eyes. "I would do anything to keep Joy safe and happy."

"So the answer is yes?"

"Why don't you ask your own mother the same question?" she said, pointing one perfect, glossy red nail in my direction as she strolled away from the register with a knowing glance.

Dammit.

What good would it do me to mend things with Dad anyway? Would it magically make me all better? And how did I expect to even try? Would I sneak around, meeting him and his little Suzi-Q for lunch on the weekends? Because no way in hell would Mom ever let me go see him with her blessing. And if she found out I'd been seeing him behind her back, it would wreck her.

It would tear my mom and me apart.

And Dad wasn't worth that risk, because she was there and he wasn't. She'd stayed and he hadn't. And that was that.

A half hour before my double shift ended, I was counting my register till in the office when I got a text from Jack: Is Nurse Katherine working a night shift tomorrow?

I replied: Think so. Why?

He texted: My parents are leaving for Sacramento tomorrow afternoon and they won't be back until noon the next day.

I reread the text several times. What was he saying? Was he . . . did he mean . . . ? Maybe it was just an opportunity for us to spend time alone, nothing more. Did I want there to be something more? I would've answered, "God, yes," to that question five minutes earlier, but now that he was putting it out there (was he?), my nerves twanged.

When I didn't reply right away, he texted again: Do *you* work tomorrow?

Setting down a stack of twenties, I leaned over my till to squint at the schedule tacked to the bulletin board. I'd just worked a double for Mary, so she could damn well return the favor. I texted: I don't now.

Jack's reply came a couple of minutes later: I can pick you up any time after 4 p.m.

"I POINTED THE CAMERAS UP THE STREET," JACK SAID when he saw me eyeing the one over the Vincents' side gate the following night. "Just don't step past the edge of the fence and you're golden."

"You take sneaking to a whole new level."

"If your father was king of the city, you would, too."

Since I had to wait for Mom to leave for her graveyard shift before I could escape with Jack, it was right at 8:00 p.m. and still light outside. "Your neighbor's watching us."

Jack waved and mumbled "nosy bastard" under his breath. "Let's go in through the front door so it doesn't look like we're doing anything wrong."

"Are we?" I asked. Because it was all I could think about since he'd asked me over—doing wrong things with him. And when he sent me his standard good night text last night, I was doing more than thinking. I considered texting him back with an explicit description but lost my nerve. Now I sort of wished I had, because maybe I'd have a better idea of his intentions tonight. The ride over here gave me no clue; we just chatted about work (boring) and how Jillian was doing (pretty good) and why his parents were in Sacramento (a fund-raising dinner for education). We didn't even kiss.

"Are we doing anything wrong?" he repeated thoughtfully. He was having trouble getting the key in the lock. He showed me his shaky hand and laughed at himself. "I guess that means a part of me must hope so. That milkmaid thing is sexy as hell, by the way."

It was the most flattering of my braid repertoire. I kept the plaits loose and pulled out a few wisps for a natural and romantic look. Knowing he liked them made heat flash through me. "I feel like there's a good joke here about the farmer's daughter, but I'm too anxious to think of one," I admitted.

"Let's just . . . uh, get inside before Mr. Martinez marshals the rest of the neighborhood watch."

He finally got the front door open. I stepped inside and looked around while he locked up behind us. We stood on dark wood floors in a foyer. Buttery-gold walls were loaded with large paintings in gilded frames. A modern wooden staircase shot up through the floors, dominating the narrow space, and because it was open, I could peer through at the floors above and below. Beyond the staircase was a living room with a fireplace and a wall of windows that looked over the decks in the back. We were on the second story, and I spied the roof of Jack's guesthouse bedroom at the far corner of the yard.

"My mom collects art," he said as I stared up a painting of a crazy-colored chair. "Mostly California artists. She really digs old chairs."

"Yes, I can see that," I said diplomatically, spotting other chair paintings farther into the home.

"It's kooky, I know. I'll give you the VIP tour. You'll see more chairs than you ever dreamed possible."

He started at the kitchen, which wasn't much bigger than ours but gleamed with top-of-the-line appliances, polished marble, and custom cabinetry. The floating wooden bridge I'd seen on the Fourth of July connected to a back door there. "We used to have a lot of cocktail parties on the deck," Jack noted.

Used to. He didn't comment on what had happened in this kitchen to put an end to those parties, but I couldn't help staging it in my head, wondering if I was standing where Jillian had stabbed her mom. We breezed through the living room and headed downstairs, which was basically one big open room divided into smaller areas: an entertainment area for watching movies, another fireplace lounge, a bar, lots of the chairs he promised (along with more paintings of chairs), and a billiards table. "No one even knows how to play pool," Jack admitted.

I gestured to a receiver behind the glass doors of a built-in cabinet. "That's some stereo."

"Music can be piped into the room of your choice, or all of them. Dad uses it for parties, so music can stream through the entire house. He has an old record collection and the turntable there."

"Gee, the mayor's a hipster. Who knew?"

"Yeaaaah, *no.* He likes the Eagles."

I laughed. "My mom still thinks Depeche Mode is cutting edge."

"How about radio instead? Pick a decade." He flipped channels featuring songs from the 1940s to the 1990s. We settled on the 1950s, partly because "Heartbreak Hotel" was playing, and I reached up and ran my fingers through Jack's Elvis hair. "Do you sing, too?" I teased.

"Not outside a shower," he said, capturing my wrists and pulling my hands to his chest. "Hope you don't have dreams of a poetic, guitar-playing boyfriend who writes you bad love songs, because I am terrible at all that."

"Do you even know me at all? I like anatomical hearts, not valentines."

He glanced down at my heart . . . or at my cleavage—hard to tell which. I was wearing a black shirt that usually tilted off one shoulder, but because I still had my jacket on, the "tilt" had shifted to the front and revealed more than I'd intended. Or just the right amount.

I felt a little self-conscious, so I pulled away and strolled around the room. I spotted a door in a darkened corner. Wrong thing.

"Before you ask, that's the door to the basement, and, no, I won't go down there. Like, ever again."

Crap. "I don't blame you."

He absently scratched the side of his neck. "To be honest, I don't like being down here on this floor, either."

I nodded, not knowing what to say. But he didn't linger on the memory. He just smiled softly and hooked his pinky around mine. "Let's go upstairs. There's something I want to show you."

Backtracking up the big staircase, we headed to the top floor, music following us all the way up. Four bedrooms were clustered around his father's office, which was one of those messy-neat rooms, with small stacks of paper and file folders everywhere. "It looks like someone cleans around the piles," I said, smiling at the vacuum-cleaner ruts still visible in the rug.

"Mrs. Weiser, every other morning on weekdays. She's our maid. She doesn't come when my parents are out of town."

Ooh-la-la, a maid. Must be nice. It took me several seconds to realize he was assuring me we were alone, and that made my stomach do a few cartwheels.

He led me up a tiny spiral staircase in the corner of the office. We emerged into a renovated attic space. White walls covered the underside of a pitched roof, making an upside-down V. Short bookshelves lined the sides. The only pieces of furniture were a small stuffed chair and a reading lamp. A light blue rug covered most of the wood floor.

The back of the room contained a porthole window that overlooked the decks, but it was the front wall that drew all my attention. It was made of glass, and two doors in the middle pushed out and folded back on themselves to open up the room onto a small balcony, where a waist-high wall of glass separated us from a stunning view of the city.

Cool night air rushed through the open doorway as we stepped out onto the balcony. The tree-lined hill of Parnassus sloped to the left (and beyond that, my neighborhood). Buena Vista Park sat to our right, and the heart of San Francisco lay before us. Darkening streets slanted toward a pink sunset. We weren't high enough to see the Bay in the distance, but it was a million-dollar view nonetheless.

We sat down side by side on the edge of the rug, legs stretching onto the balcony, and looked through the glass wall.

"Cool, right?" Jack asked. "It's the best part of the house. Jillian and I used to come out here and sail paper airplanes over the rooftops."

Minutes passed while we listened to music and watched streetlights twinkle to life under the rolling fog. I must've gotten a little too relaxed, because when he finally spoke, it startled me. "I want to know why it was so bad for you when you and that Howard Hooper guy dated."

"I told you. He was a jerk."

"No, I mean the sex," he clarified. "I need to know what he did wrong so I don't make the same mistake."

25

MY CHEEKS CAUGHT FIRE, SO I DIDN'T LOOK AT HIM. I just said, "Oh."

"What if it's bad between us, too? You might end up hating me."

"That's not going to happen. But if you're worried," I said carefully, "we don't have to . . . I mean, I'm not expecting anything from you."

He looked alarmed. "You don't expect anything from me, as in you expect it to be the same?"

"No! I meant . . . ugh." I drew my knees to my chest and hugged them. "I meant, if you're not ready, it's fine."

"Oh, I'm ready," he said so confidently, it made my chest feel warm. "I just want to know what went wrong. Like, specifically."

"Specifically?"

"If we can't talk about it, how can we do it?" He had a point. "Why was it bad?"

I sighed. "For starters, it was always in the car."

"Which was cramped?" he guessed.

Fine. He really wanted to know? I'd tell him everything. "It felt cheap. Like he couldn't be bothered to try harder. And either there was a seat belt buckle poking my rib or my head was bumping against the roof of the car—which, after I broke up with him, he apparently told some of his friends in English class about. Because a couple of them started making jokes to me, like 'Your head bruised up today, Morticia?' Or they'd pound on their desks and say 'What's that sound? It's Morticia's head hitting the roof of the car.'"

"Jesus and freaking Mary," Jack mumbled. "Are you serious?"

"That's why I hate being on top, by the way. What else? Let's see. Howard was always in a hurry, so even though he wanted to see me naked, he refused to do anything more than push his jeans down a few inches, 'just in case' we got caught and he had to make a quick getaway."

"That's hot."

Once I got going with the confessing, I couldn't stop. "So of course it always lasted like three minutes. He'd just pick me up and park somewhere, and then he'd drive me straight home afterward so he could rush back to his own house to play video games with his jerkwad friends."

"Remind me why you were with this asshole again."

"He also said he couldn't afford to take me to the movies anymore because he'd quit his after-school job, but the next Monday morning I overheard him bragging about some keg party the swim team threw, and he'd pitched in thirty dollars to help buy beer. Oh, and he never wanted to hang out with me at home because he claimed he 'didn't do the parent thing.'"

"What did Katherine the Great think about that?"

"I never told her about him."

"I see."

I hugged my knees closer. "If you want to know the truth, I probably should've known better. I ignored a lot of things I didn't like about him right from the start because . . . well, because I was lonely and just wanted to do something that made me feel like I was in control of my life."

"He was your golden apple."

I thought about that for a moment. "No, because I wasn't helping anyone in the process. I wasn't doing anything poetic or beautiful, and I didn't have good intentions. I was only doing it to make myself feel better."

"Mmm." Jack balanced a forearm against his bent knee. "Well, apart from the pitfalls of extreme douchebaggery, which I'm not even going to address, because clearly this guy is a total loser and didn't deserve you—"

"That's the truth," I mumbled.

"But what you're telling me is that you don't like to be rushed"—he began ticking off a list on his fingers—"or being on top. You *do* like making out and equal-opportunity nakedness, and you'd prefer it not to happen in a car."

"Well, what you and I did in the car was sort of nice," I admitted, glancing at him. "Really nice."

"Oh, good," he said with a soft smile. "I thought so, too."

"But a bed would be nicer. Or anywhere nonpublic."

"What about on top of some trash cans in a dark alley?" he teased.

"Gross."

"Under the bleachers, next to the empty nacho trays and cigarette butts?"

I shoved him, and we both laughed. Then I chewed on the inside of my mouth and finally said, "We always used condoms, just so you know. I might've been stupid, but I wasn't irresponsible."

"I bought some new ones," he said. "I felt weird about freeloading off your mom, no offense."

Oh, wow. That made my pulse quicken. "I brought a couple of them with me, just in case."

"You did?"

"Not that I was making assumptions."

"Make all the assumptions you want," he said playfully, his mouth quirking up. A few moments passed. "By the way, I read an entire book about the female orgasm last night."

I nearly choked.

"And I've watched a lot of porn—"

"Oh, God," I said, covering my face with my hands.

"—so it's not like I'm totally in the dark."

Some weird, twisted noise came out of my mouth. I did my best to form it into a rough "all right."

"Just promise me one thing," he continued. "If it's not good, tell me. Don't just get angry and resent me. I'd rather us not do anything and keep what we have now than screw things up between us. Okay?"

I nodded.

He nodded.

Awkward silence hung between us until he finally said, "So, how about dinner?"

Oh. I hoped I didn't look as disappointed—or simultaneously relieved—as I felt. I reminded myself that he was just doing what I told him I wanted: nothing rushed. We were just hanging out. Besides, Mom's shift didn't end until seven in the morning, which was almost ten hours away.

He stood and offered a hand to help me up. When I got on my feet, he was closer than I realized, and I bumped into him. I apologized and tried to step back, but he stopped me with an arm around my waist. "You're not freaked out, are you?"

I wanted to say "of course not," but it came out as "You haven't even kissed me today."

"You haven't kissed me, either."

I smiled, feeling sheepish. "Oh."

He traced one of my milkmaid braids and combed through the loose wisps around my temples. My gaze tracked his movements before lifting to his face. His fingers stilled. We stared at each other for a few heartbeats and then met in the middle.

His lips were warm on mine. His arms pulled me closer, and we pressed against each other, shoulders to hips. Maybe it was all that candid sex talk, but I was both extremely turned on and deliriously edgy at the same time. My hands found their way under the back hem of his soft T-shirt. He felt warm and solid and muscular, and I traced the bumps in his spine with the tips of my fingers while he trailed wet kisses against my neck. It all felt so good. Too good. My knees went weak, and I staggered against him before quickly righting myself.

"Maybe we should skip dinner," he said in a gravel-rough voice.

"Maybe we should skip the bed thing, too," I said, half kidding to cover my embarrassment over the wobbly knees.

"Okay," he said. "Here?"

Wait, here? Now? I'd only been joking. Jack, however, was not. My nerves went all jangly. "You think anyone can see us?" I asked.

"Not unless they have binoculars with night vision."

Right. Okay. "Did you bring—"

"In my pocket."

"Okay."

"Yeah?"

I could feel my pulse *whoosh*ing through my temples.

"Yeah," I finally said.

We began pulling each other's clothes off, piece by piece: jacket, shoes, socks, shirts. I nearly passed out from the thrill of seeing his bare chest bookended by those half-sleeve tattoos with their intensely saturated colors, even in the blue moonlight. And below his chest, the dark trail of hair leading to . . .

"Why do you have a 4-H belt buckle?" I whispered.

"It was my grandfather's. He loved cows."

I was loving cows right then, too. My fingers trembled as I finally, *finally*—WAS I ACTUALLY DOING THIS?—got my hands on that buckle. I was so consumed with the unbuckling that I didn't notice him struggling to unhook my bra until he growled. I laughed nervously, and he pulled me closer so he could see what he was doing over my shoulder, scolding me in a teasing voice, "You think it's funny, huh? I'm going to rip it off of you in a second if it won't—there."

Cool air rushed over my skin. For a panicked moment, I wanted to cover myself. But my shyness melted away when he touched me, softly at first, then with more confidence. And by the time we got the rest of our clothes off, he was more than confident. He was outright presumptuous.

"I can't stand up while you do that," I said, practically panting.

"So bossy," he teased. We dropped to the floor, and he kissed me in some new and wonderful places before he started touching me again. But it was—"Ow."

"Sorry, sorry," he mumbled. "What? Is this better?"

"Um . . . I think?" This was more awkward than I'd expected. Doubt crept into my thoughts. Not about Jack but about myself. What if Howard Hooper wasn't the problem? What if it was me? Maybe I was terrible at sex. Like, woefully bad. What if Jack's worries about it changing our relationship weren't wrong? What if—

"What about this?" he murmured.

I couldn't answer. Not for a while. But when I realized I could touch him, too—actually touch him! Anywhere!—I reciprocated his bold moves and marveled as he shuddered beneath my fingers.

Everything was different with Jack. More intense. Emotional. Stronger. Better . . . Him. Us. All of it. And one by one, my doubts shrank until they were more or less gone.

"Now, Jack, please."

"You sure?"

"*Yes.*"

"Are you close?"

"Maybe. Are you laughing at *me* now?"

He grinned at me with heavy-lidded eyes as he fished inside the pocket of his discarded jeans. "Only because I'm happy."

I laughed a little, too, breathless, and then groaned. "Please hurry. Do you know how to put it on?"

"If I lie and say no, will you help me?"

"You're awfully cheeky for a virgin."

"I told you, Bex. You bring out the best in me. Oh, don't do that. It's too good. Move here. . . . Jesus, you're beautiful."

"Jack . . ."

"I . . ."

"Oh . . ."

"*My God.* Am I hurting you?"

I pushed back in answer.

"You feel so good," he whispered.

"Please don't stop."

"You either."

Near the end, I turned my cheek to the rug because I was overwhelmed and afraid to let him see me lose control. He bent his head to my neck and whispered breathy encouragements until neither one of us could say another word.

THE NIGHT BREEZE FLOWING THROUGH THE OPEN doors turned brisk. Tucked against Jack's side, I huddled closer, but even his hot skin couldn't drive away the chill.

"Cold?" he asked, rolling toward me to wrap himself around my body.

"Sort of. But I also don't want to move. Like, ever again."

"We can stitch our clothes together and make a blanket."

"Collect rainwater in our shoes."

"Harvest cypress needles off the treetops for food," he suggested.

"Or fashion a trap out of books and lure seagulls to the balcony."

"Mmm, raw poultry," he said. "I renounce my vegetarian ways right this second."

I laughed and clung to him with both arms and legs, inhaling the scent of his balmy skin. "You make me so happy," I murmured against the steady drum of his heart.

"I think I've been waiting for you all my life," he murmured back.

And then we did it all over again.

WE FINALLY ABANDONED OUR NEST IN THE ATTIC around midnight. And after he'd fed me some crazy good corn chowder and cheesy muffins he'd picked up from some takeout place (my chowder had chunks of ham in it, which, as I informed him, was the ultimate romantic gesture), he locked up the main house and we spent the remaining six hours of stolen freedom in his warm and cozy room out back. Mostly naked.

We took a shower together and tried to have superhot sex standing up, but after nearly breaking both our backs trying to find a good angle—the short girl, tall boy thing wasn't exactly practical—we ended up in his bed. He let me read his comic book (Jack's humor and storytelling skills were a little better than Andy's drawings) and formally introduced me to his betta, Sashimi 3. (Both her predecessors had been given full funerary rites and buried near the guesthouse.)

But after another round of sex in a very interesting position he'd learned in his book, I couldn't stay awake any longer. So we spooned together, napping until his alarm went off and he had to drive me home.

Saying good-bye to him that morning was one of the hardest things I'd ever had to do. I cried a little. I couldn't help it. If we were older, he'd have his own place, and I could just stay over. Or I'd have my own place, and he could just stay over. It wasn't even the sex. I wanted to sleep with him and wake up with him. I wanted the whole package. I wanted more.

"One day," he promised.

He held me on the sidewalk in front of my house until we couldn't delay it any longer, and then I watched Ghost's red taillights disappear into the fog.

The light in the front window was on. Maybe Heath had forgotten to turn it off. I hoped Mom hadn't come home for a midnight lunch and noticed I wasn't in my room. The dozen steps up to my front door felt like Sisyphus's doomed hill, and when I jabbed my key into the deadbolt, the mythical boulder rolled back down: It was already unlocked.

I pushed the door open with the tips of my fingers and stood in front of my worst nightmare. A two-person firing squad awaited me, consisting of both Heath and Mom, the latter sitting on the living room sofa with her arms crossed and fire in her eyes.

26

I DIDN'T SAY A WORD. DIDN'T HAVE TO. MOM DID ALL the talking.

"Have a seat, Beatrix," she said in a strained voice.

In a daze, I sat on the sofa under the living room window, as far away from her as I could get. The floor lamp shone in my eyes like a spotlight.

"Not answering your phone anymore?" she said. "Because I've called it about a dozen times."

Crap! I hadn't looked at my phone when I was at Jack's—probably the longest I'd ever gone without checking it. Guess I was distracted.

When I didn't say anything, she demanded, "Where have you been all night?"

I quickly considered my options. Oh, that's right: I had none. I was exhausted and had just spent the last ten hours, give or take, breaking my Howard Hooper sex record with Jack in a single night.

"I was with Jack," I admitted.

"Where?"

"At his house." Should I say we fell asleep, or would that clue her in to what we were doing? I couldn't decide, so I didn't elaborate.

"And his parents were fine with you staying there until seven in the goddamn morning?"

Oh, boy. "They weren't home."

"That's wonderful, Bex. Just wonderful. You're sneaking around behind everyone's back, then?"

"It was just this once."

"Oh, really?" The color of her face matched the apples scattered over her nurse's scrubs. She was *pisssssed*. "Just this once, was it? Guess who I ran into tonight, Beatrix? Go on, guess. Nothing? Your mind's a blank? Well, let me help. I ran into Dr. Denise Sheridan, head of the anatomy lab. Ring any bells?"

Uh-oh.

"Oh, she was all kinds of familiar with you," Mom continued in the Most. Sarcastic. Voice. Ever. "Her mother has been in and out of the ER this summer because of heart problems—"

What do you know. Guess Dr. Sheridan really *had* been caught up with a family emergency that first night she stood me up.

"—and when I talked to her in the waiting room, she asked how your cadaver drawings were coming along. I, of course, looked like a complete fool because I remember that the last time we'd talked about you doing that, I specifically said you could not *under any circumstances* do any such thing. That it was gruesome and inappropriate for a girl your age to be sitting in a room full of dead bodies."

It was at this point that I noticed my sketchbook of Minnie sitting on the seat next to Mom. Hard evidence. No getting around it. I looked to Heath, quietly begging: *Help a sister out, dude!* But he just stared at the floor.

"And what's more, you got Mayor Vincent to call up Dr. Sheridan and ask her to bend her rules for you?"

"I didn't do that!" I argued. "Jack did that without me knowing. He was just trying to be nice. At the time, I didn't even know his dad was the mayor."

"*I* told you *no*," she snapped. "I am your parent—not Mayor Vincent!"

"I'm sorry," I said. "I just wanted to win the scholarship money, and I needed authentic art. I wasn't out drinking or smoking weed—"

"No, but you were running around town with a wanted vandal."

I stilled, arms clenched against the back of the sofa as my heart galloped against my rib cage. There was no way she could've figured that out. No way, unless . . .

"I'm sorry, Bex," Heath said, sounding defensive. "It just kind of came out."

"You promised!"

"And I also told you he sounded like bad news!"

"He's the farthest thing from bad news. He's sweet and caring, and he likes both of you, and you threw him—and me!—under the bus?"

Heath grimaced and shifted uncomfortably.

"I never said a word to Mom when you were cruising bars in the Castro at the beginning of the summer."

"I stopped," he said angrily. "Did you?"

"Did I what? I never spray-painted a single line. And the two of you have no idea why he's doing it or what he's been through."

"A police officer came to question you, and you lied to his face," my mom shouted. "Jack Vincent is a felon!"

"He's the most moral person I know. And I'm in love with him." There. I'd said it. Out in the open. But what I thought was the biggest news flash of the evening only elicited cruel laughter from my mother. The sound struck my chest like a hammer.

"You don't know what love is," she said. "And Jack doesn't, either, because you don't drag someone you love into the muck with you. You don't commit crimes and talk your girlfriend into sneaking around and lying to her own family."

She really shouldn't have said that. I completely lost it. All the bolts holding my brain together fell out and dinged against the floorboards. "Oh, and you're an expert? That must be why you told Heath and me all those lies about Dad, like how his new wife owned a strip club when it was really a jazz club. And how Dad refused to pay child support when you were the one who refused to accept it, because you cared more about your stupid pride than your own children's well-being."

Dead silence. Nothing but a police siren wailing somewhere in the distance.

Mom's anger-red face drained to white while Heath's mouth fell open.

Too late to take it back now.

"Yeah, I went and saw him in Berkeley that afternoon," I said defiantly. "He sent me a birthday present—the one you said you'd throw in the trash. He's been trying to see us, and you refused."

Mom's eyes brimmed with tears. "I'm your mother!" she said in a voice that was out of control, anguished and broken. "He cheated on me. He left me for *her*. He left all of us."

"He might be a bastard, but he's still our father. And you lied to us."

"What? You're on his side now?"

"No," I said. "I gave him the gift back, and I had a huge fight with him. But you could've told us he's been trying to see me and Heath. You could've told us he'd moved right across the Bay."

"He ruined my life. Made me feel worthless," she said, a single tear running down one cheek. She quickly wiped it away. "I used to tell myself I didn't want him to make you two feel that way, too. But if you want to know the truth, you were the only thing I had that he wanted. And by withholding you from him, I had control over something. I could make him suffer."

I didn't know what to say to that. Heath, either. He put his hands atop his head and paced into the kitchen. Everyone was miserable now.

"I'm sorry I didn't tell you about the anatomy lab," I said after a time. "But we both know I can't afford to go to college if I don't get scholarship money and grants. As far as Dad goes, I'm not sorry I went to meet him. He's still an asshole, if that makes you feel any better. And I don't know if I want to see him again or not. But I'm not sorry about Jack. He's going through something you can't even imagine—"

"I don't care," Mom said, suddenly snapping out of her pain. "He's a wanted felon, a troubled—"

"Please don't say 'Troubled Teen.'"

"Okay, smart-ass. But if you want to get into college so badly, think about this. You won't be getting in anywhere if you have a police record."

"I won't—"

"That's right, you won't. You won't be seeing him ever again. The only time you're leaving this house is to go to work."

"You can't do that! I'm eighteen, not eight."

"My house, my rules."

"Fine. I'll take my things right now and leave."

"You even think about it, and I'll go ring the Vincents' doorbell and tell the mayor that his precious son has been vandalizing the city."

"You wouldn't *dare.*"

"Try me, Beatrix. I would and I will."

How could she be so unbelievably cruel? "All that talk about wanting me to be happy, but when I finally am, you just couldn't stand it, could you? You had to ruin my life, too, because if you aren't happy, nobody is." I stalked off toward my room and swung around for one last dig. "Maybe that's why Dad left you in the first place."

The X-ray doors shuddered when I slammed them closed. I fell onto my bed, sinking into misery and hopelessness, and buried my head beneath my pillow to shut out the sound of Mom's crying.

27

I SOMEHOW MANAGED TO SLEEP UNTIL NOON. WHEN I woke, I stayed in bed and texted Jack to let him know I'd sent him an email about what was going on. He didn't reply, but I figured he was probably asleep or dealing with his parents' coming back from Sacramento. I listened for sounds of life outside my doors, and when I determined that the coast was clear, I made a beeline for the bathroom. When I got out of the shower and was combing my hair, a knock sounded on the door.

"Go away."

"I'm so sorry," Heath's voice said through the wood.

"Me too," I called back. "For trusting you."

"Please, Bex. I want to know what happened with you and Dad."

"You should've thought about that before you betrayed me. Go away."

I turned on the shower again to make it sound like I was getting back inside, and he finally left. He didn't make another appearance while I got ready for work, but Mom did. I saw her petite silhouette under the arch of the kitchen as I was headed out the front door. "I work from three to seven," I said to her. "If you don't believe me, you can call Ms. Lopez and verify my work schedule from now on." And with that, I shut the door and left.

Much like my life, work was a disaster. I was preoccupied and a total klutz, and I nearly started crying when a twenty-something snot of a woman yelled at me for dropping her organic eggs. I think Ms. Lopez took pity on me or something, because she quietly told me I was overdue for my break (I wasn't) and took over my register, sending me to the count-out room. Once there, I tried Jack's breathing trick, but it didn't help.

As if he knew I was thinking about him, my phone dinged with a Jack text, asking me to call him ASAP, so I did.

He answered right away with a breathless question: "Where are you?"

Relief rushed through me upon hearing his low voice. I wilted into a folding chair and answered, "At work, on a break."

"Has your mom said anything to you today?"

"Not a word."

"Think she's serious about telling my folks?"

"If she catches me sneaking out to see you, yeah. She might do it. I'm so sorry, Jack. I didn't mean to tell Heath."

"Dammit, Bex. You were the only one who knew. I trusted you to keep it secret."

He was angry with me? Worry tightened my chest and gummed up my throat. "It was after Jillian's seizure, and I didn't know if you were blowing me off, so I asked Heath for advice. He just guessed because I'm a terrible liar, and I never thought he'd betray me—"

"What's done is done," he said.

I covered my eyes with hands, as if he could see me through the phone. "I'm *so sorry*. You've got to believe me."

"Look, I have to go. I'll think of something."

"Jack—"

He'd already hung up.

I DREADED GOING HOME AFTER MY SHIFT. MOM wasn't working, which made me anxious that she'd be waiting for me. Usually on days like these, she'd hold off eating dinner until I got back, and even if it was just salad or the Ultimate Sin (what she dubbed homemade guacamole and chips when we sometimes ate it as a meal), we'd watch something trashy on the DVR and eat together.

That wouldn't be happening tonight, not after everything I'd said to her. But it wasn't like I could just text and say I was going out. My sneaking-around days were over. So I kept my head down and strode into my room, quickening my pace when I heard movement in the kitchen. But before I could hunker down and wall myself away, her footsteps stopped outside my door.

"Hey," she said, pushing inside as I stripped out of my jacket.

"Hey."

Something bounced on my bed. I glanced up to see my sketchbook of Minnie.

"You can finish up your work in the anatomy lab," she said. "But that's not a license to run around wherever you please afterward. Just to the lab and back home."

I was a little shocked. I tried to answer, but it came out as a grunt.

"Dinner's in the kitchen," she added, and then walked out. I listened to her shuffling back to her room, and the door closed.

Whatever small hope this gave me was crushed when Jack called me again later that night in lieu of our usual good-night texts. My heart raced as I answered the phone.

"I can't talk long," he said in a rush. "Mom's coming back any second."

"Okay."

"I told them."

"What?"

"I told them about the graffiti."

"Oh no. Jack? Why?"

"It was time."

"What did they say?"

"Mom cried, which sucked. Dad is furious. At first I thought he was going to make me turn myself in to the police, but he wouldn't want the bad publicity. Now he's threatening to send me to a boarding school in Massachusetts for my senior year."

"What?" Surely this was a joke or some kind of invented cover-up story, like Jillian being sent to boarding school in Europe. Only . . . it wasn't.

"Some elitist prep school," he said angrily. "It's a gateway to Ivy League colleges, but I don't want to go to Harvard or MIT, and I can't leave San Francisco. God only knows how Jillian will react—she doesn't do well with change, and Dad knows that. I can't believe he would even consider it. But I guess it's what he does with everything he doesn't know how to handle. He shoves it out of sight. First Jillian, now me."

"This can't be happening," I whispered. "This is all my fault."

"Hey, stop that. It's not. I'm glad I told them. It feels like a weight off my shoulders. And I'm not mad, so don't even think that. You hear me? I'm sorry I got upset earlier. I was just shocked. But I did this for both of us, so your mom can't hold it against you. I thought it would help, but I guess it only screwed things up even more."

I suppressed tears and sagged against the headboard of my bed. "Oh, Jack."

"You are the only thing good in my life. If he forces me to move across the country . . . ? Jesus, Bex. I'm already dying over here. One day apart from you feels like an eternity. What will happen if I can't see you for months?"

Months. I couldn't even fathom it, but I already felt the potential loss impaling my chest, a hint of things to come.

IT HAD BEEN WEEKS SINCE I'D POSTED ON THE *BODY-O-Rama* blog. Not to sound tragic, but in a way, it was pretty much the only outlet I had for conversation right now, because no one else was talking to me. Well, Jack would if he could, but before he hung up the previous night, he'd warned me that his parents were watching his every move, and they knew about his trick with their home security cameras. They were also threatening to monitor his texts. In a way, I guess I was happy for once that I paid for my own phone. Mom couldn't shut it down or anything.

With all this hanging over me, I drew a quick sketch of a human heart and added diagram labels for all the parts. It was no Max Brödel—I'll tell you that much. And maybe because it was so sketchy, or maybe because my life had been upended, I dug through the bottom of my wardrobe and found my plastic tub of Prismacolors. The scent of wood and wax wafted out when I opened the lid. I sharpened the Scarlet Lake pencil and, blowing out a long breath, set the lead against the paper.

I only meant to outline what I'd already done, but half an hour passed, and I'd softly shaded the contours of my entire sketch. I was worried all that color would look garish, but it wasn't so bad.

"Imagine that, Lester," I said to my one-armed skeleton.

A few snips in the shape of a square, and the heart, along with its diagram labels, was neatly unmoored from the paper. I carefully ripped it in two and pasted the pieces on a sheet of black paper. Done. Before I could chicken out or second-guess anything, I slapped it on my desktop scanner and uploaded the file under my BioArtGirl profile with only the date and time for a title. And, you know, it actually made me feel a little better.

That night Mom wasn't working, so she dropped me off at the anatomy lab and told me she'd be back to pick me up at 8:00 p.m. She didn't add "sharp" to the end of that, but I felt the implication clearly enough.

We were communicating only on a need-to-know basis, but at least that was better than screaming at each other, and it was certainly more communication than Heath and I had. Conveniently, he was spending the night at Noah's. Mom told me this—not him. She also told me Heath had set a move-out date: the day after my art show.

I didn't see Simon Gan in the anatomy lab lobby, but after I'd signed in and clipped on my visitor's badge, I headed into the cadaver room and spotted him in his usual spot. He saw me putting my stuff down and waved. The stand I used to prop up my sketchpad wasn't around, but several extra ones sat across the room. I headed over to retrieve one but stopped when I noticed that something was . . . off.

Laid out on Minnie's metal table was the body of a skinny old man. His leg had been opened up for dissection near a pair of bloated testicles.

"Miss Adams," Simon called out.

"There's been a mistake," I answered, scanning the other sheet-covered bodies. "This isn't Minnie."

He stopped on the other side of the cadaver and caught his breath. "That's what I was going to tell you. Minnie was cremated two days ago. This is Mickey."

"Cremated? Why?"

"They were finished dissecting her, and she'd been in the lab for nine months. It was her time."

"But I wasn't finished," I argued. "How come no one told me?"

"I asked Dr. Sheridan's assistant to let you know, just in case you wanted to be there for the cremation."

"I never got an email."

"Sorry about that," he said, looking genuinely apologetic. "But look at the bright side. At least this new body will give you someone different to draw."

I didn't want someone new. I wanted Minnie. I wasn't finished! And who was this guy, anyway? Mickey? I didn't know him. He was old and gross, and he stank strongly of formaldehyde. I didn't want to invent a new backstory for his life, and I didn't want to draw the dissection of his leg. It felt like a blasphemy—a slap in the face to Minnie.

Tears blurred my vision. I snatched up my things and raced out of the lab. I didn't stop running until I'd taken the stairs down, story after story after story, and finally ended up on the building's front lawn, planting myself against the tree where Jack had taught me the breathing trick. And I fell to pieces.

My project was unfinished.

My entry for the art show was shot.

What the hell was I going to do? I had only a week. One week! And the unfinished drawing of Minnie had taken me an entire freaking month.

Everything was shit. Two days earlier, I'd been in Jack's arms, satisfied and happy. Now I'd had my freedom snatched away, my brother had betrayed my trust, Mom and I were barely speaking, and my boyfriend might be sent to another planet—which is about how close Massachusetts felt.

And now this?

In a rage, I grabbed the sketchbook out of my bag and tore out pages. *Rip!* Sketches from the first day in the lab when I'd gotten sick in the bushes. *Rip!* All my preliminary drawings. *Rip! Rip! Rip!* Detailed studies, experimental angles, and the final sketch. I crumpled up the expensive French-milled drawing paper that had cost me several days' salary and sloppily pitched it at the bushes. People stared. I yelled obscenities at one person, until I realized how banana-boat crazy I sounded, all emotional and dramatic.

Like Heath.

Or my father.

The empty sketchpad fell from my hand. I leaned back against the itchy bark of the tree and stared blankly at the lengthening shadows on the closely shorn grass, now littered with torn pieces of Minnie's body. Plump birds pecked at the paper, searching for food. Students strolled up and down the sidewalk behind me.

When my breathing had slowed so much that I was practically meditating, I got out my phone to see what time it was. Mom wouldn't be there to pick me up for another half hour. Out of habit, emotionally numb and hollow as a beach ball, I checked my email. A comment waited for me at *Body-O-Rama*.

I clicked the link and was surprised anew at the bright Scarlet Lake in my depressing heart sketch—did I really do that?—and scrolled down past my BioArtGirl profile to read the single-line comment from a newly created profile, RockabillyBoy. It said:

Have a little faith.

I stared at that line in wonderment. And as if the words themselves had power enough to create change, an idea bloomed inside my head.

28

MOM SAYS I'M STUBBORN, AND MAYBE THAT'S TRUE. But she also taught me not to blindly follow rules without thinking. Not everything in this world is fair, and people with power don't always have sense.

If I had anything to add to that, I'd say that even good people make bad mistakes (like Mom lying about Dad, which I could forgive her for). And sometimes good people break the rules, like Jack and his golden words—which his parents had to forgive him for, too. Maybe not today or tomorrow, but if they looked at it logically, they'd eventually understand that he was doing it for the right reason.

It was a Noble Defiance.

And that's why I came to the realization that the lesson I'd learned from the jumbled mess of recent events was not that sneaking around was wrong. Sneaking around for the wrong reasons, sure. But sneaking around for the right reasons? That was a Noble Defiance. And that's why Mom continued to let me go the anatomy lab, because she knew I'd been doing it for the right reason.

That's also why I didn't tell her about Minnie's being cremated.

I just quietly picked up my ripped drawing paper, flattened it all out, and crammed the pages back into my sketchpad. And when I got into the paddy wagon, Mom pulled away from the curb and asked, "How did it go?"

"I've had a small setback," I told her. "But I know what to do to fix it."

I just needed Jack's help.

Two days later, I got it.

Mom was working, so she asked me to drop by the ER after my scheduled session at the anatomy lab. I could do that; I wouldn't actually be working in the lab that night, but I'd be only a few buildings away. At six o'clock, I waited in the lobby of the mental health hospital, pacing near some empty visitor seats.

Please don't be a mistake.

When I saw Jack's dark pompadour come through the door, all the anxious energy bouncing around in my body coalesced into an arrow that propelled me straight toward him. He didn't miss a beat, just opened his arms and picked me straight up off my feet. All his goodness hit me at once. His lemony hair wax. The rustling noise his old leather jacket made. The solid wall of his chest and the warmth of his neck, where I buried my face.

"There you are," he murmured in his low voice, the words vibrating through me as I clung to him, more grateful than I'd ever been. "Everything's right in the world again."

After a time that was too long to be polite but too short to be satisfying, I released him and slid down his body until my toes found the floor. "Did they let you come, or did you sneak out?" I asked, blinking back happy tears.

"I convinced them that suddenly stopping my visits with Jillian would be a bad idea—which is true, and they knew it. So I'm out on parole, but they've got a tracker on my phone. I told them six to eight, like you suggested, and they expect me home right after."

"That's fine," I said, curling my fingers around his and tracing the bones on the back of his hand with my thumbs. I couldn't *not* touch him. It was physically impossible. "It's enough time—that is, if Jillian's agreeable."

"I cleared it with Dr. Kapoor. He talked to her, and she's okay with it. Or she was earlier. Let's hope she's still having a good day."

"If not, it's okay. I just don't want to upset her routine."

"Me and you both, but all we can do is try." He pulled me against him for a moment and kissed me several times on my head. "Ready?"

I nodded, and we headed down the hall to check in. The ward was louder and busier than it had been before. The day rooms were just closing up for the evening, and the patients on Jillian's hall had all been fed dinner, the orderly informed us as we passed a few of them in the hallway. Even during normal business hours, the ward wasn't a chaotic zoo, the way these wards are often portrayed on TV. Maybe it was different upstairs on the fifth floor, where they kept the patients on suicide watch and the ones who were too out of control for social privileges. I remembered Jillian saying how much she hated that floor, and I wondered how many times she'd been up there.

We rounded the corner, and just like the first time, there she was, peeking out her door. Only instead of disappearing immediately, she waved at us—just once before she slipped back inside. The orderly left us with the same instructions as last time.

I could smell the cigarette smoke before Jack opened the door. She was already sitting cross-legged on her bed, with the window cracked.

"Yo, Jillie," Jack said brightly. "Cool if Bex comes in?"

"Yeah, yeah. I told Dr. Kapoor it was fine." Her eyes darted to my bag before jumping around the room.

I greeted her and asked, "Did your doctor tell you why I wanted to come? That I want to draw you?"

"Yeah. Why? Is it part of Jack's secret word puzzles?"

I was careful not to mention that he wouldn't be doing those anymore. Jack had prepped me in advance to keep quiet about that, and about the possibly of his being sent away to boarding school. "No, it's for an art show. It would be on exhibit, and if it's good enough, it could win me a scholarship."

"Why would anyone want to see me?"

"Because she wants to immortalize you," Jack said playfully.

Jillian looked at him, then at. "Is it an art show about crazy people?"

"It's an art show about science," I told her. "I usually draw people for anatomy studies, but a few things have happened to me recently, and I decided I'd rather tell the story behind the body."

She looked confused. Maybe I wasn't saying it right. I tried again.

"I'd like to draw a couple of sketches of you today, and while I'm drawing, I was hoping you might tell me stories about things you like. You can talk about anything you want, and I'll try to incorporate it into my work."

"Like art therapy on Fridays with Dr. Yang?"

"Exactly like that," Jack said, smiling. "Except you'd be more famous, because you'd get to be on display in an art gallery. I showed you Bex's art on that website, remember?"

"Yeah. It was pretty dark. I liked it." She laughed briefly and rubbed the heel of her palm against her thigh, back and forth, back and forth. . . .

"What I really want to do," I said, "is to draw you here today, and then take the sketch home and work on it some more. And when I'm finished, I'll get Jack to bring the drawing by and make sure you think it's okay before I enter it in the contest."

Jack tapped her on her shoulder to get her attention. "And if you give us the thumbs-up, the painting will go on display in Bex's art show next week. We'll take a photo of it hanging up. Just like I do with the word puzzles. Maybe even make a video so you can see how many people will be looking at it."

We'd already talked about this the night before, when Jack was able to give me a quick call: He said he might not even be able to go to the art show unless he found a way to sneak out. Even doing this today was risky, especially now that I knew his parents were tracking his phone. But I couldn't dwell on it. We just had to take one day at a time and see how things played out.

"I don't want to hide your scars," I told Jillian. "I want to show you as a whole person. Just like anyone else."

"You want to show my schizophrenia."

"Yes."

She looked at me thoughtfully for a moment. Her eyes darted away, and a small line formed in the middle of her forehead. I knew decisions stressed her out because her mind tangled up all the possible outcomes, but no way was I doing this without her permission.

After biting on her nails and taking several drags off her cigarette, she finally asked, "If you're going to im-m-mortalize me, can you make my hair longer?"

"Any way you'd like it."

"Okay, then. Jack can show you pictures of how it used to be. That's how I like it."

"Yep, I can show her," he confirmed.

"All right," she agreed with a shy smile. "I'll do it. Where do you want me to sit?"

29

AFTER MY SESSION WITH JILLIAN, I HUGGED JACK good-bye. Knowing we might not see each other for a while made leaving him excruciating. I squeezed him harder and tried to think up excuses not to let go.

"I keep going back to that first night we met at the bus stop," he said against my hair as he held me. "And, you know, I think I wanted you from the first time you laughed. But now it's so much worse. Now I need you."

"I know," I whispered.

"It scares me how much. How are we going to fix this?"

"If your father sends you away, I won't let you go without a fight. I'm willing to do something drastic."

"Like what?"

"I don't know," I admitted.

He didn't, either. His parents controlled his bank account, and I had a whopping eight hundred dollars in savings. What could we do? Drop out of school and run away? Even though my brother possessed zero pride, getting booted from community college and squatting at Mom's the last couple of years, that definitely wasn't me.

And it wasn't Jack.

All we could do was wait. And hope.

So I watched him walk to the parking garage, my heart breaking a little. Then I pulled myself together. And after checking in with Mom at the ER, I went home with my sketches and notes from Jillian, and I laid them out on my bed with the crinkled, torn drawings from Minnie. I still had a few old canvases down in the garage. One of them was barely used—just a few old brushstrokes. I remembered it well. I'd started working on it the day my parents had their big blowout. Mom had found pictures on Dad's phone of him and Suzi vacationing together at a cabin in Big Sur. Heath was still a senior in high school, and we were living in our old house. We'd stayed up half the night on his bed with our ears against the wall, listening to our parents fight in the room next door. Dad left a week later.

But even though the canvas brought back bad memories, it was still usable. A coat of gesso and it was blank again. My portable easel was still perfectly functional, and most of my paints weren't dried out. I carted them all up to my room and set them up in front of Lester. After a few measurements, I sketched out a silhouette of Jillian and started working.

Four days. That's how much time I had left until the show deadline. So I called up Ms. Lopez and explained the situation, and after a few more phone calls, I'd found three coworkers who were willing to cover my shifts.

So I started painting.

After the first day, Mom and Heath started popping in to see my progress.

On the second day, Mom opened up both the X-ray doors and watched me from the living room, bringing me tea and my favorite treat: pecan rolls from Arizmendi Bakery off Judah and Irving Streets—right down the street from the Golden Gate Park entrance where Jack painted BLOOM. She finally asked me why I was working with fragments of the cadaver drawings. "It doesn't look like the same body," she said.

"It's not." And partly because I wanted to offer her something honest as a show of good faith (and partly because I had nothing to lose), I told her the story of Jack's sister. About everything Jack and his family had gone through, and why he'd been doing the graffiti, and how he'd confessed it all to his parents, and that his father was threatening to send him away.

She quietly listened to every word without comment. No consolation. But no admonishment, either. Just poured me more tea, promising that the Vincents' secret wouldn't leave her lips, and told me to keep painting.

On the third day, I had the house to myself because Mom and Heath left to have dinner with Noah and his parents, an hour away in San Jose. I painted the entire time they were gone.

On the last day, when Mom was getting ready for work, the doorbell rang. I wiped paint off my hands and answered it, surprised to see Jack's friend Andy standing on my doorstep wearing an Isotope Comics T-shirt. His labret stud was now blue.

"Hey there," he said brightly. "Jack sent us out on a mission to find your house."

"Found me. Who's 'us'?"

He tipped his tousled head down the stairs toward the curb,

where a beat-up yellow car idled. One tiny arm stretched from the passenger window and waved. It took me a second to spot the pink-and-purple hair, and I realized it was my favorite person, Sierra.

I waved back.

"He wanted me to bring you this," Andy said, handing me what looked to be a plastic bag wrapped into a palm-sized wad and wound up with a whole lot of packing tape.

"Oh, lovely. You've brought me what appears to be a package of illegal drugs, right in front of all our neighbors. Just what I needed."

He laughed.

"But really, what is this?" I asked.

He shrugged his shoulders extra-high and held out his hands, but his smile told me he knew exactly what it was. "I'm just . . ."

"The messenger?"

"The person who's not in hot water for something that's obviously juicy and epic, because Jackson usually gets away with murder. Any idea why he's grounded?"

Jack hadn't told him? Wow. "It will go with me to my grave," I said.

"And you just happen to be grounded, too? The whole thing reeks of scandal, if you ask me."

"Good-bye, Andy."

He grinned and saluted me. "I'll let him know the package has been transferred successfully."

"Thanks." He stood there for another moment, so I asked, "Are you and Sierra seeing each other?"

"Indeed we are," he said, then added, "exclusively."

As he started down the steps, I thought of all the things the girls at Jack's party were saying about her, and I'm not sure why, but instead of hating her guts, I felt a little sorry for her. "Hey," I called out in a low voice.

He paused and turned around. "Yeah?"

"She needs someone she can count on."

"I know." He smiled and jogged down the stairs to rejoin her in the car.

Once they drove away, I headed back inside and examined the strange package. I was pretty eager to find out what was under all that tape, but it took kitchen shears and some elbow grease to get it open. Jack must've been paranoid about Andy sneaking a peek inside to have Fort Knox–ed it up like that. Why? Inside were a folded note and a small black bag.

The note was handwritten in perfect letters:

Bex,

Good news and bad news. The bad: I probably won't be able to meet up with you to show Jillian the painting, because my mom's coming with me to see her on Tuesday. But if you can email me a photo of it, I'll find a way to sneak Jillian a peek at it. The good news: I found a devious and brilliant way to attend your art show on Thursday. Don't worry! It doesn't involve graffiti.

A "devious" way? What in the world was he doing? I prayed it wasn't something risky or stupid, because him being at the art show wasn't worth it. I didn't want to make his father any angrier than he already was. But if Jack said not to worry, I wouldn't. Much. I continued reading:

As to what's inside the bag... You once gave me the choice of none of you or all of you. No matter what happens, I wanted you to know that you have all of me in return. I'm giving this to you because I trust you to keep it safe.

Love,
Jack

I opened up the black bag. The contents tumbled out. A sterling silver anatomical heart sat in my palm, suspended on a short chain. Maybe an inch tall and modeled all the way around, the pendant was beautifully cast and anatomically correct. It was also a locket, and when I opened the tiny clasp, two halves swung open to reveal a hollow compartment. My pulse leaped when I spied the jeweler's script engraving on the smooth inner wall:

Jack's Heart

I snapped it shut and looped it around my neck. It hung over the top of my breastbone, heavy and polished. I warmed the silver with my fingers and whispered a promise to him: "I will."

30

WHEN THE BIG DAY FINALLY ROLLED AROUND, I WAS A nervous wreck. I'd finished my contest entry and received Jillian's approval through Jack, and though the paint was barely dry, I got it turned in on time. Now I just had to survive the moment of truth.

The show was downtown on Geary Street, and traffic sucked. Mom, Heath, and I were stuck in the paddy wagon trying to find a parking space while I was quietly having a stroke over the fact that we were maybe-probably-definitely going to be late.

I tried to assure myself that I looked good, at least. I was wearing my most flattering dress—black and white polka dots, with buttons all the way down the front and a belt in the middle—along with the gray knee-high boots. I was also wearing Jack's heart. (When Mom saw it, she asked me where I'd gotten it, and I told her the truth; she'd only said "Hmph," but that was better than "Throw it in the trash!" so I figured it was okay.) And when I'd stopped by Alto on my way back from dropping off my painting, Ms. Lopez gave me a cloisonné ladybug for luck, which I'd pinned to the collar of my dress.

But that ladybug was already letting me down, and it only got worse when Heath casually said, "Hey, look at this *SF Weekly* article on the show tonight," and passed me his phone. My eyes glazed over as the headline attacked me from the small screen:

MAYOR'S WIFE TO SPEAK AT MUSEUM-SPONSORED
STUDENT ART EXHIBITION

I nearly choked. Heath shot me a wide-eyed look between the seats when Mom was busy complaining to herself about city parking. If this discreet silence was Heath's way of making up for his massive betrayal, I supposed I'd let him have a few points.

The article was brief. At the last minute, Marlena Vincent was scheduled to appear at the exhibition. The article described her as a "long-time patron of the arts" and remarked on her extensive art collection. (Her chair paintings? Really?) Apparently, she'd also helped raise a shit-ton of money for Bay Area art education. And *of course* the exhibition organizers were just "thrilled" to have her on board to inspire the young talent who had entered the contest.

Yeah. Bet they were.

It took me several moments of panic to connect the dots to Jack's "devious and brilliant" plan to attend the show. *He had put her up to this!* Did she even know I was entered in the contest? Because she definitely didn't know that I'd painted Jillian.

Would she recognize her own daughter hanging on the wall? Would she be shocked? Angry? Had Jack even thought this through? He'd seen the photo of the painting, for the love of Pete! He'd merely said it was "perfect," which already made me nervous enough because he didn't elaborate, and what if he really didn't like it but he couldn't tell me because he's my boyfriend and he didn't want to hurt my feelings and this is so different than any other artwork I've done over the last couple of years and why in the world did I think it was a good idea to do something so weird for a scientific art contest . . . and, and . . .

OH, GOD!

Slow breath in through the nostrils, long breath out through the mouth . . .

I abandoned the idea of jumping into oncoming traffic and calmed down about the same time Mom found a parking space. Nothing I could do about this now.

Time to face whatever awaited me.

The show was being held in a building with several floors of private art galleries, and they were all open late for some once-a-month open house. A guard sat behind a desk in front of four elevators, where signs and a map identified the student exhibition gallery. We wove though stilettos and plastic champagne glasses (private gallery openings) to join the Converse and Sprite crowd (the student exhibition).

The gallery was pretty big: one room split into three sections with white walls, wood floors, and black track lighting focused on the artwork. A small area at the far end had been set up with a microphone and chairs—for the judges, I assumed. They'd already picked the winners before the show, but the judges were around there somewhere, mingling. I scanned the room for Jack or his mom. Nada. But I did spy someone beefy and muscular and smiling: Noah.

Heath waved him over, and we all greeted one another.

"How long have you been here?" I asked him.

"Long enough to see all the entries. You're going to wipe the floor, Beatrix."

"I don't know about that."

"Saw a couple of the judges looking at it," he said. "*Everyone*'s talking about it."

Had Noah seen Jack's mom? He knew better than to mention this in front of my mom, right? Had my fall from grace come up during pillow talk? I imagined it had, and my brother's shifty eyes confirmed it.

Heath quickly elbowed Noah and cleared his throat. "Show me where Bex's painting is, then tell me everything," Heath said as he pulled Noah away.

"Good luck," Noah told me over his shoulder.

I checked in with one of the organizers and got an artist badge with my name and school listed. Crap. There were more than a hundred entries? When I'd turned in my painting, the person who took it said there were fifty. That was twice as many people to compete against.

"It's loud," Mom said near my ear. "More like a party than an exhibition."

"Heathens," I agreed, eyeing other people with artist badges. They were all boys. Like, nearly every single one. And the artwork was exactly as I imagined: magnified cells, astronomy, close-ups of flowers . . . oh, and one dissection: a frog. It was actually pretty good.

"A frog?" Mom mumbled. "*Please*. Amateur."

I blinked at her in shock.

She smiled at me conspiratorially. "Give me some credit," she said, linking her arm through mine. "I might not be happy about all the crap you've pulled this summer, but it doesn't mean I'm not a proud mama. Where is yours, anyway?"

I pushed back chaotic feelings and straightened my posture. "Must be in the middle section." Even wearing heeled boots, I had to stand on tiptoes to peer around the room. When Mom suggested we cut around a group of parents, we turned together and ran straight into the last people I'd ever expected to see.

Dad and his new wife, Suzi.

"Hello, Katherine," he said in his VP voice.

"Lars," my mom said in her *I want to rip your throat out* overly polite voice.

And before I could filter it, "What the hell are you doing here?" came out of my mouth.

"Your mother invited me."

Oh. Wait—huh?

Why?

What was going on here? Just the week before, she was biting my head off and crying over the fact that I'd gone behind her back to meet up with Dad. Now, after a three-year Dad-free zone, she was inviting him to things?

"This is Suzi," he said to us, like she wasn't the woman who'd broken up my parents' marriage. Then again, maybe she didn't. What did I know anymore? Relationships were complicated.

"It's nice to meet you—formally, this time," Suzi told me. "It was hard to hear over all that screaming your father was doing."

She smiled at me—like, a real smile. She was teasing. No way. I really didn't want to like her.

"Ah, yes," Dad said uncomfortably, then quickly changed the subject. "We saw your painting, Beatrix. It's very interesting."

Interesting. Yeah, that about summed it up. "Where is it? We just got here."

"Follow us," he said, and they began making their way through the crowd like we weren't all sworn enemies.

Mom and I sneaked glances at each other. My eyes said, *Ten dollars her boobs are fake,* and Mom's said, *Not as fake as his smile—why did I marry that jerk, again?* She squeezed my hand and everything was suddenly okay. Good, even.

Until we got to my painting.

If the room was crowded, the area around my painting was packed. I spotted the top of it, with all its bold colors, and my stomach knotted. Maybe this was the worst idea I'd had in a long time. Being grounded and forced into a celibate, Jack-free existence after our single night of spectacular sex had surely rotted a hole in my brain. And speaking of my spectacularly sexy boyfriend, his dark pompadour bobbed above the fringes of the crowd. He spotted me and smiled so big it threw cool water over my roiling emotions.

In a long-sleeve black shirt, he looked handsome and dressed up, but still very, very Jack. He cut around people and came straight to me, while Mom beckoned Noah and Heath, trying to catch them before Heath spotted Dad—which was a good thing, because all I needed was another public blowout involving my father, if Heath's reaction was similar to (or worse than) what mine had been.

But I couldn't worry about that. I just concentrated on Jack. As he approached, his gaze fell to the anatomical heart pendant at my throat, and a blissfully pleased look settled on his face.

"You look beautiful," he said, dropping a speedy kiss on my cheek. But before I could answer, he quickly murmured in my ear, "I need to tell you something."

About his mom being there, I assumed. So I whispered back, "I already know."

"How?"

Before I could answer, the crowd opened up to allow someone important to walk through. Jack's mom, looking stylish in a pink dress, and . . .

Her husband.

Jack whispered in my ear, "So sorry. He wasn't supposed to be here. Mom talked him into coming. That's what I was trying to tell you."

This was a total disaster. Why had I done this painting? I could have just made do with what I had of my final Minnie drawing instead of ripping her up in a tantrum. Or I could've re-created her. But no. I chose *now* to do something out of my wheelhouse, something weird and creative and emotional, which *wasn't me at all.* I was all about structure and control. I was black-and-white. Grayscale. This was—

This was not.

And it was too late to take it all back.

Holding my breath, I watched the crowd part like the Red Sea, and Moses himself suddenly stood a few feet away from me. He and Jack's mom were flanked by security and led by several people in suits, who had to be either the organizers or judges.

And when the mayor took his hands out of the pockets of his perfectly pressed slacks and crossed his arms, readying himself to look at my painting, I saw the *exact moment* recognition came. It struck him like a slap to the face. His head jerked back. Body went rigid. Mouth fell open. He worked to move his jaw, but no sound came out. A muscle around his eye jumped.

The span between two heartbeats seemed to stretch infinitely. I glanced up at my painting and saw what the mayor was seeing:

Jillian's round face was painted in quick strokes. I'd copied her hair from old photos, dark and bobbed and swooping over her forehead. Her big eyes were open, and she was smiling shyly. I'd tried to re-create the shape of her shoulders—the painting stopped at her waist—and I'd painted her wearing a T-shirt from her favorite band.

Minnie's dissected arm and half-chest were superimposed over Jillian. But instead of looking like the dead flesh I'd originally drawn, I'd painted it to look like the dissections were doors opening to reveal her muscles and organs—like the back of a clock removed to show the cogs and wheels.

On Jillian's arm, where the penciled dissection cutaway replaced her scars, I gave the veins and arteries life, painting them in rich red and vibrant blue, extending them into the negative space behind her, where they curled and stretched like the whorls of smoke that floated around her head as she sat at the window, posing for me.

And in place of the usual anatomical diagram labels to identify the names of bones and muscles, I substituted words from Jillian's ramblings.

Memories of her childhood cat. Her first boyfriend. Her favorite book.

Names she'd given the demons that occasionally spoke inside her head. Things that stressed her out. Regrets.

Hundreds of words. They filled the space around her, connected by diagram lines and curling veins. They were as precise and neat as I could make them, and lettered with a black paint pen. Jack would've done far better, but I liked that they flowed and curved this way or that.

It wasn't perfect. And apart from my recycled pieces of Minnie, it wasn't anatomically accurate. But it looked like Jillian. I knew it. Jack knew it.

And both Mayor Vincent and his wife knew it.

"What is this?" he murmured to her in a low voice.

"This was done by a senior at Lincoln," one of the suits offered before Jack's mom could answer. The suit stood next to my painting like a museum guide, holding a flat box beneath a clipboard. Reading whatever was attached to the clipboard, she said, "It's acrylic and pencil on canvas and paper, and it's called 'Hebe Immortalized,' which I believe is a reference to the Greek goddess of youth."

"Hebephrenia," the mayor confirmed in a flat voice. "It's another name for disorganized schizophrenia, because symptoms begin during puberty, when schizophrenics are young."

A few people in the crowd murmured, impressed with the mayor's seemingly random knowledge about the subject matter.

"Who painted this?" he asked.

"The student's name is Beatrix Adams."

I felt Jack's big hands tighten around my arms, holding me in place, as if he could read my mind and knew instinct was screaming at me to bolt. But I didn't. I stood still as a solider and watched the mayor turn around. His gaze flew straight to Jack and then dropped until it connected with mine. If he was utterly unreadable the first two times I'd seen him, now his face was a twenty-gallon tank of raw anguish.

I inhaled sharply and suffered his stare, which didn't last long. He swung back around to the painting, as if he couldn't bear to look at me any longer. Behind his back, Jack's mom leaned toward me. Her eye makeup was smudged, and she was blinking a lot. Had she been crying? I couldn't tell whether she was sad or angry, but she put a hand on my shoulder and squeezed.

That was good, right?

Before I knew for sure, before the mayor could burst into a tirade or strike me down with the emotions that made him ball his hands into fists, the suit curating my painting said, "This entry created the most discussion among the judges, and its unusual subject matter and creative use of dissection earned it the number two spot in tonight's competition."

Applause erupted around us as the woman pulled a red ribbon from the box beneath her clipboard and stuck it to the bottom of the painting's printed identification label before cheerily directing the mayor and his wife toward the next contest entry of interest.

Second place.

No scholarship money. No boost for my college applications.

I had lost.

31

IF I HAD MY WAY, I WOULD'VE WALKED OUT, BUT MOM forced me to stay through the ceremony and Mrs. Vincent's speech about the importance of art in school. I stiffened my spine and graciously accepted my prize envelope, which contained museum passes good for a year, and a bunch of vouchers for art supplies.

"Oh, gee," I said out in the hallway with my support team of Mom, Heath, Noah, and Jack. Dad and Suzi lingered off to the side, talking to someone Dad knew; no one had invited him over. "There's a fifty-dollar gift card for a chain restaurant. 'Celebrate your big win on us.' That's just peachy."

Mom took the envelope from me. "I'll keep this for you, or you'll likely burn it in some kind of angry ritual."

"Wrong child," I said.

Heath shook his head. "My burning days are over. Mostly."

"I know it doesn't help," Jack said. "But even if you'd done what you originally planned, there was no way you were beating Fractal Mitochondria Boy. That was some kind of genius. Plus, you're just a lady painter, so you're probably not serious about college anyway. Leave science to the men, whydontcha?"

I leaned my head against his shoulder. "Have I told you how much I like you?"

"Nurse Katherine is two seconds away from murdering me with her eyes, so maybe you shouldn't. What? Too soon?"

"Smart-ass," Mom said to him, half-serious, half-teasing. I guess one good thing about losing spectacularly was getting Mom to cool her rage against Jack. "Just because you're charming doesn't change anything. I'm still mad at you for putting my daughter in a situation that could've gotten her arrested."

"Don't be dramatic, Mom," Heath said.

Jack sighed. "It's fair. Guilty as charged, but just for the record, I would've taken the fall."

Mom rolled her eyes, but it was obvious she wasn't really angry. "Your romantic heroism doesn't impress me."

A crisp voice floated over her shoulder. "That makes two of us."

Crap. I immediately jerked my head away from Jack as the mayor and his wife joined our group. "David Vincent," he said, introducing himself to Mom. "And this is my wife, Marlena. She tells me you're a nurse at Parnassus."

"No need to worry, David," Mom said, like he was just some guy or a neighbor down the street and not the local celebrity she'd fantasized about having a secret love child with. "My coworkers are gossips, so I keep family business at home."

He nodded at her before turning his mayoral gaze on me.

Great. This was it. The universe had apparently decided it wasn't enough for me to waste my summer pursuing something that amounted to nothing more than a pat on the back and endless refills of soda at a chain restaurant. No, I was going to have to either eat crow and beg for King Vincent's forgiveness or defend my painting and risk making things worse for Jack and me.

Sweat coated my palms. I licked dry lips and looked him right in the eye—which was hard, because he was about the same height as Jack, and about a gazillion times more intimidating.

"Dad—" Jack started, but his father steamrolled over him.

"Miss Adams," he said to me, "I'd like to buy your painting."

Huh? Maybe I'd heard that wrong.

"You . . ."

"The first-place scholarship was ten thousand dollars. I'd like to offer you the same to purchase the painting."

I didn't know what to say. I think I might've gasped—or maybe that was Mom. I glanced up at Jack to see if he'd put his father up to this, but he was just as flabbergasted.

"Um . . ." I cleared my throat. "Can I ask why?" Was he so ashamed of Jillian that he'd do anything to make sure no one ever laid eyes on the painting again?

He inhaled deeply and took his time answering, head down, brows knit, hands in pockets, as if it were a struggle to come up with the right words. Almost laughable, really. The man who'd given a hundred and one speeches in front of TV cameras and stadiums filled with people was now tongue-tied?

When he finally lifted his head, his face was calmer. Something unguarded and honest softened his eyes. "Because," he said softly as he looked at Jack, "it made me realize I don't see my daughter as much as I should."

Oh . . .

I scratched the side of my neck. "I don't know what to say."

"Say yes, and I'll write you a check for it right now."

He was totally serious. I looked at him, and then at his wife, who was definitely brushing back tears (and trying to smile at the same time). Next to her, Mom crossed her arms and gave me a cautionary look. I imagined that the penny-scraping side of her, who wanted me to walk away with something to help my future, was at war with the proud side of her, who'd refused child support from Dad. Standing behind her, my brother had fewer moral hiccups; Heath was mouthing *Say yes* and waving me in as if I were a plane descending toward a runway and there was a pot of gold at the end.

Then I glanced at Jack, and he was just looking at me the way he always did. like I was the only person in the room who mattered. Like he trusted me to make the right choice on my own and would stand behind any decision I made.

So I made one.

"I'll give you the painting for free if you promise not to send Jack away to Massachusetts, *and* if all of you agree to let Jack and me see each other."

Total silence. *Tick-tock, tick-tock . . .*

Between us, the back of Jack's hand rubbed against mine. I slipped my fingers into his and felt a little stronger in my proverbial backbone when he squeezed my hand.

"I'm fine with it," Mom said. "As long as you're honest about where you're going and"—she skewered Jack with a warning look—"no one gets arrested. But you have to keep your grades up, Bex, and there'll be a curfew on school nights. No sneaking around after midnight."

I could've kissed her. All hail Katherine the Great.

But she was only half the battle.

I held my breath and looked to the Vincents.

Any earlier vulnerability Jack's dad had shown was now gone, and he was back to being cool and unflappable. He flexed his jaw and started to speak, but his wife silenced him with a small noise in the back of her throat. She then smiled at Mom and said, "Life is better when my son isn't moping around the house. So I believe I speak for both my husband and myself when I say that your suggestions are more than sensible, Ms. Adams."

"If we agree to this, there will be additional stipulations for you, Jack," his dad said. "You're not off the hook for the vandalism."

"Understood," Jack said.

The mayor sighed and stuck out his hand to me, the tiniest of smiles tugging at his serious mouth. "I guess that means you and I have a deal."

THE MAYOR LEFT WITH HIS POSSE WHILE MOM AND Mrs. Vincent got friendly and headed back inside the gallery together to collect my painting. I got so caught up in all the hoopla, I didn't notice that Heath and Noah had gone missing. I spotted them down the hall. Heath was talking to Dad. Noah was talking to Suzi.

"Is this the first time your brother's seen your father since the divorce?" Jack asked, watching them with me.

"Yeah. And no one's yelling. I can't believe it. Why am I the one who went nuts and Heath is taking it all in stride? He's the emotional one, not me."

Jack shuffled me out of the way of a group of rowdy students barreling down the hall. "It probably helps that Heath isn't being bamboozled into meeting your father under false pretenses like you were."

"I don't think that's a real word."

"*Bamboozled*? Of course it is. Never question my authority when it comes to vocabulary, Bex. By the way, thanks for saving me from purgatory in Massachusetts. And for saving us."

"I think it was more Jillian's influence than mine. You should go see her tonight and tell her all about it. And—hey! I can go with you." I turned around to face him, giddy with the realization.

"A week until school starts, so we've still got a little midnight oil to burn before the curfew kicks in," he said, waggling his brows as he wrapped his arms around me.

"Curfew," I said with a snort. "We'll see about that."

"Nuh-uh. Don't even start. I'm not risking Nurse Katherine's wrath again, not when I just got you back. By the way, I never got a chance to tell you earlier, but it's nice to see you wearing the necklace. Do you like it?"

"I *love* it. I'll never take it off. Well, apart from X-rays."

"Always practical. I'm glad you love it. *It* loves *you* right back."

"Does *it?*"

"Never doubt it. And when we're alone, I'd like to show you how much."

"That sounds a little filthy."

"It's a lot filthy," he assured me with a coy smile. His eyes darted over my head. "Put a hold on that filth. Looks like your father wants to talk with you."

Dad was waving me over to him and Heath. It looked

suspiciously like a trap, but considering all the crap I'd been through that night, my father was the least of my worries. "Don't move," I told Jack. "I'll be right back."

I warily approached them, checking Heath's face for signs of trauma. He just lifted his brows as if to say, *Yeah, I can't believe this is happening, either.*

Dad herded us both to the side and spoke to us privately. "I'm sorry you didn't win, Beatrix," he told me. "It was a remarkably intelligent and emotional piece of work."

That sounded like something VP Van Asch would say, but I refrained from pointing this out. "Thanks."

"Heath was just telling me about applying to his vet tech program, and I wanted you both to know that your mother and I have been talking a little this week—"

"Hello, *Twilight Zone,*" Heath mumbled.

"—and we came to a new compromise about financial matters. I've been building a little nest egg for the two of you, so I suggested, and she agreed, that I will cover your college costs. If you can secure scholarships or grants, that's wonderful. If not, anywhere you want to go is on me."

Heath and I stared at him, then at each other.

"What's the catch?" I asked.

"No catch," he said, stuffing his hands into his sport coat pockets. "Just try to pick somewhere within the state to help with the cost. And you might keep your mother's feelings in mind and look at schools in the Bay Area. Beatrix, she told me you're interested in taking both art and medical classes. Stanford's the natural choice for medicine, but if you want both, maybe you'll consider Berkeley."

"Berkeley."

He shrugged his shoulders. "I'm partial, of course, but it would certainly look great on your curriculum vitae when you're considering future graduate schools or grants. But it's up to you."

"I still feel like there's a catch," Heath said. "Mom really agreed to this?"

Dad nodded. "I'm as surprised as you are. And there's really no catch. I'd love to have lunch with you now and then, of course. Suzi and I have a pool, so if you ever wanted to come over and stay with us—"

"A pool?" Heath said.

I rolled my eyes at my brother. "You don't even know how to swim."

"Okay, okay," Dad said, pulling his hands out of his pockets to hold them up in surrender. "Let's take it one step at a time. Talk to your mother; and, Heath, discuss it with Noah. Just keep me in the loop and let me know what you decide."

At the mention of his name, Noah perked up, and he and Suzi approached us. While Heath was saying something to the two of them, Dad pulled me aside and reached inside his jacket. "I had this repaired," he said, offering me the artist's mannequin. "It might not survive another fall, so I hope you won't throw it at me again."

"Thanks," I said as I accepted it. "This doesn't mean we're bosom buddies, though. And the college thing is honorable, but I'm not sure if I've forgiven you quite yet. Money doesn't instantly erase every bad thing."

"Just as long as the door is open between us."

"Yeah," I said. "Maybe it is."

32

December, four months later

JACK AND I STOOD BACKSTAGE BEHIND THE CURTAIN, watching his father speak in front of a packed auditorium at the university hospital. The mayor probably made a dozen fund-raising speeches every year for a dozen different causes, but this was the first one that was personal. He wanted to combine city money and private contributions to fund a new outreach program for homeless people with psychiatric needs. It would add another wing to the psychiatric hospital and additional staff to diagnose, counsel, and distribute medicine to people who otherwise couldn't afford it.

People like Panhandler Will.

"Make sure you get a shot of your mom," I whispered to Jack. He was filming bits and pieces of the speech to show to Jillian later, and their mom was sitting in the front row with Katherine the Great. They saw a fair amount of each other, Mom and Mrs. Vincent. The entire Adams clan, including Noah, even spent Thanksgiving at the Vincents' house, which was surprisingly cool and fun, if not a little weird.

It was also weird to hear Jack's father talking about Jillian in public. But he was. He'd done an exclusive television interview with a local news program a few weeks earlier and told the story of the stabbing and Jillian's suicide attempt. And the world didn't fall apart. In fact, public reaction was overwhelmingly positive. People liked it when politicians were human and honest. Imagine that.

"God, they're chatty," Jack whispered as he filmed our mothers with their heads bent toward each other.

"They're probably talking about the fact that I won't get accepted to SFAI."

"Probably," he said with a grin.

I elbowed him. "Laugh it up, fun boy. If I don't, you'll be in a long-distance relationship after I end up at one of my safety schools across the state."

"Don't tease me, Bex. I can't take it."

We'd both applied to the San Francisco Art Institute. The school has a rolling admissions calendar, which means they make decisions as they receive each application, instead of having one massive deadline, and Jack had gotten his acceptance letter the day before.

"You applied almost a week after me," Jack reassured me. "Who would turn down your portfolio? It's amazing. Besides, your SAT scores are better, and your dad wrote your recommendation."

Things weren't perfect between Dad and me, but once a month he came into the city and we'd meet for lunch or have dinner—last month at Noah and Heath's place (which was sort of awkward, but sort of okay, too). And it was true that he'd written my recommendation letter.

"But he's my *dad*," I protested.

"But he didn't mention that. Besides, you have different last names. Stop worrying. You'll get in."

SFAI was the oldest art school west of the Mississippi River. Diego Rivera painted a mural for the institute, and Ansel Adams started the photography department. It's a great school. A school for serious artists, and god knew if I was anything, I was *very serious*.

The school had a reputation for encouraging students to do their own thing, so for me, that meant I could take the occasional premed anatomy class at another school in the city when I was ready. And for Jack, it meant he could attend the college where the graffiti-inspired Mission School art movement had begun. It also meant he could continue to be close to Jillian. And that was more important than ever, because she was coming home the following week.

Pretty amazing.

Jack was over the moon about it. She'd continue to go to therapy and see Dr. Kapoor several times a week, and the Vincents had hired a full-time nurse to live in the house and make sure she stuck to her routines. The new living arrangement might work, or it might be a disaster. But there was no way of knowing until they tried. And Jillian was finally ready to take that step, which was awesome. To get her acclimated to life on the outside, she'd been allowed a computer for a couple of months and had been using social media. She loved it. (A little too much: The orderlies had to stop her from staying up all night chatting.)

When the mayor's speech ended, he left the stage to thunderous applause. Jack and I were clapping, too. It was sort of exciting. His aides were walking him back to the press for follow-up questions, but he spotted us and made a detour.

"What did you think?" he asked us.

"Nice," Jack said, sticking out his fist for a bump.

The mayor bumped back and smiled. "Is that for Jillie?"

"Yep," Jack confirmed, holding up his phone. "Say hi."

"Love you, baby. Can't wait for you to come home next week," his father said to the screen. His chief of staff was calling him and motioning to his watch. "I've got to go. See you at dinner tonight, Beatrix?"

"With bells on," I replied.

He smiled and trotted back to his staff, disappearing down a hallway.

"Okey-dokey," Jack said, stopping the video recording. "We'd better clear out before this dog-and-pony show clogs up the exit."

We headed out of the auditorium and made our way toward his car, which was parked in a rare curbside space just down the hill. He'd joked that finding the premium space was "Buddha's blessing." I told him that he was going to hell for using his enlightened philosophical leader's name in vain, and that it was totally the cloisonné ladybug pin I'd worn every day since the art contest. He didn't believe in hell, but he did believe in Lucy the Ladybug, which was what I'd named the pin.

"My parents will be stuck here for a good half hour, maybe an hour," Jack said, sliding me a seductive look. "We can stop off at the guesthouse on our way out for some quickie afternoon delight."

"Gee, when you put it *that* way . . ."

We were headed to our last day of volunteer work—or, as Jack called it, our prison sentence. Every weekend since school had started up, we spent a couple of hours painting over graffiti tags on a block near the Zen Center. This was the "additional stipulation" that the mayor had mentioned after the art show. Punishment for Jack's vandalism. The SFPD, who sponsored the volunteer clean-up program, thought we were just doing it out the goodness of our hearts. No way was Mayor Vincent opening himself up to the scandal of his kid being the notorious Golden Apple street artist, so we did it on the down-low. It wasn't so bad. We painted over mailboxes, walls, windows, and sidewalks. Before we covered them up, Jack secretly snapped pictures of anything that was more than just a basic one-color tag and uploaded the images to a local graffiti online photo album. For posterity's sake.

"What do you say?" Jack pulled out his car keys and swung the key ring around his index finger. "I'll let you drive. Fast car and fast love. It's the perfect combination."

"Said no girl, ever. You sure you trust me to drive after last time?"

I nearly killed all three of us—me, Jack, *and* Ghost—when he was teaching me to parallel park. In my defense, it was a busy street and the guy behind us was making me supernervous with all the angry honking. Afterward, Jack had to do his seated zazen meditation to calm down.

"Beatrix Adams," he said. "You know I trust you with everything. The anatomical representation of my heart, my life . . . even my car."

"You must really love me," I said, matching my steps with his.

I knew he did, of course. We try not to say it casually too much, because we want it to mean something. Not just a throwaway phrase like "How's it going" or "See you later." But when I'm in his arms, when we're alone, he whispers "I love you," and those three words never stop amazing me. Never.

Without breaking our synchronized stride, he slid an arm around my shoulders and lowered his head to murmur near my ear. "Would you like me to remind you how much?"

Flutter-flutter. "I actually think I might."

"Yeah?" A slow, dazzling smile lifted his cheeks, and then he came to a sudden halt on the sidewalk. "Oh! We need to stop by the house anyway. You can see our paintings hanging together, live in person."

After the art show, Mrs. Vincent replaced her chair painting in the foyer of their house with my painting of Jillian. I got a little choked up when she showed me. I think it made the mayor sentimental, too, because he left the room awfully fast, and Mrs. Vincent says that's what he does when he gets emotional.

But my painting now had a partner. I'd seen a photo of it before the mayor's speech this afternoon, but I hadn't seen the real thing yet.

Before Jack admitted to his parents that he was the person behind all the Golden Apple graffiti, Jillian had given him one last word puzzle to decode. He'd never been able to execute the piece out in the city, obviously. When Jack found out Jillian had agreed to leave the hospital and move back in the house, he painted the tenth and final word for her as a "welcome home" gift.

BEGIN, FLY, BELONG, JUMP, TRUST, BLOOM, CELEBRATE, ENDURE, RISE . . .

And now LOVE.

The word was spray-painted onto a canvas, not a wall, and it was the smallest piece he'd ever done. But it was by far his best work. Jillian would adore it. I sure did.

"Come on," he coaxed, dangling the car keys in front of my face as he wound one arm around my back to pull me closer. "You won't ever learn to drive if you stop trying. You know you want to."

I totally did. I stood on my tiptoes, accepted the kiss he dropped on my lips, and snatched the keys out of his fingers. Feeling alive might just be a rush of adrenaline, but Jack had been right that first night on the Owl bus. It was definitely worth the risk.

ACKNOWLEDGMENTS

THIS IS NOT MY FIRST PUBLISHED BOOK, BUT IT MIGHT be my favorite. And it wouldn't exist if my extraordinary agent, Laura Bradford, had not said, "Yo! You should consider writing YA." (Or something slightly more professional.) It was excellent advice. Writing this book was like slipping into a comfortable coat. It just felt . . . right.

It felt even better after it landed in my editor's capable hands. Anna Roberto, your passion for teen fiction is infectious, and I feel unbelievably lucky to work with someone so thoughtful, smart, and talented. Thank you for making Bex and Jack even more *Bex and Jack* than they were before. Many heartfelt thanks to everyone else who works behind the scenes at Feiwel and Friends and Macmillan—including this book's talented designer, Anna Booth!—and a special thanks to the legendary Liz Szabla, for believing in this book. And a million thanks to the entire Simon & Schuster UK team for bringing Bex and Jack across the pond, including: Rachel Mann, Becky Peacock, Liz Binks, Paul Coomey and Jenny Richards. Every author dreams of working with a creative team like this.

Much love to everyone else who read the manuscript in its infancy, including Veronica Buck, Janice Ming, Ann Aguirre, and especially Karina Cooper, who, upon finishing, called me up to shout enthusiastic praise and made me feel like I'd accomplished something truly amazing. Thanks also to Taryn Fagerness, Elv Moody, and Barbara König. And to all my readers who cheered when I told them I was traveling to YA Land, I wish I could bear-hug each and every one of you.

My biggest I'm-not-worthy acknowledgment goes out to my husband. You not only help brainstorm me out of treacherous plot holes, you're also my biggest fan. Thanks for believing in me all these years, again and again and again.

A LETTER FROM THE AUTHOR

DEAR READER,

THE BOOK YOU HAVE JUST READ IS A LOVE LETTER to artists. Not only the famous ones, enshrined in museums, but also the everyday people who are brave enough to express themselves. My teen protagonists are both artists, though wildly different ones: Bex is fascinated by anatomy and wants to be a medical illustrator, while Jack is a street artist, spray-painting giant gold words across San Francisco landmarks. She's a smart loner being raised by a strong, single mother, and he's a charming, pompadour-ed boy from a different side of town. Though they're opposites – in both their art *and* lives – a mutual respect for each other's work brings them together.

I come from a family of artists. My Scandinavian grandmother was a painter, and my mother, a stained-glass artist. Expression was always encouraged and as a teen, I bounced around from (terrible) acting to (horrific) poetry to teaching myself how to play both the drums and piano (my entire repertoire included butchering a variety of Christmas carols, punk-rock classics, and "Ob-La-Di, Ob-La-Da" – which, to this day, my family can't hear without cringing).

All of that early experimentation led me to pursue two degrees in Fine Art. For me, being an artist wasn't about some sort of gift-from-the-gods talent as much as a drive to express yourself. No way was wrong, no method was off-limits. Be true to yourself. Take the risk. If you fail, get back up and try it again.

I still believe this.

At the beginning of NIGHT OWLS, Bex is struggling with unresolved family issues that have changed her artwork. Instead of using art to express herself, she thinks of it as a skill she must master if she wants a chance to escape her narrowing world. When she meets Jack – whose own family secrets are driving him in the opposite direction, bigger and bolder – he shoves her out of her self-imposed bubble. And when she shoves back, both of their worlds (and hearts!) explode in the best way possible.

I *am* Bex. I'm also Jack. And I'm betting you are a little, too. Because in a way, we're all artists, trying to communicate with each other. Trying to express ourselves while making sense of our lives and taking risks with our hearts. And I hope you enjoyed reading about two people who've hazarded to crack open their chests and bare themselves, stand or fall. Moreover, I hope they spoke to the artist inside *you*. Thanks for taking that risk with me.

Jenn Bennett